WHEN THE *Wind* CHIMES

Other Books by Mary Ting

International Sensory Assassin Network Series
ISAN, Book 1
HELIX, Book 2
GENES, Book 3
CODE, Book 4

Spirit of Ohana Series
When the Wind Chimes, Book 1

Forthcoming from Mary Ting

International Sensory Assassin Network Series
AVA, Book 5

Spirit of 'Ohana Series
The Seashell of 'Ohana, Book 2

Awards

Spirit of 'Ohana Series
Grand Prize Winner: Romantic Fiction, Chatelaine Book Awards
Gold Medal: Romance, Kops-Fetherling International Book Awards
Gold Medal: Romance, New York Book Festival
Bronze Medal: Romance, Independent Publisher Book Awards (IPPY)
Finalist: Romance, Next Generation Indie Book Awards

International Sensory Assassin Network Series
Gold Medal: Science Fiction & Fantasy, Benjamin Franklin Awards
Gold Medal: Science Fiction—Post-Apocalyptic, American Fiction Awards
Gold Medal: Science Fiction, International Book Awards
Gold Medal: Young Adult Thriller, Readers' Favorite Awards
Gold Medal: Young Adult Action, Readers' Favorite Awards
Silver Medal: YA Fantasy / Sci-Fi, Moonbeam Children's Book Awards
Finalist: Action Adventure, Silver Falchion Awards

Jaclyn and the Beanstalk
Bronze Medal: Juvenile / YA Fiction, Illumination Book Awards
Finalist: YA Mythology / Fairy Tale, Readers' Favorite Book Awards
Finalist: Young Adult Fiction, Best Book Awards
Finalist: Unpublished Manuscript, Hollywood Book Festival

WHEN THE *Wind* CHIMES

Spirit of 'Ohana, Book 1

MARY TING

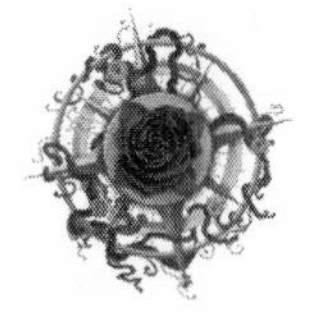

When the Wind Chimes

This is a work of fiction. Names, characters, places, and incidents either are the product of the author's imagination or are used fictitiously.
Any resemblance to actual persons, living or dead, or locales is entirely coincidental.

Cover design by Qamber Designs and Media
www.QamberDesignsandMedia.com

ISBN: 978-1-64548-204-8

Published by Rosewind Books
An imprint of Vesuvian Books
www.RosewindBooks.com

Printed in the United States

10 9 8 7 6 5 4 3 2 1

Table of Contents

Chapter One – Unexpected Passenger

"Jingle Bells" blasted at Lihue Airport on Kauai, only I wasn't dashing through the snow. I was sprinting through the terminal with a carry-on duffel bag hiked over my shoulder and a smaller one clutched in my hand.

Outside the terminal, dark gray clouds clumped like gloomy snowballs. Rain was imminent. All the travelers scurrying over the tile floor toward the doors had the same plan—to catch a cab before the downpour.

Footsteps pounded around and past me. People bumped into me as I hurried along. My duffel bag became heavier the longer I carried it. Even as I struggled to keep pace with the flow, I admired the garland adorned with red baubles, coiled around the pillars.

The beautiful twelve-foot Christmas tree with twinkling lights distracted me as I passed, and I almost ran into someone who'd stopped in the walkway.

"Sorry. Excuse me," I said. *Good grief, Kate. Pay attention before you do some damage.*

He waved a hand with an affable grin and tugged his rolling suitcase away.

I arrived breathless at the outside baggage center, sweat beading my forehead, but was soothed by the sweet fragrance permeating the air. In every direction were kiosks selling handmade leis, some with beads or coconut shells. A lady waved a pink fresh-flower lei in my face, but I politely declined and walked toward the taxi line under an awning about fifty yards away.

The cool wind kissed my cheeks and tousled my long brunette hair, and I pulled my unbuttoned sweater off. Seventy-two-degree weather didn't warrant a sweater even with the rain. As soon as I joined the line for a cab, the sky unleashed its wrath and water pelted the ground like bullets.

This line will take forever.

"A Holly Jolly Christmas" belted through the outside speakers, but the crowd and weather offered no cheer. People squeezed shoulder-to-shoulder under the awning while they waited to catch a shuttle or flag down a taxi. All the line jostling caused my neighbor to bump my arm when a suitcase slammed into him. My eyes watered as someone's strong perfume fought with the fragrant leis. I grimaced and wondered what had happened to personal space.

I had promised my sister she could count on me this year for Christmas, especially since I hadn't been there last year. I couldn't wait to spend time with her and my nephew. The last time I had seen them had been in early spring for my brother-in-law's funeral in New York where they used to live.

I pulled out my phone to text my sister to let her know I had arrived.

Abby: I'm sorry I couldn't pick you up.

Me: Don't worry. I'm on my way.

As I pushed send, a taxi pulled up and parked across the street. I had two choices: stay dry under the awning and wait for my turn or grab the taxi across the street.

Forget staying dry. Forget waiting in line.

"Taxi!" I waved frantically splashed through the puddles, as I made a mad dash toward it, lowering my head against the pouring rain. The likelihood of snatching the taxi was slim. But I had to try.

A few cars honked as I dodged past. Not a good idea. "Sorry," I bellowed, but a roll of thunder drowned out my voice.

The wind had kicked up and practically pushed me across the road. With my bags trying to take flight, I felt like Mary Poppins, only less graceful and more drenched to the bone.

Not a good idea? More like horrible, dangerous, idiotic idea. I could have been hit by a distracted driver. Or I could have slipped, and in the rain, no one would spot me until I'd been flattened. What was I thinking?

But I made it safely across.

I jerked open the door and threw my bags—and my soggy self—

into the back.

"Hi." I flipped my damp hair to the side and checked that I'd closed the door. My cold wet clothes stuck to me like a second skin, I sighed with relief and positioned the smaller bag on my lap. "Poipu, please."

Beside me, someone cleared his throat.

I gasped and jerked, my heart thundering with the storm. I hadn't expected anyone else in the backseat, especially a good-looking man with slicked-back dark hair and wide, annoyed eyes.

He smoothed the lapel of his out of place, but classy, gray tailored suit. Who flew to Kauai in business attire? He sure smelled nice, though. A scent of cedar and pine permeated the small space.

Either I was hallucinating my dream guy, or he had gotten in the cab at the same time. But I had been the only crazy person running across traffic. I'd done a quick check before I got in, but the tinted window had prevented me from getting a clear view.

He clutched a dry, folded umbrella on his lap. I waited in case he was a passenger that hadn't gotten out yet. A guy in a suit like that might be hesitant to run into the rain.

He blinked the most beautiful chestnut-colored eyes framed with thick eyebrows. The intensity of his stare drew me in and made me forget about the pelting rain, but I imagined cozy nights and intimate dinners. Then a muscle twitched in his jaw, and he wiped away the water I had flicked on his face with my hair.

I covered my mouth in horror. *Oops.*

"I'm … I'm so sorry." I swallowed, expecting him to yell or shoo me out of the cab. "I didn't see you. I'll just go." But I didn't move.

It'd take forever to get another taxi, because I'd have to get back in the long line and wait my turn. When I finally broke the gaze, I clamped my fingers around the metal door handle just as a gentle hand rested on my shoulder.

"It's fine. You stay. I was just leaving."

Combined with the tension in the car, his swoony eyes, and the unexpected touch, his smooth baritone sent a surge of pleasant electricity through me. It had been so long since I'd felt this magnitude of attraction …

Forget it!

He was probably leaving for a business trip, anyway—he was

dressed much better than the average tourist. But then the taxi would have dropped him off at the departure terminal and not across the street.

"What do you mean?" The driver twisted at his waist and propped an arm along the seat back. "You just got in. I can take you both."

The man gave an uncomfortable laugh. In spot-on timing with the song "Baby It's Cold Outside," playing softly in the background, the man said, "I can't stay."

Keep me company. I parted my mouth and the words almost escaped. I was surprised how much I hoped he would. So much for my holiday vow to forget men.

"It's okay. You can stay. I mean, you do what you want. I'm sorry I got you . . ." I winced. "Wet. I honestly didn't see you there. We can share a cab, and I am more than willing to pay."

Stop rambling.

"No need to apologize," he said in that smooth voice.

"But—"

Before I could say more, he stepped out and raised his black umbrella, shielding himself as he leaned over the door.

"Brandon, take this lovely lady where she needs to go. Put it on my tab and add the same amount of tip as usual."

"Thanks, Lee."

Did he just call me lovely?

"What? Wait."

"Have a good day. Don't worry about me. I can call my driver." He offered a gorgeous crooked grin and shut the door.

I twisted around to get a better look at him and watched him strut away like the weather was perfect. Like a dream, he faded into the pouring rain.

"Where to, lady?"

I faced the bald, middle-aged man and pulled the seatbelt strap over my chest. Then I gave him my sister's address.

"He called you Brandon. You guys know each other?"

Nosy question, but the man's kindness had been unexpected. What a gentleman to not only leave in the rain and give me the cab, but to pay for my ride. Nobody did stuff like that these days. It was like something out of an old movie.

The driver looked at the rearview mirror, green eyes glinting at me, and turned on the meter.

"His name is Leonardo, but his friends call him Lee. He calls me every time he's back from a business trip even though he could call his driver. Not much of a talker, but a big tipper. Told me once he likes to pay it forward."

I thought about asking more about Leonardo but didn't see the point. I was never going to see him again, anyway.

As Brandon talked nonsense on the way, my mind drifted to Leonardo and wondered where he lived. What his occupation was, if he had a family of his own. I didn't usually fixate on a guy just because he was attractive, but he had intrigued me and had made my crappy day a little bit brighter.

My crappy day had started before I'd even gotten out of bed. First, I'd slept through my alarm, and a horrible accident on the freeway had almost caused me to miss my plane. Then the family sitting behind me had a toddler who wouldn't stop kicking my seat and an infant who cried almost the entire trip. From the flight alone, I needed some serious spa time.

Brandon cleared his throat and turned the wheel to the left. "Where are you from, miss?"

"Los Angeles. Have you been?" I ran my fingers through my wet hair.

"No, but I'd like to visit one day, though I hear the traffic is horrible."

"It's not like Kauai for sure."

Brandon chuckled. "Got that right. There's no place like Kauai. Are you here for business or pleasure?"

"I'm visiting my sister and my nephew." I shifted to get comfortable from my sodden jeans, fighting the urge to itch through the stiff material. The rain had stopped almost as soon as we had exited the airport. Just my luck to have been caught by the deluge.

"What about your brother-in-law?" Brandon stopped at an intersection, glanced back at me, and then turned right.

"Excuse me?" I fanned my shirt from the hem, hoping that would make it dry faster.

"You left out your brother-in-law. Are they divorced?"

What's with the personal questions? I'd never met such a nosy cab driver.

"No, he passed away from cancer." I looked out the window when we got on the highway. The swaying palm trees and the grassy hills blurred the faster he drove.

Brandon sighed and shook his head. "I'm sorry."

I forced an awkward smile, but he didn't look back. I never knew if it was appropriate to tell someone casually that my sister's husband had died. I also didn't know what to say when someone apologized. Sometimes his death seemed so long ago, and sometimes like it happened yesterday.

"How long have you lived here?" I asked to break the silence.

"All my life. I've been a cab driver for almost thirty years. I meet all kinds of people, and I've learned to read people well. So what troubles you?"

I pulled my gaze away from the landscape, startled. "I have no troubles." Besides a broken heart from my ex and my brother-in-law's passing, but he didn't need to know that.

Brandon hiked his eyebrows, meeting my gaze in the rearview mirror. "That's what they all say at first. Don't worry. Whatever you say stays in this cab. I'm a once-in-a-life chance for free therapy. Something about this island makes newcomers open up. Eventually, my passengers always spill their guts to me. They can't help themselves."

I let out a light laugh. He was quite entertaining. "I'm fine, but thank you."

It was going to take at least forty minutes to get to my sister's house, so I gazed out the window, admiring the simple beauty of the curvy hills that stretched for miles.

There were no clumps of looming buildings or people hustling and bustling on the streets. As "Mele Kalikimaka" played on the radio, the six feet tall grass blurred along the long stretch of one-way road and joined forces with the sun as it peeked through the clouds.

"We're now passing through one of the famous sites in Kauai: the tree tunnel," Brandon said, breaking my trance. "A grand gateway to Kauai's South Shore."

I leaned to the middle to see through the windshield. "Wow. It's beautiful."

Trees lined on either side of the road like a canopy. Sunlight spilled through the cracks between the branches and crisscrossed the pavement in golden streaks.

"This tunnel started with five hundred eucalyptus trees from Australia." He grinned at me in the rearview mirror and winked. "I tell this to every one of my passengers."

"You're a great tour guide," I said as I admired the scenery.

A few miles on, we drove through a town. We passed by a group of boys renting surfboards and snorkeling gear at a wooden storefront. Restaurants were filled with families, and people strolled around shopping plazas.

Elation bubbled inside my chest. I couldn't wait to explore the island and spend time with my family.

As I took in the serenity of the slow-paced life Kauai was known for, no sign remained of the rain except for the beautiful rainbow that shimmered across the sky. I had no doubt this Christmas would be special.

Chapter Two — My Family

Brandon turned into a neighborhood where the houses were close enough to feel neighborly, but separated by a good-sized lot for privacy. He slowed as a family of chickens made its way across the street. Not something you'd see every day on the streets of LA.

The cab slowed to a stop in front of a house. My sister and nephew ran across the yard. Two pairs of arms wrapped around me as soon as I got out of the taxi.

I squealed and hugged them tight. "Abby. Tyler. It's so good to see you."

We held each other as if we were each other's lifeline, and I didn't want to let go. I'd felt that way when I'd had to go home after Steve's funeral. The guilt of leaving had never subsided, but I was here now. We were together and that was all that mattered.

"I'm so glad you're here, Auntie Kate." My four-year-old nephew's voice was muffled, his face pressed to my stomach.

It was still so strange that Steve was gone. One less person to greet, one less hug. I could almost feel him with us. Any second now, my tall and lean brother-in-law would casually walk out the door and, being his usual shy self, would wait for an invitation before joining the hug.

My sister took the large duffel bag from me, and my shoulders welcomed the relief.

She narrowed her eyes. "Why are your jeans damp?"

I let out a light laugh and waved a hand. "A long story. I'll tell you later." Then I turned to Tyler. "Wow, look at you, Ty. You've grown so much." I ruffled his fine hair. "You're almost as tall as me."

He laughed, his brown eyes beaming. "No, I'm not. You're being silly."

Tyler had grown an inch taller and lost a little bit of his baby face. His features were similar to Steve's—sharp nose and square jaw—but sometimes when he smiled, he resembled my sister.

I dropped a big, fat, exaggerated kiss on his forehead and took his hand, leading him to the one-story house. Pampas grass and coconut trees ringed the front yard. We passed between two plumeria trees with yellow and white flowers on either side of the front walk.

The scent of sweet, ripe peaches embraced me when we entered. White plumeria flowers floated in a round glass bowl on the entryway table.

I slipped off my shoes and placed them next to Tyler's on a shoe rack. It felt strange not to see any of Steve's shoes, but my sister wouldn't leave his things around. I'd never thought about something like missing shoes being part of grief.

My sister had lived in an upscale apartment in New York City, but when Steve passed away, she'd moved to Kauai, where they'd gone for their honeymoon. Being here seemed to give her peace.

"I love what you did to the place." I glanced about the airy family room and set my purse on a wooden end table. "The pictures you sent didn't do it justice."

Abby waved a hand toward the hearth by the bookshelf. "I painted the stark white walls a warmer beige and put in hardwood floors before we moved in. It gave the house a new feel."

"It does, and your oil paintings look absolutely breathtaking." I went closer to examine a sun-soaked beach scene hanging beside the fireplace.

My sister had emailed me pictures of the landscapes of Kauai she'd painted but they were even more impressive in person. On the other side of the fireplace was a tropical mountain with a misty waterfall that gave the whole scene a pensive, slightly sad aura.

"I wanted to fill up the empty space. What's an artist if they don't display their work somewhere? Let me show you your room." Abby took my other bag and carried both down a short hall. "This is your room." She dropped my bags beside the bed. "It's small, but so is the rest of the house."

I sat on the bed, ignoring the damp and heavy material still clinging to me like a second layer of skin. I smoothed the flowered bedspread beside me. It had been a long day.

"It's perfect," I said. "This home is perfect. I'm glad you made the move. Steve would have loved it."

The room was only big enough for a queen bed and a dresser, but that was all I needed.

Abby's chest rose and fell as she breathed slowly. First Christmas without Steve was going to be hard for everyone but especially her and Tyler. He had passed away sooner than the doctors had expected.

Cancer, like everything in life, was a mystery. Even the experts couldn't predict the outcome. Illness not only ate away the victim's body, but it damaged the loved ones' souls.

Sometimes things happened when you least expected them to, both the good and the bad. But regardless, we had our health and each other. Though grief plagued our hearts, we found a way to move forward.

"Thank you. I needed to hear that." She blinked her teary eyes before meeting my gaze. "Sorry."

"It's okay." I put a gentle hand on her arm, but I wanted to do more than that. I wanted to take away her pain. "You're allowed to be sad. I'm here."

She nodded with her lips pressed tight and leaned her back against the wall, her arms crossed over her chest.

Even the strongest people need to be vulnerable.

Tyler stepped into the doorway and glanced between Abby and me with a serious expression. Then he dashed the short distance to his mother and linked his arms around his mom's waist.

"It's okay, Mommy."

His gentle voice nearly broke me. Such a brave boy. At such a tender age, no child should experience the loss of a parent. I wanted to put him in a bubble and keep him safe from the world.

Seeing him comforting his mother told me Abby was raising him well. Whatever she said or did to help him through his grief showed he was capable of empathy, no matter how cruelly life treated him.

I needed to change the subject before the three of us ended up in a crying session. Abby and I could talk later and sob in each other's arms if needed, but not in front of Tyler. Though we spoke often on the phone, Abby typically wasn't as emotional as she was being now.

I understood. Holidays were hard when a loved one wasn't around. It hadn't been that long since Steve had passed away. Christmas was supposed to be the happiest time of the year. I was going to make sure it was for them both.

"So, Ty, do you have a girlfriend?" This question should break up the sadness.

"Auntie *Kate.*" Tyler turned away from his mother and tilted his head, as his cheeks turned color.

Abby made a funny noise that sounded between laughter and choking and wiped the corner of her eyes with her knuckle.

"Oh. My. Goodness, you do?" I bent lower to be face-to-face with him. I loved seeing him flustered. He looked so adorable.

"No. She's just a friend." He curled his shoulders inward, shifting his stance from side to side, avoiding my eyes. "Mommy says it's okay to have a friend that's a girl." He peered up at Abby to confirm.

"She is absolutely right. Your mother is smart, but not as smart as me." I winked. "You should always listen to her."

"Yeah, Mommy says that all the time."

"Well …" Abby clapped her hands to get our attention. "Would you like something to drink? I was in the middle of making dinner. Let's go to the kitchen. We can talk there. You can unpack later, right?"

"Yes, I would love some tea." I rose from the bed. "And I can unpack my beautiful ballgown later."

My sister rolled her eyes and the corner of her mouth tugged a little, then she slipped out. Her footsteps headed toward the kitchen.

"But let me change first. I'll be right out," I called.

"Ballgown? Like Cinderella?" Tyler shook his head and strolled out of the room.

I took out a pair of jeans and a T-shirt from my duffel bag, changed, and tied my hair back.

While Tyler played with his building blocks on the living room rug, I leaned against the light wooden cabinet by the stove while Abby opened a cabinet. The appliances were white and minimal—unlike the state-of-the-art, stainless-steel stove and refrigerator she'd had in New York—but they fit the simple look.

"Here. Good for your soul." She handed me a steaming, fragrant mug and got back to stir-frying slices of chicken breast.

"Mmmm." I sighed deeply, savoring the warmth and the flavor. "You make the best tea." I flinched when the rice cooker beeped.

Abby threw cabbage and broccoli into the pan, sizzling with oil and garlic. "I'm sorry I couldn't pick you up at the airport."

"Would you stop apologizing? Just because you're older than me doesn't mean you have to take care of me. Besides, I'm here to take care of you and Tyler, not be an added responsibility."

"Thank you." She dashed some salt, chili powder, and hoisin sauce into the vegetables and mixed up the ingredients. "I had to meet a client at the gallery and I couldn't change the time." She lowered her voice so Tyler couldn't hear. "I really needed this sale."

Abby had worked in an art gallery in New York. When she'd moved to Kauai, she'd decided to open up a small one. I used to love painting too, but after Jayden broke my heart, I'd lost my confidence.

Abby had some of my oils on canvas hanging in her Kauai gallery. She'd even sold a couple. A long time ago, I'd pushed away the dream of being a painter and became a graphic designer so I could get a steady income; however, I did paint every chance I got. Or I had, before Jayden.

Sometimes I wished I could take the leap as Abby had and pursue my dream. If I knew for sure it would pay the bills, I just might quit my job and paint full time.

I took another sip of the passionfruit green tea and let out a long breath. "Like I said, I understand. Can I ask you a personal question? You don't have to answer if you don't want to, but I'm worried."

My sister gave me that stare but surprised me when she nodded.

I looked over my shoulder to make sure Tyler wasn't listening and then set my eyes on Abby. "Are you in financial trouble?"

Abby divided the stir-fry onto three plates, scooped some rice, and then handed two filled plates to me. "I have some savings. I'm okay for now. I've got enough rent money for the gallery, thanks to the person who purchased one of my paintings today, but who knows how long that will last."

I set the plates on the table. "Ty, dinner is ready."

Tyler peered up from the block tower he had been building, his big brown eyes wide and alert. The blocks toppled to the ground when his heel knocked against the base on his way to the table. He eased into his chair next to me and picked up a fork.

Abby grabbed her tablet off the counter, turned on background music, and sat across from me. A soft Christmas melody filtered through the house, filling my soul with peace.

"You've made it this far," I said. "You'll be fine, but if you—"

"Nope." She raised a hand. "I'm fine. But thank you."

If she needed financial help, she would reach out to our parents. Her pride wouldn't let her ask me. For her, it would mean she had failed because I was the younger one.

"But just in case." I wanted to stress my point.

We weren't little anymore. The little difference between our ages was nonessential. We should lean on each other through troubled times. Yes, we were sisters, but we were more than that. Best friends.

Abby shrank into her seat and smiled. "Thanks. I appreciate your concern. The future is unsteady and impossible to predict. That's the hardest part of this business. Sometimes I wish I had taken your route and opted for the steady income."

I took a bite of the delicious chicken and savored the sweet sauce. "Sometimes I wish I hadn't."

"Well …" Abby regarded Tyler with affection. "Let's put aside our worries for now and eat in peace. I'm glad you're here."

"Me too. It's going to be the best Christmas ever," Tyler said around a mouthful of rice.

He glanced up at me, then back to his plate. He did it a couple more times. When I pretended I wasn't looking at him, he quickly placed a few pieces of broccoli from his plate to mine. I smiled at his attempt at being inconspicuous and made a mental note not to feed Tyler broccoli.

At the mention of Christmas, I realized I hadn't noticed any holiday decorations. I glanced around to see if I'd missed them, but there were none. No Christmas tree. Not a single holly leaf or twinkling lights.

Simple furniture took up the cozy family room. A large family portrait of the three of them hung over the mantel and a few framed pictures of Mom, Dad, Abby, and me when we were younger sat on the end table.

Abby and I looked similar and yet different. We both had our father's eyes and our mother's smooth, pale skin, but I had inherited our mother's narrow jawline.

"So …" My sister cleared her throat, bringing me back to the present. "I didn't have a chance to get a tree."

Two cardboard boxes sat by the TV, marked *Christmas*. I jerked my head toward them.

Abby scrunched her nose and swallowed. "I haven't had time to unpack."

She meant it was too painful to look at the Christmas things she had collected over the years with Steve. Though I knew my sister was making an effort to be in the Christmas spirit for her son, her heart wasn't there. I didn't blame her.

"Leave that up to me." I poked through cabbage with my fork. "I'm good at unpacking."

"You don't have—"

"I know, but I want to help. What are sisters for?"

I meant it with all my heart. I also wanted to make up for when I hadn't been there for her. Jayden and I had been going through rough times and I hadn't been in a good mindset to help anyone.

Abby nodded and picked up a piece of broccoli with her fingers, but didn't eat it. "Have you spoken to Jayden lately?"

I knew Abby had been dying to ask that question. She hated my ex. Even before he had cheated on me, she'd always said he wasn't good enough for me.

I chewed on some cabbage and looked at Tyler, who smiled at me with curious eyes. Sometimes I didn't know what was appropriate to say around a child his age.

"I'll explain more in detail later, but …" I lowered my voice. "He called me before I left for the airport today and begged me to take him back again."

My sister's face contorted into something wild and dangerous as she dropped the sprig of broccoli. She could probably kill someone with that expression.

"You didn't, right? *Please* tell me you didn't."

Her volume and passion shocked me into silence. Even Tyler stopped chewing.

"No, of course not. I learned my lesson … twice."

Last Christmas, I'd spent the holiday with my boyfriend. The very next day, I'd found out he'd cheated on me. He'd begged me to take him back, and I had. A big mistake on my part, because he never left the other woman.

This Christmas, I planned to do things differently. Like forget him for good—forget all men in general. I didn't need love in my life—for now, at least. I just needed my family.

Abby lowered her shoulders, her voice softening. "Well, you shouldn't have had to learn that lesson, and once is plenty. Maybe you'll meet someone nice over the holiday and move here permanently." She offered a sly but hopeful smile.

"I don't think so. Besides, I don't need a man to convince me to stay. It'll be on my own terms if I decide." I sipped my warm tea. "Anyway, when are Mom and Dad coming? I know they're going on a cruise but I forgot the dates."

"They'll be here before Christmas. They plan to spend a week here and then fly back home to LA."

"So what's the plan for tomorrow? You don't work on Sunday, do you?"

"No, I'll show you around." She waved a forkful of chicken through the air. "But I might go in for a little while to do some work."

"Sounds like a plan." I held up my fork as if I was giving her a thumbs up.

After dinner, while my sister did the dishes, Tyler and I played a game on Abby's tablet. The object was to splash paint over the other player's territory. Sometimes, on my bad days, I wished I could make that kind of mess on my canvas. But I never had the courage to cut loose. Not in life or in art.

Chapter Three – Poipu Shopping Plaza

Tyler pounced on my bed far too early and begged me to get up. After breakfast, while Abby went to work, I helped Tyler build a city with building blocks and read him several books. When my sister came back, we went to Poipu Plaza and had lunch at a quaint restaurant.

"Look at all the decorations," Tyler said as we strolled down the plaza after lunch, bouncing at my side.

Wreaths adorned with baubles coiled around the poles. Strings of lights framed the shop windows. A tall Christmas tree was stationed in the middle of the plaza, covered with gold trimmings and oversized ornaments. The festive embellishments lifted my spirits, and for a moment all my worries were nonexistent.

"When do we get to decorate our house?" he asked.

I squeezed Tyler's hand. "Very soon. I promise."

Tyler, sandwiched between Abby and me, peered up at his mom. "What about the Christmas tree?"

"We'll get one today," Abby said.

"Yippee." Tyler jumped and swung his legs forward, pulling on our hands for support.

Abby and I stumbled forward, and I nearly dropped the camera hiked over my shoulder. The three of us laughed as we meandered past the bakery, jewelry, and clothing shops.

"Wow. Look at the view of the ocean." I let go of Tyler's hand and took a step back. Releasing my lens, I aimed to get the perfect angle shot between the ice cream shop and the small market.

I took pictures of the sparkling ocean reflecting golden hues and the puffy white clouds decorating the blue canvas like swirls of whipped cream. Then I focused on my sister and Tyler. My camera clicked almost continuously.

"That's enough, Kaitlyn. Stop taking pictures." Abby waved a hand, annoyed.

"Okay. I'm done. I'm thinking I can blow them up and you can sell them." I carefully covered the lens and walked beside Tyler.

Abby halted, her forehead creasing as if she were in thought. "That's a good idea. See what you can do."

I appreciated my sister trying not to talk me into painting again. She knew I would do it when I was ready, but her quick acceptance of my idea took me by surprise.

"Can I have shaved ice, Mommy?" Tyler asked.

"Sure. I think your aunt would like one too."

"Shaved ice, you say? I've always wanted to try it. Do they actually taste like snow?"

Tyler let out a cute sound. "No, Auntie Kate. You're silly."

He laughed, swinging his arm along with the rhythm of our steps. While we stood in line, I glanced at the list of flavors attached to the door. Strawberry, mango, and the list went on. After I picked out the flavor, I released the cover on the lens and prepped my camera.

The vibrant colors caught my eye. I raised my camera and took pictures again. In the middle of the outdoor shopping plaza, local vendors set up their displays of fruits, flowers, handmade jewelry, candles, and many more items on individual tables.

I took pictures of the fruits: mangos, papayas, pineapples, and lychees. The massive lens I'd gotten from my parents last Christmas came in handy when wanting to take pictures from a distance. I also took some of the surrounding shops and the Christmas decorations.

When I focused at the greatest distance, the background blur resolved into a restaurant we had passed on the way. Then I zoomed out a few yards and focused on a man wearing a white, long-sleeved button-down shirt, sitting on a bench with one arm resting on the top. Only his profile was visible.

Curious about the woman next to him, I continued to invade their privacy. It was through the lens, after all. No harm in that, right? I couldn't see her face, only the long, blonde hair hanging down her back and the ankle-skimming violet dress she wore, billowing with the soft breeze.

They seemed to be in a heated conversation. The woman turned in her seat, and I got a glimpse of her beautiful face. She pointed to a store and said something. Then the man shifted to look in the same direction, giving me a clear view.

I blinked.

Leonardo.

I lowered my camera, flushing volcano hot. Then slowly I raised my camera again. His face made my heart skip as it had in the cab.

What was I doing spying on him? And worse, I felt a tiny tinge of jealousy when he caressed the woman's face.

"What are you doing?" Abby placed a gentle hand on my arm.

Click.

Crap. I'd accidentally taken a picture.

I jerked guiltily and dropped my camera to my chest. Had it not been for the strap around my neck, the camera might have fallen and shattered.

As if Leonardo had sensed me watching, he had chosen that moment to look straight at the camera. Or at least it seemed he had.

"Nothing. Just checking my view." Heat suffused my face again.

"Mommy, we're next." Tyler pulled on Abby's arm.

"What can I get you ladies?" a young guy asked, smiling.

Abby leaned closer and took out her wallet. "Two please. One strawberry for my sister …" She looked at me to confirm. When I nodded, she continued. "Another one with mango." After Abby paid, she grabbed some napkins. "My treat," she said.

I didn't argue. I would return the favor next time.

"Yummy." Tyler took a small bite and exited the double doors.

"This way to the Farmer's Market." I tipped my head to the side and stole a quick glimpse at Leonardo, who still sat on the bench with the woman. I had to look away, so I distracted myself. "Let's buy some fruit."

"I like the mangoes." He poked one. "Can we get mangoes, too, Auntie Kate?"

"Ty, keep your hands to yourself, please." Abby gently pulled back his arm and looked at me. "You were always the fruit lover. I'll hold your shaved ice for you."

"Thanks." I picked out a few papayas and mangoes and handed them to the lady running the shop.

The seller placed my purchases in a brown paper bag. "That'll be fifteen."

"You didn't buy any passionfruit. Have you ever tried those?" Abby picked up two and handed them to the lady. "They were Steve's favorite."

The vendor leaned closer. "People say that it increases your sex drive." She winked. "That'll be twenty."

"Oh, no." Abby shook her head, flushing pink. "Not me. I don't need … I haven't … I mean … never mind." With cheeks burning red and wetness in her eyes, Abby rushed to the next table selling flowers.

At that moment I realized my sister wasn't herself. She was always the confident one. She could give anyone a straight answer, even if the topic was awkward.

Ever since we were little, she had been my voice, the one who spoke up for me. I was the shy one, and I couldn't remember ever seeing her flustered before. Yes, she was still grieving, but I didn't want her pain to drive her into depression.

I had no one to tie me to Los Angeles anymore. I didn't love my job. Perhaps it was time for a change.

My sister and I had both been born and raised in Los Angeles, and we'd graduated from USC with degrees in illustration. City life was what made me stay in the first place. Something about the bustle made me feel young and vital.

Shops, theaters, restaurants, and bars—anything you wanted was right there. The night life was alive and fun. In Kauai, stores closed early. Besides water sports, there wasn't much to do.

"My sister is … Thank you." I didn't know what to say to the lady as I handed over the money and joined my sister by the flower vendor.

"Tyler. Come here. You're spilling all over your shirt." Abby wiped his mouth with a napkin, sounding irritated.

It seemed the fruit vendor had touched a nerve.

"I can't help it. It's melting." He licked faster, orange-yellow juice smeared over his chin.

"Let's move away." I gave an apologetic smile to the middle-aged gentleman who seemed nervous Tyler would get the sticky liquid on the hibiscus. "So, I was thinking," I said as we strolled past more shops. Perhaps I could put her in a better mood.

"About?" Abby threw the used napkins into the trash, her tone still sharp.

I handed her the bag of fruits and grabbed the shaved ice from her.

"I'm thinking maybe I'll look for a job in Kauai. Then I can move here permanently and be close to you," I said and took a bite.

The icy treat numbed my mouth and speared through my forehead. I held up a hand as I shivered through the brain freeze. The chill passed and tangy, sweet strawberry flavor melted on my tongue.

I proceeded along the sidewalk, but when I noticed she wasn't beside me, I grabbed Tyler, who was oblivious to everything except his shaved ice, and waited for Abby to catch up. She had been looking at something through the jewelry store window.

"Are you serious about moving here?" Her eyes widened with a happy glow as she matched my slow steps.

It was a picture-perfect moment. I was tempted to take a photo of her, but I knew she would bite my head off.

I hiked a shoulder. "I'm thinking about it. I have two interviews lined up."

Living from paycheck to paycheck was arduous and stressful enough. If I wanted to live in Kauai, I needed to find a job.

"What?" She squealed and then lowered her voice. "Why didn't you tell me?"

"I didn't want to get your hopes up. Even if I get an offer, I might not take it if it doesn't feel right. You know how much I love the city. I also want to be close to you, but I don't know how long I can handle being surrounded by water. You understand, don't you?"

"Of course I do." Abby softened her voice. "I don't want you to feel like you have to live here on account of me. I'll be fine. Ty and I will be fine. We'll be."

My heart cracked at her uncertainty. It sounded like she meant to convince herself, not me.

"When's the interview and where?" Her lips flattened in a thin line, hindering her smile.

"Tomorrow, late afternoon, at Poipu Design." I took another bite.

"I was going to take you to my gallery but that can wait. Do you need a ride?" She placed the bag of fruits in front of her chest and wrapped her arms around it.

"No, I'm fine. I'll call a driver. Besides, you need to be at your gallery. Someone has to pay the bills. Geesh, look at you trying to get out of work. Slacker."

Abby shoved me lightly and then linked her arm with mine as we continued our stroll. On my other side, Tyler slid a small, sticky hand into mine.

"I'm so happy you're spending Christmas with us this year," she said as we passed the bakery.

My heart swelled, easing the guilt I still carried for spending Christmas last year with my ex.

Jayden and I had been having problems and I'd decided to stay to work things out. If I'd left to be with family while things between us were unsettled, I would have been a Grinch. I wouldn't have wanted to go anywhere or do anything, aside from sulk in bed. I'd thought I was sparing them the annoyance.

Jayden and I had talked about visiting my sister together. We'd planned to go snorkeling, drive along the beach, and eat all the shaved ice possible. But now I was here without him. Life was unpredictable that way.

I reminded myself I was there to lighten the mood for all of us, not wallow in the past. "Let's get out of here and get our Christmas tree. What do you say?"

"Yes. Yes. Yes." Tyler whooped and pumped a fist in the air.

Before I turned toward Abby's car, I glanced over my shoulder, hoping for one last glimpse at Leonardo. But he was gone, and so was his beautiful companion.

Chapter Four – The Interview

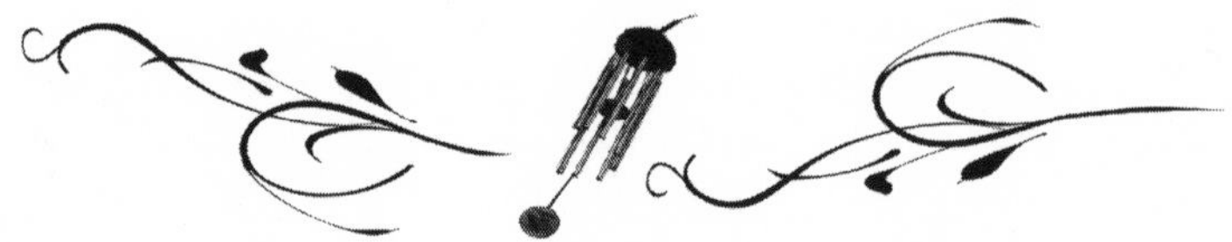

Abby left to take Tyler to daycare and then go to her gallery, while I had the morning to myself.

The scent of fresh pine filled the air from the Christmas tree. I felt like I was standing in the middle of a forest. Christmas always brought out the kid in me. I couldn't wait for Abby and Tyler to see the fully decorated house.

After I made some coffee, I blasted Christmas music on my phone. "Deck the Halls" played and I sang along while opening the boxes marked *Christmas.*

I placed a couple of snowmen made out of socks by the six-foot tree we had set up by the hearth. Any bigger and we wouldn't have been able to lug it on top of Abby's minivan.

I reached inside the box and picked up a photo of Steve, Abby, and Tyler in front of a brightly lit tree, and then another one with a Santa Claus in the background. As tears pooled in my eyes, I placed them back in and decided to ask Abby what to do with them. She might not be ready.

Next, I took out three plush red stockings, each embellished with a name: Tyler. Abby. Steve. I traced Steve's name over the soft material as an ache squeezed my lungs. I missed him, and I missed my sister's joy. I placed his stocking back and hung the other two on the mantel.

My brother-in-law had been the sweetest. He had the biggest heart, and they were a perfect team. Where Steve lacked creativity, Abby made up for it, and where my sister lacked financial knowhow, my brother-in-law excelled at it. I wished things had turned out differently.

I placed Santa Claus on the end table and tucked reindeer trinkets on bookshelves. Then I covered the front door in metallic silver wrapping paper with a big red bow on it. It looked like a huge present. I couldn't wait for Tyler to come home and see it.

As a child, I'd found decorating the tree the most memorable part of Christmas besides opening presents, so I decided to wait for Tyler and Abby. It should be a family activity, anyway.

By the time I had finished decorating, I still had time to spare. I picked up Tyler's blocks scattered in the family room and piled them into a plastic container, tidied up the house, ate lunch, and dressed up for my interview.

Poipu Design was in a low, flat building—nothing like my tall, gleaming office in Los Angeles—but the interior was well designed and modern. Everything in the office space was white and spic-and-span clean.

"Hello, may I help you?" the young woman at the front desk asked.

"Hi, my name is Kaitlyn Chang. I'm here for the four o'clock interview."

The woman glanced at her clipboard and looked back to me. "Oh, yes. I have you down. Please have a seat."

I inhaled a deep breath, settled into the white leather sofa, and scrolled through the pictures on my cell phone to pass the time. Pictures of my parents, Abby, Tyler, and Steve, my friends, and even Jayden.

Jayden had his arms wrapped around me from behind, his chin resting on my shoulder. I'd thought he was the one. I'd thought we were going to get married and have a family. Tyler wouldn't have been the only grandchild.

I closed my picture app so I didn't have to see his blue eyes and cocky smile. What on earth was I doing at a job interview an ocean away from my home? Was I running away from Jayden? Perhaps I didn't have a clear direction in life.

Just as I seriously considered bailing, a middle-aged woman walked out from a closed door with a kind smile.

"Ms. Chang?"

"Yes." I stood, focusing on the present.

"I'm Judy Jones. It's nice to meet you." She shook my hand. "Please, follow me to my office."

"Honey, I'm home," I belted as I entered Abby's house.

"Auntie Kate." Tyler charged across the room and grabbed my waist in a hug. "Look at our house." He pointed out the Santa Claus and reindeer trinkets. "I love the door. It looks like a present. Mommy said you did it." He tugged at the red ribbon as if he might be able to open it after all.

I snickered, loving the joy on his face. At first, I'd debated waiting for them to decorate the house, but now I knew I made the right decision. "Do you like it?"

"I love it. Thank you." He squeezed me tighter. "It's so cool. It feels like Christmas, finally."

I relished the warm tug in my heart. "Good. That makes me happy." I kissed his forehead and stroked his back. "Hey, Ty. How was your day?"

"Good until Bridget went home. She got a fever." Tyler touched his forehead and frowned.

I kicked off my shoes by the door as I inhaled the scent of the plumeria inside the glass bowl. It was soon replaced by the aroma of miso salmon the farther I walked into the house.

"Bridget is …?" I took his hand and followed the delicious smell to the kitchen.

"Bridget is my friend from school." Tyler hiked himself up on the stool.

A bottle of red wine and two filled glasses were on the granite counter. I peeked into the oven and watched as Abby broke apart butter lettuce with her hands.

"Don't worry about Bridget, Ty," I said. "All she needs is medicine and a good sleep. She'll be fine. I promise. You've been sick before, right?"

"Yes." He arched his eyebrows as he tilted his head. He looked confused, but brushed it off. "Mommy, when's dinner? I'm hungry," he said with a whine.

Abby stopped arranging the salad on the plates and furrowed her brow. "Excuse me, young man. Is that how you ask for dinner?"

Tyler dipped his head. "No. Sorry. When's dinner, *please*?" He flashed all his teeth with an exaggerated grin.

Abby perked her lips, trying not to laugh. "Much better. How about you help me put the salad plates on the table?"

Tyler hopped off the stool, and Abby handed him the plates from the counter. He shuffled away holding himself stiffly as if his task was vitally important.

Abby picked up the tray of baked salmon from the stove and then faced me, holding out the platter. "Your turn. Put this on the table. And … how was your interview?"

"Fine," I said quickly and headed to the dining table to avoid the topic.

"Did they say anything after the interview?" Abby sat across from me and handed me a glass of wine. She then scooped up a piece of salmon and placed it on Tyler's plate. Absent-mindedly she cut his fish into bites with her fork.

I took a bite of my fish and hummed. "Yummy. You make the best miso salmon."

"Don't change the subject, Kate."

I poked my fork in the air toward her and narrowed my eyes. "I didn't. And my interview … It went well, but …" I cringed.

She stilled, her fork stabbed into a cucumber. "But …"

I released a frustrated sigh. "She said I was over-qualified."

"What do you mean *over-qualified*?" She knew what I meant. It was a rhetorical question. "Maybe start off doing simple things and then she can change your job description as she gives you more responsibility?"

She hoped I would get a job so I would stay, but what she was suggesting was ridiculous.

"She won't be able to pay me the same salary or even close to it."

"Oh." Her tone pitched lower. "I guess it's a no then."

I took a big bite of butter lettuce. "I have another interview tomorrow. Maybe it'll be better."

Her eyes lit up. "Okay. Well, good luck."

"Thanks." I took a sip of my wine and savored the light, fruity taste. "How was your day? Did you sell any paintings?"

Abby scooted her lettuce to the side of the plate, her attention elsewhere, and then met my gaze. "No, but we had a few customers stopping by—mostly tourists. They loved the paintings, but either they didn't want to pay for shipping or it was too expensive. Maybe I should have a sale."

"*No*." I winced and lowered my voice. "People don't understand the time, sweat, and passion you pour on the canvas. You're not a student. You've had your work displayed in well-known New York galleries. You are worth every penny, Abby. Don't sell yourself short. If they don't want to pay the price, then too bad for them. They don't deserve a piece of your soul."

At least that was how I felt after I finished a painting, like I had given a slice of my soul. Every stroke of the brush was a glimpse of my thoughts, hopes, and dreams. All that time and energy spent, I fell in love with all my creations and hated selling them.

My sister chewed her bottom lip, taking in my words. "You're right. Thank you for the reminder."

"You've sold many paintings in New York and your prices were pretty high, competitive to others of your caliber. Don't downgrade yourself."

"Okay. I get it." She sighed and smiled at her son sitting next to me.

Her love. Her life. Everything she did was for him. I could only imagine how difficult it must be to raise a child by herself. All the more reason I should try to help her in any way, including financially.

Tyler rested his chin on his knuckles, his elbow planted on the table. With his other hand, he flicked the salmon with his fork.

"Ty. You okay?" I asked.

He had been quiet during dinner and wasn't listening to the conversation like he usually did.

"Is Bridget going to be okay?" Tyler's lips curled downward, his shoulders slumping.

"Bridget is going to be fine. You'll see." I rubbed Tyler's hair. "How about after dinner we decorate the tree?"

"Okay." He sat up taller and began to eat again.

I cleared my throat to get Abby's attention. My sister was staring at the two red stockings hanging on the mantel. She must be thinking about the one that should have been there. Her glassy eyes made mine fill with tears. When she shifted her attention to me, her lips spread—only a little, but a smile nevertheless.

"Kate, thanks again for brightening up this house." She lowered her voice to a whisper. "I don't think I could have done it."

"I know. It's okay, Abby. I'm here. Let me be your strength as long as you need."

Abby nodded and dabbed the corner of her eyes. "Having you here makes a difference. You're all I need."

Chapter Five – Sick Day

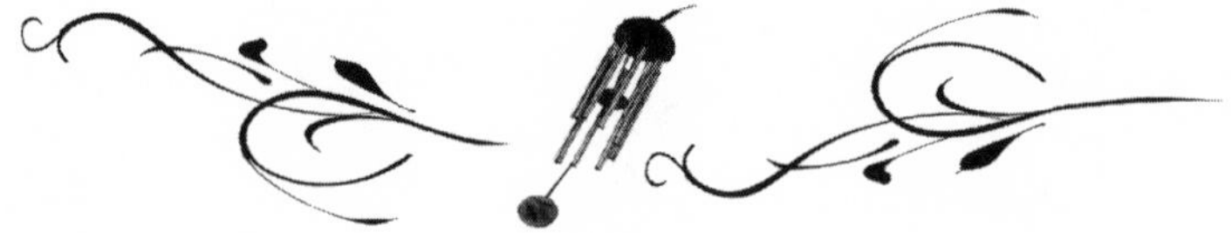

"I'm sorry I'm late for dinner," I hollered into the house the next day and leaned my damp umbrella next to the entryway table. After the second interview, I'd decided to stroll on the beach and take pictures. It had sprinkled at first and then the rain had come tumbling down. Luckily, there had been a convenience store nearby with umbrellas in stock. I didn't mind getting wet, but I didn't want to ruin my camera.

"Hello?" No one had come to greet me. Not even Tyler.

Abby dragged her feet out of her bedroom wearing a white bathrobe, sipping from a mug I had gifted her for Christmas two years past that read *Mother Knows Best.*

I furrowed my brow and laid my camera on the side table. As I headed for the kitchen, Abby's slippers slapped along the hardwood floor.

"Are you ready for bed already?" I stopped beside the sink, blocking her way. "Aren't you going to …"

She ran her fingers through her messy hair as if she'd just woken up. Then she rubbed her watery, red eyes, and itched the pink and raw area around her nose.

"Oh, Abby, you're sick." I gave her a sympathetic frown, and then I took out a teabag from the cabinet and a mug from the dish rack. "You were fine last night. What happened?"

She leaned against the wall by the stove and rubbed at her neck. "I woke up with a sore throat. I took some medicine but it kept getting worse. I picked up Tyler early from daycare. I think he gave me whatever is going around his class."

Last night, we decorated the tree with ornaments and strung the multicolored flashing lights. Tyler had been running a slight fever at bedtime, so we'd given him medicine and put him to bed early, and he had been fine in the morning.

I had warned my sister not to sleep with him, but of course she hadn't listened. Abby was prone to catching colds; she had missed more school days than I ever had.

"I told you he would get you sick. You should have told him to sleep in his own room." I didn't mean to sound like a scolding mother, but this could have been avoided.

"I know, but he was scared." She rubbed the warmth from her mug as she shuffled to the dining table. "It's just that he's growing up so fast, and pretty soon he won't need me."

I couldn't claim to know how she felt, but if I felt helpless, I could only imagine her distress. "How's he feeling?" I poured hot water into the mug and watched the steam rise.

Abby eased into the dining chair, and the vinyl squeaked as she shifted. "He doesn't have a fever. He's in his room watching cartoons. I told him he had to sleep by himself until I get better."

I sat across from her and took a slow drink. "Good. And if he gets scared, I'll have him sleep with me."

"Thanks." She massaged her temples.

"What are sisters for?" I flashed an exaggerated smile.

She twisted her mouth to the side. "Speaking of what are sisters for … I need a favor."

"Of course, just let me know." I sipped my tea and placed my mug on the table with a light thud.

"I need you to work for me tomorrow. Stella will be there to answer phone calls. I just need you to answer questions for the customers, if there are any. And hopefully sell a piece."

"Stella?"

"She's fairly new and recently graduated from college. She wanted to take a year off before jumping into grad school. She's trying to figure things out."

"Aren't we all," I murmured.

Secretly I had always wanted to own my own gallery, and I wanted to see hers. I traced the palm tree design on the mug with my thumb. "Sure. I can be there as many days as you need."

"Thank you. Do you have other interviews lined up?"

"No. I only had two."

"Are you sure you can work for me tomorrow? I hate to ask, but—"

"It's fine, Abby. You were going to take me with you tomorrow anyway."

Abby nursed her tea, holding it close to her chest. Her gaze darted to the Christmas tree by the hearth. "True, but not to work there. But if you had other plans, you don't have to change it. I can arrange—"

"I said it's fine." My tone went sharp with annoyance.

She offered a tender smile. "Thank you. I owe you one."

"You don't owe me squat."

I shifted my attention to the window, where movement caught my eye. I'd thought I'd seen a cab, which made me think of Leonardo. Actually, every cab made me think of him, and there were plenty on this island, especially since Abby's house bordered an area with several hotels.

I hadn't expected to see him again, but there he'd been at the shopping plaza with a beautiful woman. Poipu wasn't a big city and I wondered if I would run into him again. If I did, what would I say? Would he remember me?

A guy who paid for strangers' cab rides without expecting anything in return wasn't the kind of person you met every day. Everybody had a story to tell. I wondered what his was.

Being a painter had enhanced my natural curiosity. In one of my college classes, I'd had to people-watch for a project and capture their emotions on the canvas. I always imagined people as paintings and tried to read their emotions. But Leonardo was hard to read, and his aura of reserve intrigued me. He didn't seem to be the type of man that wore his heart on his sleeve.

"How was your interview today?" My sister's weak voice pulled my gaze away from the window.

"The interview went well. We'll see. Anyway, have you ever had anyone pay for your cab before?" It didn't make sense to keep thinking about that brief encounter, but if anyone, I could talk to my sister about it.

She leaned closer, her deep brown eyes locked on mine. "Why do you ask?"

"To make a long story short, when I got in a cab at the airport, a good looking guy was already inside. I tried to get out, but he insisted I stay. He even paid for my ride."

I skipped how he'd made the air hotter and how I'd wanted him to share a ride with me so I could savor the feeling a little longer.

My sister gave me a sidelong glance and narrowed her eyes at me. "Why did you get in when there was someone else already inside?"

I jerked a shoulder. "Like I said, it's a long story."

"To answer your question, no. No one has ever done that, handsome or not."

"It's no big deal."

My sister opened her mouth to speak, but then footsteps pattered into the room.

"Auntie Kate. You're home." Tyler dashed over and nestled his head on my shoulder. He smelled of vanilla and honey, the kids' soap Abby had used since he was a baby.

"Hey Ty." I kissed his cheek and laid my palm against his forehead. No fever. *Perfect.* "You feeling better?"

"Yes, but Mommy is sick." He peered up through his long eyelashes at my sister, a rueful pout on his face, and then he pulled out a chair and plopped next to me. "That makes me feel bad."

Sometimes Tyler surprised me. Maybe I didn't know much about kids, but he seemed older than four years old.

"I coughed with my mouth closed and I washed my hands like Mrs. Fong told us to," he added. "I didn't mean to get Mommy sick."

"Your mom will be fine. We'll take good care of her. Sound like a plan?" I ruffled his hair to lighten the mood. "Besides, it's your mom's fault for loving you too much."

He arched his eyebrows at me and gave in to my silliness. "Can loving someone too much make you sick?"

It does when he doesn't love you enough back. It hurts like hell.

I squashed those thoughts and simply said, "Not that kind of love. Come on, I'm starving. Want to help me make some chicken soup?"

"Can I stir it in the big pot?" He tugged me out of the chair.

Chapter Six – Game Time

While Tyler and I made chicken soup and turkey and avocado sandwiches, Abby went to her room to lie down.

"What's an interview?" Tyler tried to talk and slurp at the same time, and dribbled broth down his chin.

I wiped my mouth with a napkin and handed him one across the table. "An interview is like a meeting. You meet the person who is doing the hiring and you talk. For example, she asked me questions about where I worked before, and I answered. I asked them questions too. Now I wait to see if they want to hire me."

Tyler stuck out his tongue in concentration, carefully peeling the crust off the bread. "What if they hire you? Are you going to leave us?"

"No, silly. That's a whole different story. Drink your soup before it gets cold." I jerked my chin to his bowl.

He relaxed his shoulders. "Oh, good. I like it when you stay with us. Mom smiles more. And you play video games with me."

Something warm tugged my heart. "I like staying with you too." I tapped his nose. "And I like playing video games with you."

Tyler offered a huge grin. "Is Mommy going to eat?"

I glanced at the closed bedroom door and took a bite of my sandwich. An avocado slice squeezed out the other side and fell on my plate. I picked it up and shoved it in my mouth.

"She's resting right now. I'll check up on her later. She'll eat when she's hungry. Don't worry about her. You got better, right?"

"Yup." He kicked his dangling feet and got back to eating.

I stared at Tyler, surprised how much he had grown up. He was close to five. A year ago, he'd answer my questions and the conversation was mostly one-sided.

Abby was right. He was growing up quickly. It felt like a blink of an eye. I wanted to spend as much time with him as I could before heading back to my life in LA. I still hoped something would come out of the two interviews, but the first one hadn't panned out.

In truth, I probably wouldn't take the second job if they offered. The salary wasn't close to what I was getting paid, and they hadn't factored in the cost of living adjustment. But I didn't have the heart to tell Abby.

"After dinner, after we clean up, we can play your favorite game. What do you think?"

"Okay." He furrowed his brow. "Auntie Kate, have you heard of a game called *Unicorns versus Skeletons*?"

"Yes. It's one of my favorite games. I have it on my phone."

"You do?"

"It might be hard to believe, but grown-ups play games too." I swallowed a spoonful of hot soup.

"But Mommy doesn't play any games."

"Some grown-ups don't and that's okay."

Tyler ran the crust of his bread around the plate like a train. "My friend Jace, his dad plays video games with him. Do you think my dad would have played with me?"

Oh, my heart. I had to pause because my breath caught. "Yes, Ty. He would have done many things with you. You two would've had the best time." I kissed his forehead, blinking away the tears pooling in my eyes.

I had spoken the truth. Abby had told me Steve had been a hands-on dad. He'd helped with changing diapers and even burping his son. And when Tyler had gotten older, he'd taught him how to catch a ball and had read to him often.

Steve had been an ideal husband and dad, the kind I hoped to find one day when I was ready to settle down. I'd thought Jayden might be the one, but turned out he was more into getting noticed by other women.

"Can you show me how to play better?" Tyler nibbled on his sandwich.

"Sure." My heart hurting for his loss, I would bring down the stars for him if it would help him feel better.

"Am I going to school tomorrow?"

"Yes. I'm going to take you."

"You are?" Tyler opened his mouth wide. "Yippee. I can't wait for you to meet my friends."

After we cleaned up, Tyler followed me to my room and stood in front of me while I sat on my bed.

He beamed like sunshine and handed me Abby's tablet. "I practiced a little when you were at your—what's that word … inner … no—interview. My friends are good at it, especially Jace. And Bridget started playing it and she's really good too."

"That's okay. Everyone is different. Maybe Jace is better because he played longer than you. Let me show you some tips." I patted my comforter.

Tyler plopped beside me and leaned closer, his brown eyes wide and his long eyelashes blinking. When he looked at me like that, I saw Abby. She wore the same expression when she was uncertain.

I tapped the home button. Then I pressed the *Unicorns versus Skeletons* app. The game popped up with a catchy tune.

Tyler and I laughed and bobbed our shoulders to the music, sometimes bumping lightly into each other. There were unicorns on the left and skeletons waiting to attack on the right. In between were flowers lined in rows.

"Attack." Tyler clutched his hands together in anticipation.

I rapidly tapped the screen. The unicorns' horns touched the flowers. After the flowers turned golden, they opened up their petals then swallowed the nearby skeletons.

"The trick of the game is not to panic and to concentrate only on the flowers that are in front of the unicorns," I said.

"Ohhhh." Tyler's eyes grew wider and moved his fingers near mine, mimicking my movement.

"Would you like to play?"

"Nah. I'm not good at it." He shook his head and curled his lips downward.

"Just because you're not good at something, does that mean you stop trying?"

"No." He dipped his chin lower, as if embarrassed.

"I can help you."

Furrowing his brow, he chewed on his bottom lip. "Okay."

I guided Tyler at first, but he began to maneuver the unicorns on his own. Tyler whooped in the air when he cleared stage one. A glowing rainbow arched across the screen.

"I did it!" He bounced on the bed, so I seesawed next to him.

"See, you can do anything. You just have to try." I gave him a high five.

"You're right," he said with the same excited tone, passing the tablet to me. "It's your turn, Auntie Kate." When the flowers ate the skeletons, he chanted, "Eat it, eat it, eat it."

Tyler and I cackled with exhilaration and we moved onto a higher level.

"Eat it. Eat it. You piece of …" I bit my tongue just in time when the screen went blank. "What happened? Sh—" I slapped my hand over my mouth. "I meant … sham."

Tyler crossed his arms. "Sham? That's not a word. I know what you were going to say. I've heard it before, plenty of times from you and Mommy."

I snickered and frowned.

"That's okay. Mommy says it all the time and asks me not to say it out loud." He brought his voice to a whisper, his eyes glinting with mischief. "But I say it when I'm in my room alone."

We shared a laugh.

He's the cutest.

"But seriously, did you forget to charge this or did we break it?"

He jerked a shoulder. "I'll go charge it. Can we play later?"

"Sure. I'm going to work on a few things on my computer. Let me know when you're ready." I needed to return emails and look for other jobs, then perhaps read an urban fantasy novel about the Greek gods I'd bought for this trip.

"Okie dokie." Tyler skipped out of my room.

Chapter Seven – Carousel Art Gallery

"You're taking me to school, right?" Tyler leaned his elbows on the dining table and scooped up a spoonful of cereal I had poured for him.

I massaged his shoulders, tickling him. "Yes. And I'm going to pick you up, too."

Tyler giggled and squirmed. He went back to his eating, swinging his legs, humming to the tune of *Unicorns versus Skeletons.*

That kid. He has my heart.

I weaved around the dining table, put my coffee mug on the counter, and headed to Abby's room.

"I'll be right back," I said. "I'm going to check up on your mother."

Abby lay with multiple pillows supporting her back and her eyes closed. Nyquil and a water bottle were on the bedside table beside her cell phone, a blown-glass lamp, and a photo of Steve. She seemed to be sleeping, so I took a step out of her room.

"Hey. You ready for work?" Her voice sounded dry and hoarse.

I leaned against the door and crossed my arms. "Just about. Don't worry about anything. I'll take care of Ty, take care of the gallery, and I'll even get dinner ready … or I'll pick up something on the way home."

She closed her eyes halfway and lowered her voice to a whisper. "Thank you. You're good for something, I guess." She tried to laugh, but she coughed instead.

I gave her a half-hearted smile. "Guess I am. I gotta go. I'll call you later."

"Thanks, little sis." She closed her eyes and grunted softly. "I hate being sick, but I'm so glad you're here."

Me, too. If I weren't here, she would've had to rely on someone else. Abby had made some friends in Poipu, but I didn't know how close she was to them.

I eased the door closed and went to my room. I wished good things for her. Hopefully, her gallery would do well and she wouldn't have to work so hard.

Maybe I should create some pieces for her to sell, but I needed to get my creative juices back first. Not sure when that would happen. It had been a year since I'd picked up a paintbrush. After the first breakup, I had no desire to paint.

"Ty, you almost done with breakfast?" I shouted from my room.

"Yes," he yelled.

I slung my purse over my shoulder and headed toward his voice. No Tyler at the dining table. Where had he gone? I turned to head toward his room and heard a squeak.

"I'm right here." He giggled.

Tyler was standing in front of the door. I didn't know how I'd missed him.

"I'm proud of you for being ready." I helped him put on his light jacket and opened the door.

"Yeah. Mommy says that all the time."

"She should." I winked.

I called a driver and led Tyler outside. We waited on the sidewalk by a coconut tree. When the car came, we hopped in. After about a ten-minute drive, we arrived at Poipu Preschool.

A Christmas tree stood in the corner of the front office, and flashing lights adorned the wreath around the receptionist's desk. Pictures of snowmen, Santa Claus, reindeer, and stockings on fireplaces, illustrated by the children, hung on the large bulletin board.

Some kids waved at Tyler and a few mothers smiled when our gazes met.

"Auntie Kate, you have to sign your name." Tyler pointed at a paper on a clipboard on the table next to the office desk.

I had been drawn to the cute pictures and forgotten to check Tyler in.

"Oh, sorry." I scribbled my name on the sheet and set the pen down. "There. I'm done. Now what?"

"Bye." He gave me a high five and dashed inside the classroom.

My focus shifted back to the bulletin board and then to a smaller board next to it, plastered with notes and fliers that looked unofficial. A *wanted* post caught my attention with a phone number listed below.

Requiring a nanny for two weeks. Call Mona.

I fished out my cell from my purse and took a picture of the ad. *Maybe.* I was good with kids. Just as long as they weren't infants.

Since the interviews hadn't panned out, I'd started considering my other options. Rather than looking for the perfect job, I'd started wondering about *any* job, even if I had to hop around for a while. I also could help my sister at the gallery.

The idea had come to me that morning, but I didn't know if I wanted to carry it through. It might derail my career, or it could lead to something I hadn't even imagined yet.

I peeked at Tyler and smiled through the glass door. He was chatting away with two friends on the carpet with books open. They must be Jace and Bridget. I imagined him telling them how he'd beaten his own high score in *Unicorns versus Skeletons.* With a quick wave, I left.

I strolled down the sidewalk with the warm sun on my face, admiring the quaint bakeries and shops selling hand-made jewelry. A few minutes later, I'd arrived at Abby's gallery.

I stood in front of a huge, bold blue sign that read Carousel Art Gallery and inhaled a deep breath. *Baby steps, Kate, baby steps.* Just because I'd have access to brushes and canvases doesn't mean I had to paint.

I pushed through the double glass door and entered.

Beautiful paintings adorned stark white walls—a mixture of landscapes, portraits, and abstracts in both oil and acrylic. Two paintings stood out: *Tree Tunnel,* a dreamy portrayal of the eucalyptus tree tunnel on Maluhia Road, the one Brandon the cab driver had pointed out to me. And *Wailua Falls*, a rainbow arched over a lush mountain and sparkling waterfall.

Sculptures of angels, fairies, and fantasy characters were displayed on shelves by the front window.

A wooden tea table sat between two white leather sofas in the center of the gallery. And against the side wall, a coffeemaker, water bottles, assorted box of teas, and other amenities were on a rectangular table under a black-and-white woodcut print of a sea turtle.

"Hi, Stella." I waved to the cute young woman at the small

reception desk with a pale complexion and shoulder-length dark hair.

I glanced at her desk when she didn't respond. Besides a laptop and a land line phone, she had a napkin perched like a tent over the open book to the far left.

Stella had been working for Abby for two months. I gave her kudos for being here the longest, as every other person before her had left after a month. I didn't blame them. I'd leave too if all I did was answer the phone—which hardly rang—and greet the rare customer.

Stella flinched and straightened her spine. "Oh, hi …"

Engrossed in a novel, she must not have heard me walk in.

"Kaitlyn," I finished for her. "I'm Abby's sister. She called to let you know I was coming, right?"

"Oh, yes she did. Would you like any coffee or water?" She tugged her dark hair behind her ears and patted the napkin down.

She was trying to be sly about the book, but she didn't know I had hawk eyes and a knack for observation. An artist never misses the smallest details.

"No, thank you. I'll be in the back." I headed to the back room as I hollered, "Ring if you need me, and you can go back to reading your book."

I could have sworn I heard Stella grumble a foul word.

Big, clear plastic bins filled with art supplies were set in the right back corner with untouched canvases of various sizes, next to the restroom. Exactly where Abby said they would be.

I put my purse on the desk at the left back corner and browsed through a stack of unfinished paintings, trying to get some inspiration, but nothing came. I even flipped through some art magazines Abby had collected. After tossing the last one back on the stack, I leaned against the cabinet and stared at the huge, untouched canvas mounted on the back wall—the thing probably measured eighty by eighty inches at least.

A small spark inside me nudged, enough for me to run my fingers over the primed surface—tight as a bowstring and smooth as paper. I would have to stand and paint. No big deal.

My heart palpitated. A good sign. But the canvas wasn't mine.

I texted Abby and asked her if I could put the canvas to good use. When she gave me the green light, I opened the bin and picked out the brushes and paint tubes. After organizing them, I placed them neatly on a tall rolling tray. Though I had no idea what to paint, I decided to take a dab at it and see what happened.

Sometimes you have to just go for it.

I did have time to kill.

I decided on oil instead of acrylic. *Let's give it a try.* After I squeezed the various paint tubes on a large palette, I laid out a sheet to protect the floor, shoved in my ear pods, and set my music.

I couldn't decide which brush to use, so I opted on none. As I stood, I dotted gold on the blank white with my fingertips in a circle.

Today wasn't about creating anything sellable. Today was about liberation and getting reacquainted with my artistic side. Today was about to hell with men, to hell with Jayden. It was about me.

As I listened to Ed Sheeran croon, I added red and green next. The cool, soft buttery texture greased my palms. I caressed the canvas in a rhythmic pattern from side to side.

There—Christmas colors. I laughed at the childlike creation. Tyler could have done this. I had switched to another song when the land line phone beeped.

I scurried past a collection of easels leaning against a wall to the desk, loaded with catalogs. With my elbow, I hit the speakerphone button. "Hello?"

"Kaitlyn." She dropped her voice to a whisper. "There's a man here."

"Oh. Well, show him around. I'm busy."

"It's Mr. Medici. What do I do?" She sounded nervous.

Had she never given a tour of the gallery before?

I sighed. "Stella, show him the paintings we have available. There's a price tag on each one. If he has any questions, then I'll come out. If he likes a painting, then he'll buy it."

I pushed the same button again with my elbow and went back to the canvas. I didn't mean to sound like a grouch, but she'd been there for two months. If she didn't know how to do the job, she should be fired. Then guilt wrapped itself around my conscience. If she called again, I would go out.

I pressed on "Beast of Burden" by the Rolling Stones and began to sing. This time I stamped my paint-coated hands on the canvas to the rhythm of the beat. Then I added blue and yellow and smeared it all over.

My gooey hands moved in circles while colors mixed. I didn't care that it looked like someone had vomited on it. Art was art. I sang and swayed my hips from side to side, paint splattering on the sheet, having the time of my life. I hadn't sung and laughed so hard in a while.

Then …

I thought I heard a door slam. No one should be back here unless Stella needed something. I turned and smacked into something hard. Not something, but some*one*.

My hands smeared with multicolored paint, had splatted flat against on a pristine, white dress shirt, right over a set of nice, hard pecs. I peered up into familiar chestnut-colored eyes growing wider and angrier, as the scent of cedar and pine enveloped me.

Crap!

How long had he been standing there? Mortified, I flushed with heat and released a soft whimper.

Chapter Eight – Mr. Medici

"I'm so sorry." My heart ricocheted inside my chest as I stared at my trembling hands, wondering what in the world had just happened. Of *all* people, Leonardo walked right into my paint-covered hands.

The universe hated me. My timing was horrible. How could I have gotten so carried away in Abby's workplace?

He didn't speak as I slowly peeled my hands away. His silence couldn't mean anything good. I had to rectify this fast.

"I'll-I'll pay for dry cleaning. No, that won't really work. Oil paint on fabric is … it's pretty much ruined. I'll pay for a new shirt. Oh my goodness, that's an expensive shirt. I'm so sorry."

I couldn't stop babbling. I unbuttoned his top button, getting more paint on his shirt. "If I do it right now before it sets in, I can at least try to get the paint off with turpentine. But that would stink a lot and would probably ruin the shirt anyway. I can't believe I'm paying it forward like this."

What am I doing?

Around the third button, his fingers locked around my wrist and he cleared his throat. His hands were warm on my skin and I wanted to melt. Partly to just disappear and the other half … well, I had to take my mind out of that naughty place.

"I'm so sorry. I don't know what I'm doing." I could probably die right here, right now.

I should definitely die right now.

I wanted to cry. I wanted to start today over. I wanted him to yell at me or say something, but he'd kept quiet. All I'd wanted was to take my mind off things, to do something I loved. Didn't I at least deserve that?

"You." He squinted, his voice soft. "You were in … the cab."

He remembers me? And that voice, his smooth baritone sparked fireflies in my stomach, and made me feel so alive that it scared the living daylights out of me. How could this stranger inflict such want in so few words?

I bit my bottom lip and ran a hand down my hair. Oh, that wasn't good. I hunched my shoulders.

His eyes grew bigger. "You got paint in your … hair."

I said nothing, unable to meet his gaze, and nodded frantically—my way of thanking him for letting me know.

"You got some on your face." He extended his hand toward my cheek but dropped it instead.

Please leave before I make a complete fool of myself. Well, too late for that, but maybe just leave before I do worse.

He kept glancing between the colorful canvas and back to me.

I finally met his eyes, eyes that looked intently back at me. His stare gave me the shivers, stripping me bare. I didn't know what it was about him, but his presence made me nervous. He sucked up all the air in the room—in a good way—and I couldn't breathe.

I let my eyes roam about his face, memorizing the details—my artist's habit, or so I told myself. I wanted to run my fingers along his dark brooding eyebrows, down his perfect nose, curve around his high cheekbones, and caress those kissable lips. I had the urge to create a sculpture of this perfect Mr. Medici. This flawless being that looked and stood like a Greek god.

His impressive physique made me imagine him as Zeus, or perhaps Poseidon, who had walked straight out of a romantic fantasy novel, with a taste for mortal women. I really needed to stop reading those books.

I took a step back, composing myself with the little dignity I had left. "Mr. Medici, how may I help you?"

He stood silent, just examining me. I wasn't sure how much time had passed when he broke away.

"I think you did enough." He pivoted sharply, his dress shoes tapping against the tile.

I shook my head in disbelief as I watched him strut out the door. I was the unicorn and he was the skeleton. He'd just eaten me alive, taken all my glitter power and magic with him. I didn't know why I cared.

Oh, yes I do. He might be one of Abby's biggest customers. This could cost her.

"Mr. Medici. Wait." I sprinted after him, but he was already out the front door.

A warm breeze wrapped around me like a cozy blanket and the door closed. Wind chimes tinkled faintly—soft and soothing, like the caress of an invisible hand on my back.

I rubbed my arms. Funny, I'd never noticed the door chime. I'd almost swear the chime hadn't sounded when I'd walked in.

I released a long heavy sigh, almost forgetting about Stella at the desk, as the peaceful melody lingered on the air.

Stella looked away from the computer screen to me with her mouth open and her gray eyes glistening. "What happened? And what happened to you? What did you guys do?"

I wanted to ask myself the same question, but a laugh burst out of her as if she'd held it a bit too long. Then I joined her because, why not?

"I got paint on him. Did you see?" I eased on the sofa in the center and extended palms out, careful not to touch anything.

"I did." She snorted. "He looked like he had been attacked by an artistic octopus. And so do you. Or it looks like you two were having some fun together." She waggled her eyebrows.

I flushed. "Oh, no. Not what happened." I almost shoved my hands to my face but stopped myself. "I should wash this off. Please tell me he's not one of Abby's big clients."

"If I told you that, I would be lying. This is my second time seeing him, but then again, I've only been working here for two months. Abby said something about Mr. Medici stopping by once a month to check out the new paintings. Don't you know who Leonardo Medici is?"

"No. Should I?" I kicked my feet up on the coffee table and leaned back with my hands away from the white sofa.

Stella folded her arms on the desk. "He's twenty-eight, but he's a billionaire. He's the Medici Real Estate Holdings heir. I think he buys paintings from Abby to display at their properties. Also, he's been on the cover of a few business magazines. And before you ask, no idea if he's single or not. He keeps his private life private."

I stared at the painting of a waterfall and groaned, releasing my frustration. "I don't care if he's single, but you should have warned me."

I wanted to start today over again for screwing up a possible deal for my sister. Then I realized Stella had tried—the reason why she had sounded nervous.

She turned back to the computer screen and clicked away on the keyboard. "I'd thought you knew. I figured your sister would have told you."

"Nope." I stared up at the high ceiling, wishing for the hundredth time I could start over today. "Do you have any suggestions on how I could fix this?"

Stella twisted off the cap from her water bottle and took a sip. "Pray?" Then she snorted. "But seriously, I think it'll be fine. I'm just glad you'll be the one telling Abby you finger-painted on Mr. Medici and not me."

I blew out a long breath. "Do I have to tell her?"

She shrugged. "Your sister, not mine. Good luck."

Time to be a grown-up and clean up the mess I made. But first, I went back to my painting and tried to finish up my amateur work. I thought I might name it *Mr. Medici's Shirt.*

Chapter Nine – Confession

Once the gallery closed, I picked up Tyler and went home. Since not a sound came from Abby behind her closed door, I told Tyler to play in his room while I took a long hot shower. I needed to wash paint out of my hair.

Distracted by today's events, I decided to call for delivery. Pizza for Tyler and me, but leftover chicken soup for Abby.

When I peeped in Abby's room, she was lying on her bed awake. So I told her how I got paint on Leonardo's shirt.

She slapped her forehead and closed her eyes. "You did what?" My sister's voice came out barely a whisper, but I heard the frustration.

"I'm so sorry. It was an accident. I feel horrible." I plopped on the edge of the mattress and shoved my face into my hands.

My sister scrubbed a hand down her cheek and sighed. "What did he say to you before he left?"

I raised my chin and pushed back my shoulders, imitating his deep voice. "I think you did enough." My playfulness all gone, my pitch rose with concern. "Oh, Abby, did I ruin your deal? I feel horrible. I'm supposed to be helping, not making a mess."

She fluffed the pillows supporting her back and frowned. "I honestly don't know. He might never come around again."

"Just because I accidentally painted on him? Are you serious?" I clenched my jaw and glanced at the photo of Steve on the bedside table. "Can't you tell him I'm your idiot sister who took over for a day because you were sick? Besides, it was his fault. He came into the room unannounced. He shouldn't have been in there."

"You know how snobby rich businessmen are."

"Yes. I do. That's exactly why I don't associate with"—I curved my index and middle fingers in air quotes—"'snobby, rich businessmen.' They're so full of themselves. So what? He can afford another shirt. He probably has hundreds."

I didn't mean that all rich men were snobby, but Jayden's friends were, and none of them were even close to billionaire status. I had dated a hedge fund manager before Jayden and dumped him for that very reason. They weren't pleasant to be around. All they talked about was themselves and how they flaunted their money.

Abby smacked her comforter. "I can't do this anymore." She began to laugh hysterically, her voice fading to a squeak.

"Do what?"

"I'm just playing you. It's all good. He called to let me know he wanted to purchase one that was hanging near the front door."

My nostrils flared as I marched to the opposite side where she lay. Abby and I were the best of friends and sometimes we acted more like teenagers than adults. My high school friends used to envy our close friendship. Abby and I just *got* each other.

I snatched up a pillow and pounced at her as I spoke. "You're mean." The pillow bounced off her shoulder. "You're so mean." The cushion smacked her arms she held out to cover her face. "I was so worried and here you are …"

"Ahhh … I'm sorry, Kate." She laughed, swatting her arms to block my blows. "But you should have seen your face."

She waved her hands as I gave her one more blow with the pillow.

"You have to learn to relax girl, or you'll have a heart attack."

I pushed back the pillow and something thumped on the hardwood floor. I looked down, panting. The water bottle had fallen off the bedside table and rolled five feet to the master bathroom.

"I'll give you a heart attack." I poked her ribs, her side, her waist. "I bet you're not sick. You're probably playing me about that, too."

"Stop. Stop." She giggled until she started to hack and cough.

I picked up the water bottle I had knocked over and handed it to Abby. After she'd gulped down enough, I placed it back on the bedside table.

"You're a terrible sister, you know that?" I said.

"I know." She gave me a tight-lipped smile and tossed a pillow at me. She hit the closet door instead.

I slid next to her and rested against the headboard while she laid on her stack of pillows.

"He was the one who paid for my cab ride when I arrived here," I said.

"What?" Her eyes rounded, her mouth an O shape. "Why didn't you tell me?"

"I just did." I snickered. "I didn't know he was *Mr. Medici* in the cab. I thought I would never see him again. And I certainly couldn't have predicted Mr. Medici would stop by your gallery." I said his name with a hint of sarcasm. "Do you know anything about him?"

Abby faced me and arched her eyebrows. "Not much. I don't know if he's here on a business trip to look over his properties or if he's lived here for years. I don't get out much. He did tell me that he buys a lot of paintings because he wishes he could paint, but that's as much as I got out of him. He's very private."

I picked up the pillow Abby had thrown and hugged it. "He seems like it."

"Medici Real Estate owns properties in Europe, China, Singapore, Korea, Los Angeles, and Kauai, and that's just a few. You could say his family lives up to their famous last name."

"I suppose. Anyway, I'm glad he's a bigger man than I thought, and I'm glad I didn't mess up anything for you. How much did you sell the painting for?"

Abby's lips spread a bit wider and her eyes lit up. "Three grand. Only because it's a smaller one, but he's bought others for five and ten before. He said he'll be back again after he gets the measure of the wall."

I jerked forward and faced her. "What? Three grand for that piece? I saw the painting and it's—"

She gave me a light sock on the arm. "Not as good as yours. I agree."

"No. That's not what I was going to say, but thank you very much."

"He's been my saving grace. So, he paid for your cab?"

I didn't like her playful tone. "Yes. It doesn't mean anything."

"He might be available," she sang. "He's only four years older than you."

I shifted my legs to get comfortable. "He paid for my cab. No big deal. He would have done it for anyone." My mind drifted. "He's got beautiful eyes though." My voice became soft and dreamy. "Strong jawline and nice biceps. You can tell he works out."

My sister sat up and pinned me with her sharp gaze. What was meant to be a casual comment had my sister at attention.

"I agree and I'm glad you said that," she said.

"What? You agree on what? I didn't mean anything by it. I hardly know him, and besides, he probably hates me. And it's just an innocent comment and—"

She grabbed my hand. "I know, Kate. I'm just saying that it's okay to feel something. It's okay to think a man is handsome or notice if he makes you feel something. I'm not just talking about Mr. Medici. It's okay to move on if you're ready. Just because Jayden hurt you doesn't mean the next guy will. That's all I'm saying."

I wanted to tell her the same, but it was too soon to bring up moving on. One day, maybe.

"I know." I dipped my head lower and stared at our intertwined fingers. "I'm not ready to open my heart yet."

Abby stroked my hair and pulled me into her arms. Talking about Jayden had me all worked up and I found myself tearing up a bit, my healing heart ripping at the seams.

I had put up a barrier and acted like I no longer cared for him. Jayden and I were not meant to be together, I got that, but breaking up wasn't easy. In losing him, I'd also lost my friend. It felt almost like death.

"It's fine. I'm sorry I brought it up. I just want the best for you." She caressed my arm.

"I know." I drew back and wiped my tears. The truth was, the thought of moving on with someone new scared me.

"Love is easy when it's with the right person," Abby added. "So, you got paint on him … does that mean you're going to start painting again?"

She sounded excited and I didn't want to let her down.

"Sort of. I painted on the huge canvas and it looks like something Ty would paint, but I'll eventually get there."

"Something I can paint?" a small voice asked. "Is it okay if I come in?"

I had asked Tyler to stay in his room until I finished speaking with his mother. I patted the comforter. "Sure. Come here, you, and join our hug."

"Come here, baby. I've missed you." My sister threw her arms open.

Tyler jumped on the bed and flopped between us. We both hugged him and planted kisses all over his face.

"We should stay like this," I said, my arms still around Tyler.

"But I'm hungry." On cue, the doorbell rang. Tyler bolted out of the room and waited by the door. "The pizza guy is here."

He knew better than to open it, so he eagerly waited for me. I grabbed the exact amount and tip out of my wallet and handed it to the pizza guy.

I closed the door and placed the box on the table as I savored the comforting aroma of melted cheese and the spicy tang of pepperoni. Tyler set the table with paper plates and napkins for the two of us. I dumped two pepperoni slices on his plate and grabbed the other side with all the toppings on it. Just the way I like it.

Tyler gave me a goofy smile and stuffed his face. "Can we play *Unicorns versus Skeletons* after dinner, Auntie Kate?"

"Sure, only if you tell me why you looked sad when I picked you up." I grabbed an apple juice box from the fridge and placed it in front of him. Then I went to the family room.

The lights were turned off so I switched on the Christmas tree lights … There. Red, blue, green, and violet lights twinkled along the wall. And the star on top glowed the brightest. It perked up the gloomy atmosphere.

I went back to Tyler and poked the straw through the juice box for him as I waited for him to answer. He pointed to his mouth, letting me know he was chewing. That sly boy, he was buying time.

"I already told you I had a good day," he said with a hint of annoyance.

"You did, but I know you. Something is wrong." I took a warm bite, watching the string from the cheese stretch.

"How do you know?" He furrowed his brow.

"Because I have a feeling."

He nibbled on the crust, slowing down. "That's what Mommy always says. Grown-ups must have some kind of feeling power or something. Fine. It's no big deal. Bridget is on level five. Jace is on level six, and I'm on level four. They're moving up too fast and I can't keep up."

"I'll tell you what. If you wash up and do everything your mom expects you to do before bedtime, then I'll help you move up, but we have to leave time for a bedtime story. Deal?"

His eyes bulged. "Deal. You're the best."

After dinner, while Tyler washed up, I warmed up Abby's dinner. Secretly, I couldn't wait to play the game with him. It was our special time together.

"Can we play now?" Tyler walked into my room in his PJs, holding the tablet, and then bobbed on the balls of his feet.

"Come." I patted my bed.

He crawled under the comforter beside me.

"Watch where my fingers move. Remember to touch the plants in front of you then move to the sides."

"What if two come out at the same time?"

"Then you have to shift your fingers faster and touch the one nearest to you first, and then the second, okay?"

"Got it. Thank you." He kissed my cheek and smiled.

After we played for half an hour, I read Tyler a bedtime story and tucked him into bed. I checked up on Abby and then opened up my portfolio website for some inspiration.

There were photos of my sketches and paintings in various media during my college years, and also of the ones I'd given to Abby to sell in the New York gallery. She had sold my favorite, an acrylic on canvas with stars on a violet-blue background. I called it *My Soulmate*.

I enjoyed going down the memory lane but it also left me frustrated, so I shut down my laptop. After I washed up, I crawled in bed and read my novel. Maybe I'd find my spark tomorrow.

Chapter Ten – Poipu Preschool

I'd offered to take Tyler to Poipu Preschool the next day and told my sister to stay home. She needed at least one more day to recover from her twenty-four-hour bug.

"Have a good day, Tyler. Do I get a kiss?" I leaned lower for him by his classroom door, but he frowned and pointed at two kids beside him.

"Auntie Kate. These are my friends, Jace and Bridget."

I straightened. "Nice to meet you," I said and smiled at the few parents stopping by the check-in table.

"Hello," Jace said.

Bridget smiled and waved her small hand at me.

"Hey, guess what?" Jace said, his brown eyes gleaming. "I went to level seven last night."

"I moved up too." Bridget raised her chin, her blue eyes clear and shiny like marbles, just like the unicorn's horn on her shirt. When she rocked on her heels from excitement, her long braided hair with blue ribbons bounced.

Tyler's smile grew wider and he looked at me like we shared a secret. "I'm on level five now."

It made me happy to see Tyler smiling and confident.

"Kids." A young lady with short brunette hair clapped her hands. "It's time to get to class."

"Oh, gotta go. That's my teacher, Mrs. Fong." Tyler waited for his friends to leave before he gave me a quick kiss on the cheek and dashed off.

Working parents had left, but some moms stuck around to talk to each other in the parking lot. Having some time to spare, I read through the message board again. Movie and Popcorn night, Saturday at seven p.m., at Poipu Community Center caught my eye, and the nanny position was still available.

Should I call?

Abby was feeling better, and though she could use another day of rest, she planned to work tomorrow. Then what would I do? Wait for the phone to ring with a job offer?

"Mr. Medici. What can I do for you?" The front desk woman's voice perked up and she adjusted her glasses.

My muscles went rigid. My heart raced a mile a minute. I fished my cell out of my purse, pressed it to my ear, and pretended to be on a call. I kept my gaze on the board while peeking from my periphery.

Leonardo Medici towered over the reception desk, clad in a navy suit, form fitted to his broad shoulders.

"I forgot to drop this off." He handed her a pink blanket.

A daughter? *He has a daughter? Then he probably has a wife.* Not that I cared.

"It's a good thing you came back. She would have been sad without it. Have a nice day, Mr. Medici."

"Thank you. You too, Mrs. Hall."

Thump, thump, thump went his dress shoes, then silence.

I couldn't move. I couldn't breathe. He stood behind me and I felt the warmth of his presence. Did he notice me? Or was he reading the message board too? *What do I do?*

After I'd ruined his shirt with oil paints, he'd definitely remember me. Better I stand still and wait for him to leave.

"Mr. Medici, is there anything I can help you with?" The front desk lady again.

Thank goodness for her. But he didn't move. I stiffened, afraid I might do something else foolish.

Both of us stood unmoving, staring at the message board. Another minute passed and I couldn't take it anymore. I bolted out the door and sprinted for my sister's gallery.

After a few minutes, I slipped inside the front door, breathless. Then I wondered why I had run.

Because I ruined his expensive shirt and made a fool of myself.

But he'd bought a painting from Abby, so all was forgiven and forgotten, right? I passed the reception desk and stopped beside the sofa.

"Hey, Stella." I dabbed the sweat on my forehead with my hand and unbuttoned my sweater. "It's hot in here, no?"

Stella started and looked up from her desk with wide, surprised eyes. She must have been reading.

She cleared her throat. "Why are you panting?"

Good question, but you don't need to know.

"Oh, I thought … Um, anyway, everything good?"

She hiked up her eyebrow. Nope, she wasn't distracted.

"You had a customer this morning, but I told him you would be in a little later."

I stopped shrugging off my sweater, one arm still trapped. "What customer? I don't have any friends here and I certainly don't have any customers. I don't have any new pieces." My babbling gave away too much.

Her lips tugged at the corner. "I didn't say he was your *friend*, Kaitlyn."

The coy tone and the curl of her lips implied she had more to tell.

My flats slapped the tile floor as I walked to her desk. "Who is it, Stella? Does this customer have a name?" I used the same mysterious voice back.

"Mr. Medici. He asked for you." She sipped coffee from her paper cup and placed it down by the office phone.

I furrowed my brow. "What? Why?"

"I don't know." She lifted her shoulders.

"Did he look mad?" I adjusted my purse strap and placed a hand on the corner of her desk, eyeing her cute floral dress.

Stella squinted with a speculative gleam in her eye. "No, but is there something going on between you two?"

"No, no, no." I shook my head. "I don't know him. Why do you ask?"

She gave me a side-long glance. "Well, he seemed … nervous. I don't know how to describe it, but he walked in and out of the store a couple of times, and when he finally stopped to talk to me, he asked if you were working today. When I told him you were coming back later, he seemed relieved, I think."

Whatever. Perhaps he wanted me to pay for his dry cleaning. But that shirt had been unsalvageable. Maybe he wanted me to buy him a new shirt—that didn't sound right either. If he could spend three grand on a painting, he could afford to replace a shirt.

"Well ..." I stopped talking because I had no answer and backed away. "I'll be finishing up my painting. Just ring if you need anything."

She twisted her rolling chair to face me. "Sure. That's what I did the last time and you told me to take care of it."

A mistake that got me into a mess.

Sarcasm must be the reason Stella had lasted longer than the others. I stopped halfway to the back room and cringed.

"Sorry. I won't do that again."

Stella continued, "Do you want me to get anything for you during my lunch? I'm going to get a chicken salad and a strawberry smoothie."

I opened the door and looked over my shoulder. "Sure. I'll have the same. Thanks."

After I set my purse on the desk, I tapped play on my earbuds and set up my painting area in front of the huge canvas named *Mr. Medici's Shirt.* A laugh burst out of my mouth at the memory of my creation on his white, crisp, expensive shirt.

This time I let my paintbrush do the work. No more hands for a while. I thought about Tyler as I added white over the red and green I had smeared on yesterday.

The paint blended on the canvas, creating new colors and shades. Oils had been the right choice since they didn't dry overnight. I had no plan for this masterpiece, but it might turn out to be something Abby could sell.

Perhaps I should consider the nanny position. I could be a nanny for two weeks and paint at the same time. At least I'd be making money.

I grabbed my cell from my back pocket of my jeans and punched the numbers before I could change my mind. A woman with a sweet voice answered the phone—Mona.

After Mona and I set up the date and time of the interview, I got back to painting. When Stella came back from her lunch break, she brought a salad and a smoothie for me as I'd asked. I took a few bites and got back to working on my piece. An hour later, Stella beeped me.

"Yes," I sang, trying to sound polite since the last time I'd nearly bitten her head off.

Her voice dropped to a whisper. "Can you come out? Mr. Medici is here."

I nearly choked on my smoothie. My heart leaped out of my chest and crashed back in. "What did you say?"

"Mr. Medici. You know, the man you painted on."

I'd thought I heard someone clear their throat in the background.

"Tell him I'll be right out."

Taking a peek in the restroom mirror, I ran my fingers through my hair, straightened my pink sweater, and dusted off my black jeans.

Presentable enough. I walked out.

Mr. Medici stood by the paintings and focused on the one called *Wailua Falls*, a mountain waterfall with a rainbow glittering in the spray.

As a ray of sun highlighted him through the window, he looked like a glorious angel without wings. A perfect portrait. I wished I had my camera to capture the moment.

I cleared my throat. "Mr. Medici. We meet again."

We meet again? How lame is that?

I extended my hand. "It's nice to meet you—I mean to see you … again. How can I do you? I mean …" I cringed and dropped my hand before he could touch me. *Let's try this again.* "How can I help you?"

Stella snickered quietly, and I almost told her to walk away. I seemed to lose my tongue and my brain around him.

Leonardo's lips perked, like he was holding in a laugh. He scrubbed the back of his neck and said, "I bought a painting from Abby Fuller yesterday over the phone. I'm supposed to pick it up tomorrow, but I thought I'd stop by and get it now. Is it ready?"

It took a second to process his words as I admired those beautiful brown eyes with thick, long eyelashes, perfect nose, and manly yet pretty lips.

"Yes, it's ready." I wasn't sure, but I didn't want him to think I was incompetent. "Stella and I will help you." I rushed over, tugged Stella out of her chair, and whispered sharply, "Do you know which one?"

Abby told me Leonardo had bought one near the front door, but there were three.

Mr. Medici narrowed his eyes at us. A smart man like him could see through my awkwardness and realize I didn't know what I was doing. When I caught him looking our way, he glanced to the small sculptures on the shelf by the front window.

Stella murmured, "Abby places purchased art in the back and wraps it up, but she wasn't here yesterday. Did she say anything to you?"

"No, because she's planning to work tomorrow. Mr. Medici came a day early. Call her."

"I'll go do that and you keep him company."

I swallowed nervously and turned to Leonardo. "Stella is going to get it for you. She'll be right back."

"Perfect. It's the painting of the ocean and palm trees, and there's a couple in the background," he said loud enough for Stella to hear.

I assumed Abby had gotten confused, and the painting was in the back room and not in the front. We had to communicate better.

He called to let me know he wanted to purchase one that was hanging near the front door.

Was and not currently. Abby liked to shift her paintings around, putting the newer ones in front the way retail stores redressed the dummies in the windows with the newest merchandise. Sometimes she grouped them according to the size of the canvas, color theme, or the artist.

"Would you like to sit down?" I waved to the white leather sofa like a game show hostess.

"No, thank you. I'm good." He focused back to the clay figurines.

I wasn't sure if he was genuinely interested in the sculptures or if he was trying to avoid small talk. He seemed a bit nervous, unlike the first time I'd met him. But the longer the silence remained, the more anxious I became.

"Would you like something to drink?" I asked, inching toward him.

Leonardo eyed the table with small water bottles, coffeemaker, and boxes of Hawaiian tea.

"No, thank you," he said, and strolled away to a display with several small figurines about a foot tall. "Is that for sale?" He pointed to a half-naked, cute figure holding a bow and arrow.

"Yes. It's Cupid."

"I assumed so." He chuckled lightly and looked at me from the corner of his eyes.

I nearly died of stupidity.

"Oh, sorry. I didn't mean you didn't know." My face flaming, I picked up the statue and looked at the bottom. "It's two hundred."

"Two hundred?" His eyebrows pinched together.

"Not my price. It says on the tag." I should really stop talking.

His lips curved into a small grin. "I'll come back another day for it."

I put the Cupid statue back down. "Sure. Not a problem. You're welcome to put a small deposit and I can put it on hold for you. I don't mean to sound like a pushy salesperson, but it might be gone by the time you decide to buy it. If you change your mind, you can let me know and I'll refund the deposit. We can hold it for three days."

He rubbed his chin, his brow furrowed. "Fine. I'll purchase it now." His eyes gleamed. "I know where I'll put it. Credit card okay?"

"Sure," I said cheerfully, happy to make a sale. "Follow me, please."

Very aware his eyes were on me, I walked faster.

I picked up the card-reading gadget from the drawer and swiped Leonardo's card when he handed it to me. After he signed, I'd extended my arm to give the card back when it slipped out of my hand.

I bent down quickly to retrieve it, but I smacked my head into something hard. Air whooshed out from my lungs as I landed on my butt with a thump. Pain shot up my spine.

Crap!

"I'm so sorry." Leonardo bent to one knee and picked up the card. "Let me help you," he said and extended a hand.

I let him pull me up. Our bodies were too close for comfort and he wrapped his arms around my waist to steady me. My heart skipped a beat and butterflies fluttered in my stomach. When his eyes locked on mine, they sparkled to life for just a second, and then he backed away in a hurry.

"Are you okay?" His baritone voice was smooth and pleasant. "Did I hurt you?"

I rubbed the side of my head and leaned against the desk for a moment. "I'm fine, but did I hurt you? I have a hard head."

He chuckled. "It would be impolite for me to agree." He winked. "But I think mine is harder. I'm fine, thanks for asking."

Oh, goodness that wink. He looked so playful and sexy. Silence filled the air, and I tried to think of questions.

"My nephew goes to preschool with your daughter." The words flew out before I could stop them. *Oops.* I shouldn't know that about him.

He hiked an eyebrow. "How do you know I have a daughter?"

Heat flushed up my face as I made up a lie and I was surprised how quickly I'd thought of it. "Abby told me."

"What's your nephew's name?"

"Tyler Fuller."

"Tyler?" he said as if mulling the name. "Oh, yes. Bridget and Tyler are friends. She talks about him all the time."

My breath caught for a moment. "Tyler talks about her all the time too."

I wouldn't have guessed. Bridget had blonde hair and blue eyes so unlike Leonardo's dark eyes and dark hair. The blonde woman he was with at the shopping plaza must be his wife or girlfriend. All speculation, of course, but it made sense.

Leonardo shoved his hands inside his front pockets and rocked on his heels. "They should have a playdate sometime. If Tyler is available."

"That sounds nice. I'll let my sister know." I pushed my hair behind my ear and clasped my hands together.

Why is Stella taking so long?

"Your sister?" He gave me a sidelong glance.

"Abby is my sister. I'm in town for Christmas. She was sick yesterday, which is why I was here and not her."

"Oh, that's right. You said Tyler is your nephew. Now that I know, I see the resemblance between you and Abby. I spoke to Abby on the phone. I hope she's feeling better."

"She'll be in tomorrow."

I debated whether to ask him about the shirt, but the sound of someone clearing their throat interrupted me.

"Here it is. Sorry it took so long." Stella brought the painting out, all encased up in bubble wrap. She had done a great job.

"Thank you, ladies." He glanced between the two of us. "See you next time." He gave a tight-lipped smile and headed for the door.

"Oh, wait. Mr. Medici, you forgot—" I rushed after him.

When he whirled, we would've collided yet again had I not skidded to a halt.

I stepped back and pointed. "Your Cupid."

"Could I pick it up another day? My hands are full." He glanced from me to Stella and back to me.

"Of course. I'll hold it for you, and you can pick it up at your convenience."

"Thank you, Miss—? Missus …?"

"Miss Chang."

"I'll likely stop by tomorrow. Have a good evening, Miss Chang." He tilted his head and walked out the door.

"He's so gorgeous." Stella slumped into her seat with dreamy eyes. "And he's such a gentleman. It's hard to find a man like him."

"I didn't notice." I picked up Cupid from the shelf to put him in the back for safekeeping.

Stella gawked at me. "You'd have to be blind not to notice him."

I shrugged as I passed the sofa. "I wasn't looking at him. I mean, I had to look at him to talk to him obviously, but not like that."

Stella's eyes beamed while she rocked back in her chair. "Not like *how*, Kaitlyn?"

"What?" I halted half way to the back room and pivoted toward her.

"Never mind. Whatever you say," she murmured and pulled up the computer to input something. "I'll finish the invoice of the transaction."

"Thanks. I'll be in the back room."

"Yup. It looks like Cupid did his job."

"Excuse me?"

"Never mind. Happy painting," she said. "Too bad you didn't get paint on him this time. He was one sexy mess yesterday. Someone to dream about."

I shook my head and snorted, though I had thought the same thing.

Chapter Eleven – The Beach Front House

After I dropped off Tyler at his preschool, I called a cab and went to the interview for the nanny position.

A family that could afford a nanny was obviously well off, but I didn't expect a private beach where all the homes were within walking distance to the ocean. I'd have brought my camera if I'd known I'd be looking at this view.

Families strolled along the shore, their children laughing and kicking up white sand. Dogs on leashes trotted beside their owners, and a few braved the cold water to swim.

As the cab drove off, I shivered when a cool breeze brushed my neck as I walked up the curvy driveway. Yellow, white, and red hibiscus bloomed on either side of the front porch, and their sweet scent spiraled around me.

A Christmas wreath hung on the front door, adorned with gold baubles and one big red ribbon on the top. One of the double doors opened after I rang the doorbell and a woman peeked out.

"Hello. I'm Mona. You must be Ms. Chang?"

Mona smoothed a hand down her long-sleeved, flower-print dress that brought out the blue in her eyes. Strands of loose white curls had come undone at her temples. She was older than she'd sounded on the phone.

"Yes, I am, but you can call me Kate."

She nodded. "Come in."

As my shoes clicked on the beige marble floor, I peered up at the high ceiling. A crystal chandelier with teardrop pendants glistened against the sunlight beaming through the window. Farther in, I admired the sweeping staircase with a festive garland curling around the handrail, then the giant Christmas tree decorated with silver ornaments dominating the foyer.

"Please, follow me." Mona led the way as I continued to marvel.

The family room was three times the size of Abby's. A smaller

Christmas tree was stationed in the corner with a few presents under it. Across the mantel stretched a paper garland made from a cutout of a child's handprints. My heart tugged at the sentimental touch.

I realized then that I never asked how many children I would be watching over, and there were no photos of the family displayed in this room. Perhaps in another room? Also, there were no toys.

In Abby's house, Tyler's toys and books were always scattered about. But then again, Abby didn't have a nanny or a huge house to set boundaries.

"This is the family room," Mona said. "Let me show you the other rooms."

We strolled into the kitchen—my dream kitchen—with white cabinets and cream granite counters. All stainless steel and state of the art appliances, top quality no doubt.

"It's lovely." Not a spot stained the stove. I wondered if they had a side kitchen.

"Come, come."

Mona escorted me to the guest room and an office with only a bookcase and a desk. I eyed every fixture, every space. Again, no photos of the family. So strange. But the painting hanging … I went closer.

Mona cleared her throat to get my attention.

"Sorry. Did you say something?" I asked.

"No, but you've been staring at the painting. It's beautiful, isn't it?"

Dreamy clouds backed by the day sky hung over the glistening ocean. It reminded me of Kauai.

"Yes, it is." I always appreciated the work of a talented painter.

Then we climbed the stairs. She skipped the master bedroom, but showed me other bedrooms and bathrooms

The last bedroom contained all-white furniture: the bed frame, desk, bookcase, and the dressers. A pink unicorn comforter blanketed the bed and a giant stuffed unicorn with a rainbow-colored horn sat in the opposite corner.

On the bed were two more stuffed unicorns, and pink and white throw pillows. We both loved unicorns, so I had that in common with this child already.

"I just want to make sure—there's only one daughter, correct?" I asked from the doorway. "I should've asked you how many children in this household before."

"Yes. This room belongs to Roselyn." Mona opened the shutters to let in a flood of sunlight on the hardwood floor, across the white rug, and onto the marble bathroom floor.

I furrowed my brow. "Roselyn? Does she attend Poipu preschool?"

I'd gotten the phone number from the board, but maybe the parents put the number in all preschools. I would if I were desperate to find one quickly.

"Yes. She's four years old, soon to be five. A very sweet, lovely girl."

One child, about Tyler's age. How bad could it be, right?

"Let me show you the backyard." She went past the hall, down the stairs, and through the kitchen.

"Wow," I muttered under my breath.

The front yard was breathtaking with the view of the ocean, but the backyard was another island on its own.

Palms trees lined either side of the walkway. A three-tiered gray stone fountain gurgled in the center. Past a garden of Hawaiian flowers was a grand swimming pool with manmade boulders and a super cool water slide.

Tyler would love to swim here.

"It feels like a whole new world out here." I followed Mona alongside a dining table with a fire pit in the middle. "I love the built-in barbeque," I said.

Then I followed her under an awning, past a set of sofas with outdoor pillows, and between a pool table and a ping pong table.

"You can vacation here instead of going to a resort." I chuckled.

"This is very true. Come. I forgot to show you one more place."

She took me to a room next to the kitchen. The bed was made, but the cell phone on the nightstand and the robe on the bed suggested someone slept there.

"This is my room. Nobody touches my room." She gave me a pointed look. "If you were offered the position, you'd be sleeping in the other spare room. Come."

Wait. What? Sleeping in the other spare room? Had I heard her correctly? I wanted to ask her questions but she hurried along.

We scurried through the kitchen to the other side, near the garage and closer to the front door. This room was just as nice as hers. It also had an adjoining bathroom and a spacious closet.

I'd be sleeping in this room, she said, so the family *was* looking for a live-in nanny. Watching the child was one thing, but having to take care of one twenty-four/seven was another.

Standing on the threshold I asked, "I don't know—did you require—did you request a live-in nanny? I don't remember."

She tilted her head and fluttered her eyelashes. "I don't recall. It's only for two weeks, so you might not be required to stay every night. The parents might be home on some days. And Roselyn is easy to care for. She's truly a joy."

"What are my duties?"

"Give her snacks. Spend time with her. Read her stories. Make and feed her dinner. Give her baths. Not much to it."

"What about taking her to and picking her up after school?"

"The family driver does that."

Lucky little girl.

I leaned back on the doorframe. It was only for two weeks. While she was at preschool, I could paint and help Abby at the gallery.

"You'll get paid four thousand," she added, and squeezed past me into the hall.

"Excuse me?" I rushed after her.

"Did you want more?" She halted by the sweeping staircase and squinted as if disappointed.

I flashed a glance at the towering Christmas tree and said, "Oh, no. I-I didn't know if you were offering me the position. Wait, are you?"

This woman was confusing.

She met my eyes with a stern gaze. "Yes, I am offering it to you, or else I wouldn't be showing you the house."

"But you don't know anything about me. I didn't even give you my resume."

Why was I trying not to get hired? Four thousand dollars was a lot of money for two weeks. Maybe I should change professions.

She crossed her arms. "Kate, I need to find someone fast. And I know enough about you. My sister is a retired cop, and my younger brother is one currently. I asked them to look you up for me. I learned enough to know you can be trusted, and from this interview, you seem like a nice lady."

I tucked a lock of hair behind my ear and dipped my head a little. "Well, thank you."

"To tell you the truth, I've interviewed a handful of nannies already." Mona walked back toward the foyer. "Either they were too old, too young, or my gut told me they weren't the one. It's a small island and the pool of suitable people is not large."

I matched her slow steps across the marble floor.

She added, "I've been a nanny my whole career. I can read people well, and I know what sort of person gets along with children. I can tell you have a kind, genuine heart and common sense."

My face warmed a little. "Thank you, but if you're the nanny, then why am I needed?"

"Look, Kate. My sister just got out of the hospital and I need to take care of her."

"I'm so sorry." I readjusted my purse strap and stopped walking.

She waved a hand. "Thank you. She's doing better. Anyway, I'm not trying to pressure you in taking the position, but I need to find someone right away. The payment is high because it's last minute. I need you to start on Monday, if you are willing. I can ask for higher pay if that's what you want."

I put out a hand. "Oh, no. I'm fine. Four thousand is plenty." Any more than that would be ridiculous. "I have a question, though. Don't the parents want to meet me?"

"They're out of town. They'll be coming home Monday evening and then leaving again. They trust my judgment. I've cared for Roselyn as if she were my own ever since she was born."

"I see. And I have no idea who I'll be working for." I snorted.

She patted my arm in a steady rhythm. "Last name is Banks. That's all you need to know. Just concentrate on Roselyn and you will be fine."

Two weeks. Nothing to it besides the fact I had to take full responsibility for a child and live in a stranger's home.

Mona clasped her hands together under her chin as if in prayer. "So does this mean you'll take the position?"

I had nothing better to do. I might as well work. I could give half of it to my sister to save for a rainy day.

"Sure. I'll take the job," I said with a smile.

Mona released a sigh of relief and shook my hand.

Chapter Twelve – Surprise

Abby's eyes bulged. "You did what?" Her voice rose to a near shriek.

I had sprung the news about accepting the nanny position on her out of nowhere. I would have been shocked, too, had I been in her shoes. She'd only known I had interviewed for regular jobs in my career field.

my career field.

"Four thousand for two weeks?" Stella gazed out the window from her desk.

She certainly wasn't getting paid that much here.

I paced around the sofas and stood in front of the clay models by the window. "It happened kind of fast. Besides, you don't need me, and I have nothing else to do."

Abby leaned her hip against the amenities table and crossed her arms. "That's true. And I'm fine with whatever you decide to do in your free time. I was shocked, that's all. What are their names? Maybe I know them." She poured hot water in sturdy paper cups and handed me one with a tea bag in it.

"Thanks." I took a tiny sip, savoring the warmth as I enjoyed the sweet mango-flavored tea.

"Maybe I'll know them." Stella's gray eyes glistened as she opened her water bottle to take a drink. "I've lived in Poipu, Kauai all my life. It's a small community. Everyone knows everyone."

I eased into the sofa and kicked up my feet on the tea table. Likely nobody was stopping by the store during the lunch hour, so I could get comfortable.

"Do you know the Banks family?"

"Banks? What are their first names?" Stella narrowed her eyes as if I were purposely withholding information.

"Just Mister and Mrs. Banks. A woman named Mona interviewed me."

Abby sat across from me, her fingers clasped around the cup. "And who is Mona?"

"The nanny." I sipped my tea.

Stella gulped down her drink and wiped her mouth. "She must have some power over the family if she's allowed to hire you. And if she's the nanny, why do they need to hire another one?"

"Mona said her sister just got out of the hospital and she needs to take care of her. And the parents are away often. She—Mona—has been the girl's nanny since she was born, apparently. I'll get to meet the parents on Monday. No big deal. It's not like they're wanted criminals and you'll never see me again."

It was supposed to sound absurd, but once I said it out loud, I wondered if there was a possibility of that scenario coming true. Either I needed to stop watching crime shows, or I needed to call Mona and tell her I'd changed my mind.

Abby must have read my expression. "It's fine. I'm sure it's fine. Just call me every day so I know you're not dead." She frowned and brought the paper mug to her lips.

"Their daughter goes to the same preschool as Tyler, and she's the same age. That should make you feel better."

"Really. What's her name?"

"Roselyn."

"Roselyn?" Abby peered up to the ceiling thoughtfully. "Tyler has never mentioned a Roselyn before."

"Maybe they're not friends." I crossed my legs. "Tyler can't be friends with everyone. Aren't there like fifty kids?"

"A bit more. There aren't that many preschools nearby."

"Where's the house located?" Stella scrolled through some pages on her phone.

"More like a mansion." I should have brought that up first. I wasn't going to stay overnight at some sketchy place.

"On Skyshore?" Stella's voice went an octave higher and shifted her gaze to me.

"Yes." I raised an eyebrow.

Stella squealed. "No wonder they're paying you four grand."

Abby bit her bottom lip and cupped her mug with both hands. "I don't know, Kate."

Stella raised her hand. "If Kate doesn't want the job, I'll take it."

We both turned to her for different reasons.

"I need you, Stella." My sister pointed at her. "You're staying. When I hit it big, you're getting a raise."

"A two thousand per week raise?" Stella let out a belly laugh.

Abby turned her lips downward in a pout.

"Awww, Abby, I'll never leave you," Stella said with a mocking tone. She placed her elbow on the table and propped her chin on her fist. "At least for now. But I might go to grad school or actually get a job related to my major."

I took a last drink of my tea and placed the paper mug on the table. "Did Mr. Medici come today to pick up that Cupid figurine?"

"No, he didn't." Stella shifted her attention to her fingers dancing across the keyword. "I packaged it this morning since he left a voice message saying he was coming today."

"Maybe he'll come later or tomorrow." Abby hiked a shoulder.

"Maybe he wants to make sure Kate is working," Stella said with a playful tone as she stole a quick glance my way.

"What? Why would you say that?" I gave her an evil eye.

She waved a hand. "Oh, nothing. Just my observation. Cupid did his job, that's all."

Abby glanced between Stella and me, just as confused as I was. I frowned. She was making more of it than had really happened, but I let it go.

I took the paper mug and refilled more hot water. "By the way, Abby, are you taking Ty to Movie and Popcorn night? Do you know about it?"

"Yes, I was going to ask you to come with us."

I dunked the tea bag several times and tossed it into the trashcan under the table. "Sure. What are we watching?"

"I have no idea. Something animated. That's all I know." Abby pulled her phone from her back pocket and kicked up her feet on the table. Then she shot back up into a sitting position while scrolling through her phone. "Oh, darn it. I told my friends I was free on Saturday night. I was going to ask you to watch Ty for me."

I mixed honey into my tea and stirred the hot liquid with a mixing stick. "Definitely. You go out with your friends and I'll take care of

Tyler."

"I don't know." She bit her bottom lip. "I should spend time with him."

"He'll be fine. You spend almost all of your time with him—one night isn't going to hurt. Besides, when will I ever get to take him to a function alone without you? It'll be quality auntie-nephew bonding time."

"As long as Ty is okay with me not being there, then I'll take your offer. It's been a while since I did adult things."

I was ecstatic to see my sister wanting to go out with her friends. She deserved some fun too—needed to move forward without Steve.

"Well, break time is over." Abby rose and stretched her arms to the ceiling. "I'm going to the back room so I can fix something." She directed her words at me with an accusing squint.

She meant the hot mess called *Mr. Medici's Shirt.*

I shrugged sheepishly and plopped down on the sofa. "I told you I was sorry." I pouted.

When I had told Abby I had painted the huge canvas, she'd thought I'd painted something worth selling. Little did she know I had made a mess. When she'd seen the masterpiece, she'd scolded me over the phone.

She rolled her eyes. "It's fine. Actually, you should come with me and fix it." She pulled me up from my seat.

I pointed at my chest. "You want me to fix *Mr. Medici's Shirt*?"

"Yes. You made the mess. You fix it. And you actually gave that monstrosity a name?"

I raised my hands, palms up, as if to say *who cares?*

We sounded like two kids in a fight. It reminded me of the days when we argued over clothes, makeup, and art supplies. She was right though. I did make that mess and no painting was set in stone.

"Fine." I frowned.

Stella swiveled her rolling chair to face us. "Awww. You two are so cute. I wish I had a sister."

I grabbed my tea and dragged my feet, "Are you sure you'd want what I have to deal with? You might want to take that back, though we are cute."

Abby shook her head and wrapped her arms around my shoulder. "She's not as cute as me."

We laughed like little girls as we entered the painting room.

Chapter Thirteen – After School

Abby and I decided to surprise Tyler by picking him up together after work. Abby had already signed him out and we were waiting by the bulletin board for Mrs. Fong to excuse him.

"Mommy! Auntie Kate!" Tyler rushed out from this classroom and tackled his mom first and then me.

I squeezed him tight, and he made a gruff sound. "How was your day?"

"Good. We made a Christmas ornament with our picture on it, but I can't take it home yet. We can go home now." Tyler clutched Abby's shirt, practically dragging her out.

"Hold on. Let me ask a question." Abby spun to her right, leaving Tyler with me, and stopped at the front desk. "Mrs. Hall, is there a student name Roselyn Banks at this preschool?"

I shoved my fists on my hips and snarled at Abby. I didn't care if anyone saw me act childish. She couldn't leave it alone.

Mrs. Hall adjusted her glasses and blinked. "Mrs. Fuller. Let me take a look, but the name doesn't sound familiar. Is she new?" She thumbed through the files and then scrolled on her computer. "No. We don't have a student named Roselyn Banks. Are you sure you have the right name?"

Abby flashed a glance my way, schooling her face into an *I told you so* expression before she shifted her attention back to Mrs. Hall. "Perhaps I got the name wrong. Thanks for checking."

"You're welcome. Is there anything else I could help you with?"

"No, but thank you. Have a good evening. And thank you for all you do for our children and this school."

"Kiss-butt," I whispered to Abby when she joined us back at the bulletin board.

"Yeah. Yeah. Yeah. Call me whatever you like. Something doesn't feel right."

I furrowed my brow. My sister might be older, but no way would she tell me what to do.

"I'm going there Monday because I made a commitment. If anything feels strange, I'll back out. Maybe Mrs. Hall didn't check the records well, or maybe people who live in a house like that require more privacy. I'm just saying people make mistakes."

"I'm just looking after you, but fine, go get yourself killed." She stabbed me hard with her gaze.

"Mommy." Tyler pointed at a poster on the bulletin board. "Can we go to Movie and Popcorn night? Oh, please, please. They're playing *The Littlest Christmas Tree*, and Jace and Bridget are going. They want me to go too."

Abby lowered to her knees as she did when she wanted his full attention. "Ty, would it be okay if Auntie Kate took you instead of me?"

"I don't mind. Does that mean I can go?"

Abby had been stressing, but Tyler wanted to go so badly he probably didn't care who took him. Sometimes we gave kids no credit.

"Yes," Abby said and kissed his forehead.

"Yah! It's going to be fun." His brown eyes gleamed. "I've never been to one before."

Abby rose and looked at me. "I've taken him to school fundraiser events before, but we never stayed long. So thank you."

"What are sisters for?" I gave her a pointed look.

I understood Abby not wanting to socialize. Having to be polite while she explained repeatedly that her husband was dead would be torture.

Tyler tugged on Abby's shirt, leading her out the door.

Abby turned to me to whisper, "Ty won't hold my hand at school." Then grabbed his arm to prevent him from bumping into another parent. "Whoa, hold on Ty. Why are you in such a hurry?"

"Well, hello there," a sultry voice said.

A gorgeous woman and a handsome boy were also heading to the parking lot.

Tyler scowled.

"Oh, hi Jessica," Abby said nonchalantly. "This is my sister, Kaitlyn."

When she introduced me as Kaitlyn, I knew she didn't like this woman. It had been our secret code since high school.

Jessica's auburn bobbed hair was immaculate, not a strand out of place. The flawless makeup brought out her blue eyes, and the red dress fitted to her curvy body made her look like a Victoria's Secret model.

"Nice to meet you, Kaitlyn." Jessica eyed me from head to toe.

Her scrutiny unnerved me. When she raised her eyebrows, I knew she didn't approve of my faded jeans and loose-fitting T-shirt.

"Same here." I gave her a polite nod.

"Oh, this is my son, Jarrad." She laid a hand on his head proudly. "We're going shopping for the movie night. He's so excited. He wants to wear a new outfit. He's so mature for his age." She giggled. "Will you both be there?"

Jarrad wants new clothes, or you do? Seriously, who shops for new clothes for a movie night?

"I-I—" Abby seemed lost for words.

"I'm taking Tyler. Abby already made plans," I interjected.

"Oh. Okay. Then I'll see you, Kaitlyn. Have a nice evening to both of you and …" She finally looked at my nephew. "And him."

"Tyler," I said, accentuating his name.

"Yes, of course, Tyler." With that, she strutted to a shiny black Mercedes-Benz.

"Wow. Nice friend." I rolled my eyes as we headed to Abby's minivan.

Abby gave me an evil eye. "Not my friend, but I can see you two becoming best friends." She opened the rear door for Tyler.

"You're funny." I faked a laugh.

"I don't like Jarrad," Tyler grumbled and climbed into the car seat.

Abby clicked Tyler's seat harness and tugged at it. "I told you this before, Ty, but you don't have to like everyone. Just treat others as you would like to be treated. Remember that?"

He scrunched his face into a sour expression.

I squeezed my shoulder behind Abby to get a better look at him. "Is he bothering you? Did he say anything to you?"

I swore if Jarrad was bullying him I was going to raise Cain. Sure, I wasn't his mother, but I could be the bad cop when Abby might feel pressure to be nice. No child should ever feel unsafe.

Tyler crossed his arms and scowled. "No. But he likes to show off his new toys and tries to get Bridget's attention."

Abby sighed and patted Tyler's thigh. "You can all play together. We discussed this already."

He let out a huff. "I know, but he only wants to play with Bridget. He doesn't want to play with me."

"What about Jace?" his mom asked.

"Jace ignores him."

"Then you should do the same."

It wasn't my place to tell him what to do, but I felt defensive on Tyler's behalf. "Forget him, Ty. He doesn't deserve your friendship. You're better off without someone like him. Play with nice humble kids. Play with kids like you."

Tyler bopped his shoulders. "Okay."

Just like that, all seemed fine.

Abby turned to face me. "Why does he comply when you say it, but when I say it, it's not okay?"

I hiked a shoulder and smirked. "Because I'm the cool aunt."

She shook her head as she closed the door, and went around to hop in.

Abby started the engine. "Ty. Do you know anyone named Roselyn at your school? Maybe someone's nickname?"

"Roselyn?" Tyler squinted in the sunlight beaming on him and pulled back. "No. Is she going to go to my school?"

Abby looked over her shoulder at Tyler and backed out of her parking spot. "No. I was just wondering. Never mind."

I clicked my seatbelt and released an annoyed sigh. "There are reasonable explanations. I'm still going."

"Stubborn," she said and slid into the lane with oncoming traffic.

I flicked her cheek and leaned back against the door. She knew how much I disliked being called that, just as much as she hated being flicked.

"Ouch." She glared at me, and then looked at the front window and sang, "Stubborn. Stubborn. Stubborn."

Tyler curled in on himself and threw his head back, laughing. "You act like kids in my class," he said, catching his breath.

We cracked up. Just like the good old days, bickering one second and laughing the next.

"Sometimes your auntie acts like one."

"And so does your mother." I turned on the radio and we three fa-la-la-la-la'd all the way home.

Chapter Fourteen – Movie Night

Abby zipped up her jeans in the bathroom, tucked in her tank top, and shoved her arms through the sleeves of the matching magenta cardigan.

Her light makeup enhanced her brown eyes, high cheekbones, and plump lips.

"You look pretty, Mommy." Tyler peered up at her, blinking his long eyelashes, and plopped on Abby's bed.

"Thanks, Ty. You look handsome." Abby glanced at the mirror and pushed back a loose strand she had curled.

I wanted him to look his best for the Movie and Popcorn event, so after dinner, I had gelled his hair back and outfitted him with jeans and a button-up blue and black plaid shirt. Yes, I had a competitive side. If what's-her-name was going to doll up Jarrad then I would do the same to Tyler.

Abby came out of the bathroom and reached down to kiss him.

Tyler backed away. "No, Mommy. You have on lipstick. I don't want you to mark my face."

Abby frowned.

"I'm not wearing any lipstick." I went to the other side of the bed, grabbed his face, and kissed him repeatedly as I inhaled vanilla and honey from his hair.

Tyler pushed away and put out a hand. "Auntie Kate. Once is enough."

I held in a laugh.

"Ready, people?" Abby shouldered the strap of her purse.

"Where are you going?" Tyler slid off the bed and shoved his hands inside his pockets, hiking his shoulders upward.

Abby bent lower to give him her full attention. "I already told you. Out with my friends."

"I know, but where? To a restaurant, or park, or where adults hang out?"

"To a restaurant to eat. We're going to eat and talk. Sometimes mommies need time with their friends. You're okay with Auntie Kate, right?"

Tyler grinned at me. "Yes. I love her."

"Awww. And I love you too." I stood beside him and raised my hand to his head.

"Not my hair!" He jerked backward and almost knocked the photo of Steve off the bedside table.

Abby and I exchanged glances and laughed.

"When did he get big enough to care about his hair?" I frowned, making a sad face.

"In the blink of an eye," Abby said, admiring her son. "Come on. If I don't take you both now, you're going to be late."

We hopped in the minivan. Abby dropped us off at the community center after a quick ride and left to go meet her friends.

Not a cloud in the sky. Countless stars twinkled and dotted the dark canvas. The full moon cast a warm glow over the swaying palm trees and water shimmering like gold glitter.

A rush of cool wind picked up a few strands of my hair as I smelled the ocean scented air. The center sat on a hill, but the tall pampas grass limited some parts of my view of the ocean.

This serene, picturesque moment, I could paint this.

"Let's go in, Auntie Kate. I don't want to miss it." Tyler dashed ahead of me to the ticket booth in front of the entrance.

"Ty, wait. It's fine. We're not late." I speed-walked to catch up as the wind tousled my hair.

Mrs. Hall sat behind a table, collecting tickets at the front of a small line. After a few minutes wait, I pulled out two tickets from my purse and handed them to her.

"Hello, Tyler. Look at you." She lowered her glasses. "You look handsome."

Tyler giggled, but he held up his chin. "Thank you."

"Where is your mom tonight?"

"She couldn't make it. This is Auntie Kate. She's here from Los Angeles to visit us for Christmas."

She smiled at me and said, "You have a lovely auntie, Tyler."

"Thank you," I said.

I'd curled my long hair and put on some light makeup. I'd worn dark jeans and a long-sleeve pink sweater. It was warm during the day, but it got cooler in the evening. I didn't look any different than I did every day, but I appreciated the compliment.

"Enjoy the show." Mrs. Hall smiled and turned to the family behind us as we entered a large square building.

Chairs were lined up in rows in front of a giant screen that took up the back wall. Most of the seats were filled toward the front but there were plenty of seats left. No need to hurry.

Two tables at the back, by the entrance. sold cupcakes and popcorn. The rich aroma of butter popcorn dominated the air.

Lights hung around the room gave it a festive feel, and Christmas songs played softly in the background.

"Let's get some popcorn first before we sit down." I placed my hands on Tyler's shoulders to lead him to the short line. I recalled Abby's words and didn't hold his hand.

"Tyler!" Jace rushed over from one of the rows. "Do you want to sit with me? I'm in the middle. I'm saving a seat for Bridget, too."

If Bridget was coming, then Leonardo and likely his wife would be here. Two adults could be friends, right? I let out a snort, thinking about how I'd fallen on my butt after we bumped heads. Two clumsy friends, that's for sure.

"We can sit with Jace and Bridget, right?" Tyler asked.

"We can sit wherever you want. This is your night. You can go with Jace, I'll find you."

Tyler left in a hurry. I should have asked what flavor he wanted. The list was long, like the menu for shaved ice.

"May I help you?" said a smooth baritone voice.

Too busy deciding which flavor Tyler would like, I hadn't realized I was next. But that voice. I knew that voice. My heart leaped when my gaze met his chestnut-colored eyes.

Leonardo sat in the center with a small cash box in front of him. Plastic buckets of popcorn piled on top of the table according to the flavors: chocolate, white chocolate, butter, plain, caramel, and kettle corn.

"I—hi. Um—" My tongue twisted suddenly and I lost the ability to speak.

Leonardo's eyes grew wider. He looked just as surprised to see me and rose from his chair. "It's nice to meet you—I mean to see you … What flavor are you? I mean …" He blinked. "What flavor would you like?" He rubbed the back of his neck and gave me a crooked grin.

I let out an awkward laugh as I recalled how I had said similar words to him at the gallery, and he chuckled as well.

Leonardo wore jeans and a button-up shirt, casual and less intimidating, but nonetheless attractive. He could wear grubby sweats and he would still look good.

"Which one do you recommend?" My hand hovered first over the caramel corn, and then over the butter flavor.

"Do you like chocolate?"

"I do very much," I said.

"I recommend that one." His lips curled upward.

He had such a charming smile, the kind that created a false sense of bliss. The kind that made you believe in fairytales and treasure waiting for you at the end of the rainbow.

His grin deepened. "Sorry to rush you, but you should hurry. The movie is going to start soon."

"Then two buckets. One kettle corn and the other chocolate. Please." I pulled a wallet from my purse.

"That'll be fifty dollars."

"Fifty dollars?" I winced and looked around to see if anyone heard me raise my voice.

He leaned in closer, and I got a whiff of the cologne that was already familiar. I could drown in his smell.

"I said the same thing," he said. "But it's also a fundraiser. Twenty-five dollars each. Can you believe that?" He placed the two buckets in front of me.

Abby hadn't told me it was a fundraiser or I wouldn't have said anything. I felt like an idiot.

"Well, it's for a good cause." I handed him cash.

Our stare lingered for a few heart beats longer until he lowered his head. "Enjoy the show."

After I got the popcorn, I searched for Tyler as I popped a piece in my mouth. The melting chocolate over the puffy, lightly salted kernels tasted heavenly.

Tyler waved at me frantically. "Here. Here, Auntie Kate."

The whole world could have heard him. To make matters worse, practically all eyes flashed to me as I inched sideways to him in the middle of the fifth row. After I placed my purse strap over my chair, I sat, handed him the kettle corn, and introduced myself to Jace's parents.

An older lady with dark hair walked to the front and spoke into a mic in her hand.

"Good evening, everyone. I'm Hilary, the president of Poipu Preschool. I want to thank you for spending your Saturday night with us and supporting our fundraiser. We are working to expand our program, which includes hiring music and art teachers. All the profits will be going to that account. I would like to thank Mr. Medici for renting this spacious room and the chairs, or we would have been cramped and sitting on the floors at the school."

Laughter filled the room.

"Mr. Medici, please stand up." Hilary searched through the audience. "Oh, there he is."

Leonardo waved from the back. He must be on his way to his seat. But where was Bridget? Jace had told Tyler that he had saved a seat for her.

Hilary continued, "And I would like to thank Mrs. Conner for donating her time in organizing the event and getting the popcorn donated. Mrs. Jessica Conner, please stand up so the audience can see you."

Mrs. Jessica Conner was that pretentious woman I had met. Auburn hair and blue eyes. She not only waved like a beauty pageant queen, but giggled and lowered in a quick bow.

"Please give these two awesome parents a hand."

Parents clapped politely, and children cheered.

"Without further ado, let's start the movie." Her voice boomed through the mic.

The lights went out and the movie began. I grabbed a handful of popcorn and ate one piece at a time. Not a minute later, a child sat next to me. I looked over to see Bridget and her father by her side.

Leonardo leaned back with his eyes trained to the screen. A child occupied a seat on his other side. Where was his wife? I supposed I could have said hello, but I kept quiet and ate my popcorn.

"Hi, Tyler." Bridget leaned forward to get a better view of him.

"Bridget. Why are you late?" Tyler whispered.

"I was helping. Jace was supposed to save me a seat."

"I did." Jace pointed at me. "Tyler's aunt is sitting on it."

Great. My fault.

"Shhh," someone said from behind us.

"Auntie Kate, can you switch seats with Bridget?"

I licked the melted chocolate from my finger, savoring the sweet taste, as I glanced between Tyler and Bridget. Bridget stared at me with pleading eyes. Of course I wouldn't refuse.

"Sure, but do it fast so we don't bother people," I whispered to her. "Ready?"

She nodded.

"Okay. Now."

Bridget stood and stepped around me while I slid into her empty chair. Nothing to it except I bumped into Leonardo when Bridget almost knocked my bucket out of my hands. Popcorn would have not only made a mess all over the floor but would have spilled onto Leonardo's lap.

"Whoa." Leonardo grabbed the back of my chair so he wouldn't collide into the kid next to him.

"I'm so sorry," I whispered.

"It's a bit dark to play musical chairs." He chuckled, his voice soft in my ear. His eyes twinkled in the darkness, reflected from the light from the screen.

I straightened in my seat as heat rose up my neck. "The kids wanted me to switch seats." I leaned closer to keep my voice down and inhaled his scent.

We broke away to watch and I stuffed popcorn in my mouth. The audience laughed at the movie, but I had no idea what had happened.

"How do you like the chocolate?" Leonardo asked a minute later.

"It's very good," I whispered. "Thanks for suggesting it."

"It's my favorite too, but …" A song started in the movie, and the kids sang along.

"What did you say? I couldn't hear." I shifted closer, tilting my head to his.

"They ran out," he repeated over the song, but not loud enough for the people around us to hear.

"Oh, here. We can share." I held the bucket between us.

"I'm fine." He placed a hand on the tub. "But thank you."

"No, I insist. I can't finish it all."

His hand went to his lap, then back to the bucket, then to his lap again, and then finally to the bucket. "Okay. Thanks."

We focused back to the movie, picking out the popcorn a few pieces at a time. I tried not to reach inside at the same time he did, but a couple of times we bumped hands. Each time I felt a jolt to my core. We apologized, exchanged small smiles, and got back to the movie.

The animation was fantastic, and the heartfelt story drew me in. Near the end, when the little Christmas tree who had ran away had found his way home, it was unexpectedly moving. I sniffled, trying to hide my tears.

"Do you need one?" Leonardo handed me a napkin.

"Thank you." Embarrassed, I hid my face and took one from him.

Shedding a few tears in front of anyone was mortifying enough, but I had to do it in front of this man of all people. But I liked that he was observant and engaging with me. For a little while, I'd forgotten he might be married, and I brushed away any attention he had given me. He was being nice—that was all.

Lights went on when the movie ended. I squinted in the brightness. Some parents left in a hurry, while others gathered to talk to each other as their children chased each other around the room.

After we filed out of our row, I waited by the entrance door with Tyler. He wanted to chat with his friends before we left.

"That was awesome," Tyler said. "I want to see it again."

Leonardo and I stood next to each other and waited patiently for the kids to give us a green light to go home. While we listened to the kids' conversation, occasionally our gazes met, and then I looked away with a smile.

"That was fun," Bridget said.

Leonardo cleared his throat. "I'm glad you had fun, Bridget. But, it's time to go home."

Before he could take a step, I said, "Thank you for the popcorn suggestion again." I raised my voice amidst the voices and shuffling of chairs. "Oh, you forgot to stop by to pick up Cupid."

Leonardo blinked as if he remembered something. "Thank you for the reminder. I had meetings all day and I couldn't make it. You're still holding it for me, right?"

I wrung a strand of hair around my ear. "Yes, of course. You already paid for it. We can hold onto it as long as you like. Pick it up at your leisure."

"Thank you. Well, have a nice evening." He dipped his head, a goodbye gesture.

I pivoted to leave when someone came between us.

"Oh, there you are, Lee." Jessica linked her arm with his. "It's hard to find people when they're all bunched up together." She stroked his arm, batting her eyelashes.

Either she was single or not a very good wife. Looked like shopping with her son meant shopping for herself. Jessica wore a stunning black dress, showing more than she should at a family event. A crystal necklace and earrings sparkled on her neck and at her ears, and a Louis Vuitton purse hung over her shoulder.

Leonardo stiffened and slowly retrieved his arm. "Can I help you with something?"

From his professional tone, they weren't lovers or even friends.

"You already have." She giggled. "Just having you here at our little soiree makes me happy. You make people smile, Lee. It was wonderful of you to donate your time and this place. I love charity work. It's so rewarding. We should host something together. Can I call you?"

I wanted to puke at her fake voice and her transparent pickup line. Leonardo met my gaze with a panicked *help me* look. I snickered at that. Poor guy. I had turned to sneak away when Leonardo spoke.

"Have you met Miss Chang?"

"Yes, I have. Hello." Jessica gave me a one-second glance before turning back to her main goal. "So, what do you say, Lee? Put our efforts together for a good cause?"

"My name is Leonardo, but let me see if I can fit it in my schedule. My assistant will contact you if I have time."

His name is Leonardo, but his friends call him Lee. The cab driver's words. Clearly, she was not his friend.

She drew back her shoulders, surprised. "I see. That's fine. When you're not busy then." Jessica glimpsed my way, her cheeks coloring. "Well, I better go find my son." She hurried off in her towering heels.

Leonardo rolled his eyes and scrubbed a hand down his face. "I'm sorry about—"

"Don't apologize." I let out a light laugh. "I'm sorry I didn't save you, but you did fine on your own."

He offered a crooked smile and gazed into my eyes. We stayed like that for who knew how long until a man stepped between us and introduced himself to Leonardo. I backed away a step. The more people surrounded him to thank him, the farther I retreated.

My vision narrowed until I saw only him. Even as he chatted with the other parents, he met my gaze often and gifted me that gorgeous smile, as if he didn't want to let me go.

I fought the urge to stay and finally broke away from this spellbinding moment to search for Tyler, leaving Leonardo alone to deal with the appreciative community.

He might be taken, I reminded myself. But even if he weren't, and even if I was ready for a relationship, someone like him wouldn't date someone like me—a temporary nanny who didn't know what she wanted from life.

Chapter Fifteen – First Day

"You didn't have to drive me," I said.

Abby looked over her shoulder to her right and turned the steering wheel. "I want to know where I should pick up your body just in case I don't hear from you."

"Seriously? You're going to go there?"

Abby glared at me. "You're my baby sister. I care about your safety. Someone has to. I mean, who—"

"Okay, Abby. That's enough." I gritted my teeth as I stared out the window at the ocean.

I loved her, but she could be overbearing and in my business. I wanted her to be my friend, not a mother. I'd thought after high school she would lighten up, but her older sister duty never went away. Even our mother had never been this attentive.

"Turn left up there, after that palm tree," I said quickly. "Right there." I pointed. "Skyshore. You'll see the house."

Abby slowed the car to turn and then parked on the curb in front of a two-story mansion. "Wow. Very nice. Well, good luck and call me."

I got out of the car and opened the back door to get my duffel bag. "It's only two weeks. Besides, I'll only be spending the night when the parents are away for whatever the reason. You'll see me soon. Don't miss me too much. Give Ty my love and kiss him for me." I blew her a kiss and shut the door.

Abby's tires on the gravel sounded loud in the quiet of the posh neighborhood. I watched her leave and then knocked on the front door. The longer I waited, the harder the knots formed in my gut. I inhaled a deep breath and released an even a bigger one.

A door opened.

"Miss Chang." Mona stepped back with a relieved smile.

She must have worried I wasn't going to show up.

"Come in." She opened the door wider and took my bag. "Let me put this away for you. I'll be back with Roselyn. We want her to meet you before the driver takes her to school."

Mona left, leaving me to stare at the crystal chandelier and the grand Christmas tree. I stiffened when a man jogged across the foyer, unbuttoning his shirt.

He must be Mr. Banks.

"Mona, where's my dry cleaning?" he hollered by the stairs, his back to me.

I retreated and watched from the doorway. We hadn't met, and I didn't know if he knew I was there. I'd wait to be introduced by Mona.

Mr. Banks had his hand on the banister, his shoulder muscles taut and defined. When he peered upward, the sunlight cascaded down on his dark hair from the window high above.

"Mona, where are you?"

My heart somersaulted in my stomach. That voice. I knew that voice. I swallowed hard … twice. Surely I was wrong. To prove myself wrong, I came out of hiding and strutted toward him.

"Mr. Banks?"

He spun around and his face registered the same shock I felt. More shocking, his unbuttoned shirt gave me a peek-a-boo of his muscular chest.

I sucked in a breath. "Leonardo? Um … what are you doing here?"

"What am I doing here? I live here. *You're* Kaitlyn Chang? You're the Miss Chang Mona hired?"

He clearly knew my name. He had said it like he didn't know?

"Yes," I said.

"Why?"

What is he implying, exactly? I crossed my arms.

He read my expression well enough to lower his voice. "I didn't mean that. Mona told me the new nanny's name, but I didn't know it was you. I thought it must be a strange coincidence. I didn't know you were a nanny. You work with your sister. Why would you need this job?"

Leonardo was merely explaining, and there was nothing technically wrong in what he said, but somehow it made me mad. Should I be mad? When it came to that man, everything was confusing.

"Would you like me to leave? I can fire myself." I certainly wasn't going to be fired by him.

When he just stared at me, looking perturbed, I walked away. Here I'd thought we'd gotten along just fine at the Movie and Popcorn night. We weren't on bad terms. We hardly knew each other. But his tone made it clear he wasn't happy to see me.

To make matters worse, I felt ridiculous for storming out, but I didn't care if he thought I was rude. Abby would be happy. She didn't have to worry for my safety, but she might need to nurse my ego instead.

"Miss Chang."

I passed the grand Christmas tree.

What was taking Mona so long? But I was glad she wasn't there to witness that scene with … Roselyn? Or was it Bridget? Did he have two daughters? But Mona said I'd be taking care of one. And what was Leonardo's real last name—Banks or Medici? I shook my head, confused.

I was trying to get out of there before a child saw me. If it was Bridget, she'd be shocked.

Bridget, Roselyn. Whoever.

"Miss Chang."

I passed under the chandelier.

Thinking of Mona reminded me she had my bag. Great. I had to turn right back around and ask if she could give it back. So much for the dramatic exit.

Perhaps I could just storm right back in, stomp up the stairs, and swoop back out with my bag, all the while ignoring Mr. Medici.

"Miss Chang."

Making up my mind to get my bag without asking his permission, I whirled just before I reached the front door. Unaware he had caught up and was right on my heels, I collided with him.

My hands somehow slipped through his open shirt and my palm smacked against his warm skin. His arms wrapped around my back to keep me from falling.

Oh, heavens.

Words fled me. The surf rushed in my ears. I saw stars and fireworks around the edges of my vision. I knew he experienced the same intensity when his gaze pierced through mine. Time seemed endless as neither one of us looked away until the fog over my mind vanished.

"I'm so sorry." I backed away as my fingers laced through my hair. "I was going to get my … Mona took it and …" I leaned sideways as if I could point to Mona there.

Surprisingly she stood at the top of the stairs with her arms crossed, looking giddy as a child holding cotton candy with her lips spread in a delighted smile.

If I didn't know better, I'd call her smug. Next to her was Bridget, her eyebrows arched upward in confusion. Had they been there all along, watching us?

"Mona?" I clenched my jaw and walked toward her, Leonardo behind me. "Where did you go?" Then I mustered a sweet smile. "Hello, Bridget."

"Hello, Tyler's aunt." Bridget waved, keeping the same flustered expression.

Mona took one step at a time down the stairs. "I put your bag away in your room as I said. I was going to introduce you to Mr. Medici, but you two were already … talking." She pursed her lips, suppressing a laugh.

So Medici and not Banks. Why had Mona lied to me?

My face burned. I took a quick peek at Leonardo next to me—Mr. Medici, now that he was my boss—and he was rubbing his neck.

"I was trying to explain to Miss Chang that I was confused, that's all." Leonardo's grin tugged up at one corner.

Was he laughing at me?

"It didn't sound like he was," I said to Mona.

"Well, if Miss Chang would just stay put like a grown-up and let me explain, we wouldn't be wasting time." His voice was soft and calm, but his brow furrowed. Then, as if he realized his daughter was present, he said, "Bridget, everything is fine. This is Miss Chang. She'll be taking care of you in place of Mona until she returns. We talked about this, remember?"

Calling Abby to pick me up did cross my mind, but now that I knew who I would be working for and this unnerving situation had settled, I decided to stay. Two weeks. Nothing to it.

Bridget nodded. "Yes, I remember. Does that mean Tyler will be staying over too?"

Her blue, glistening eyes made me think of the ocean.

"No, sweetheart. Just his aunt. Are you ready for school?"

"Yes." She bounced on the balls of her feet on the marble floor.

She looked adorable in jeans and a purple shirt with unicorns on it. Her hair was braided in two sections tied with pink and white ribbons. Her white Mary Jane shoes reminded me of the ones I'd had when I was little.

"Wait. Who is Roselyn?" I asked Mona.

Her eyes widened. "Oh, that. Mr. Medici will explain. Well, I have to go, my ride is here. Mr. Medici, your dry cleaning is in your room. Look again in your closet. I set it to the side. And Miss Chang, Mr. Medici can tell you everything I was going to tell you. Unfortunately, I'll be late if I don't go now. And Bridget, you need to get to school." She shouldered her purse and scurried to the front door.

Mona sounded like a mother who had just given strict orders to her two children before leaving for work.

"Have a good day, sweetheart. I'll call you tonight." Leonardo got to his knees and embraced his daughter. "I love you."

Bridget nestled her head into the crook of his head and neck. "Have a safe trip. I love you, too."

The tender loving interaction tugged my heart and my vexation eased.

"Come on, dear. I'll take you to Phillip. He's waiting for you outside." Mona took Bridget's hand and guided her toward the door.

"Is Miss Chang going to pick me up?" Bridget asked, her feet scurrying to keep up with Mona.

Before I could answer, Mona said, "No, Phillip will. Everything stays the same. Oh, Miss Chang, don't forget to put the chicken in the oven at four and take it out by five thirty."

Mona closed the door, but it sounded more like a slam in the dead quiet. Then they were gone, leaving Mr. Medici and me by the stairs.

"Let's start over?" Leonardo's eyes widened, almost pleading, and then he extended a hand.

"Sure." My traitorous gaze settled on his unbuttoned shirt when I shook his hand. I lowered my eyes so he wouldn't notice.

But he did.

He began to fasten buttons as he spoke. "Mona started dinner for you and Bridget. I won't be home for dinner. Actually, I'm not going to be home for a couple of days. When I come back, I'll be home a day or two. You're welcome to go home during those days if you'd like."

"Great. Thank you." I paused to figure out how to ask what I needed to know. "How about Mrs. Medici? Will she be around or on the trip with you?"

I didn't know how to ask about his significant other. Nobody had mentioned anything about Bridget's mother. I hadn't seen anyone besides the three of them, but perhaps Mrs. Medici was packing for the trip.

"No. There is no Mrs. Medici," he said flatly.

Strange. Mona had indicated during the tour that the household had two parents.

"Oh." I tried to make nothing of it and keep my tone neutral. "So, Banks? Roselyn? Could you explain, please?"

His gaze lowered to the marble floor and then back to me. "I'm sorry for misleading you, but if we had told applicants my real name when they interviewed, news would have spread fast. I wanted people to apply with genuine interest for the job, not curiosity about me."

A man of his status and money probably got a lot of attention from people, including those with an angle. I'd already seen how women, like Jessica Conner, worked hard to get his attention.

"Anyway, I left my cell number with emergency contacts just in case on the kitchen counter. If you have any questions, please don't hesitate to call. Also, if you wouldn't mind, please text me your number."

"Of course."

"Thank you." He gave a polite nod and finished buttoning up his shirt.

"You were asking Mona for your dry cleaning, right? Did you want to change your shirt?" I pointed at his shirt pocket.

He glanced down at the small yellow stain, the reason he'd been taking off his shirt in the first place.

"That's right." He furrowed his brow. "That's what I get for being in a hurry. Thank you for the reminder. I'm going to change and then leave. Have a good day."

"You too." I watched him strut up the stairs maybe longer than I should.

My pulse finally slowed to a steadier beat, but the warmth from Leonardo Medici's skin lingered on my hands.

Chapter Sixteen — Snooping

After Leonardo left, I wanted to check out the chicken Mona wanted me to bake. As I headed to the kitchen, I did a double take in the family room.

A large framed photo of Bridget wearing a white ruffled dress hung over the mantel. A small beaded tiara crowned her long locks that flowed over her shoulders. It hadn't been there the last time, and neither had the photos in the cabinet.

One that caught my eye was a picture of baby Bridget and Leonardo hugging. I smiled, then wondered about the mystery of Bridget's mother.

When I had come for an interview, there had been no photos, which I'd thought was strange, but now it all made sense. If an interviewee recognized the people in the photos, they would know who lived here.

I went to the kitchen and opened the fridge. A silver baking tray sat on a tidy shelf, and I pulled it out to sniff. Not only had she seasoned the chicken, she'd left me simple baking instructions and the times to put it in the oven and when to take it out.

"You are good at your job, Mona," I said.

Having time to kill, I washed the frying pan and a few dishes. Then I roamed about downstairs, opening all the doors. There was a fitness room Mona hadn't showed me before. The last door led to a laundry room as big as my sister's family room. Then when I thought I knew every nook and cranny of the first floor, I went to the second.

I took the sweeping staircase and glanced between the left and right hall. The left led to the master bedroom Mona hadn't offered to show me the last time I was here, and the right led to the other rooms.

I gravitated toward the left. No one had told me I couldn't go in Leonardo's room. A quick peek wouldn't hurt. Besides, I was the nanny and I needed to know every inch of this mansion.

Just as I swung the door open, I wondered if there were cameras in the house. I also wondered if Leonardo had some kind of app on his phone to monitor the cameras that might be scattered about.

Some of my friends had doggie cameras. They'd shown me the funny things their pets did when owners weren't around. Not only could they monitor the rooms, but they could broadcast their voices through a smart speaker.

Too late.

My pulse kicked up, but I told myself Leonardo was on his private plane and too busy to spy on me. Bridget wasn't even home yet, and Leonardo had things to do, like not be late for his meeting. Wherever he was going. I hadn't even asked—not that I needed to know.

There was no portrait in his neatly made master bedroom. Only the king-size bed, cherry-wood dresser to the right, a large flat screen television across from the bed, and a painting hung to the left.

I marveled at the painting, so familiar that I knew every detail of the colors and strokes. I went closer and sure enough, my signature was on the right corner.

Leonardo had bought my painting? He thought my painting was worth hanging in his bedroom? I couldn't believe this.

I'd felt like half of me was missing when Abby had told me she'd sold it a couple of years ago in New York, but she hadn't told me who had bought it. But then again, I hadn't known Leonardo then. If she had told me the buyer's name, it wouldn't have meant anything.

An artist pours their heart and soul into their craft, and it was always difficult to part with any creation, but this one, *My Soulmate*, meant the most to me.

I recalled the night that had given me the inspiration for the piece. The night sky had been filled with stars and I'd pulled over on my way home to study them.

The leftmost star was me, and the farthest right star was my soulmate, whoever he might be. I'd once believed it was Jayden. How wrong I had been. I wasn't sure if I believed in soulmates anymore.

Abby had sold a handful of my paintings before, but never to someone I knew. It felt strange knowing he had my favorite.

Do I tell him?

Feeling like I had overstepped my boundaries, I made my way out and shut the door. I went to Bridget's room next, which was awash with sunshine, the window facing the grand backyard.

The giant stuffed unicorn with a rainbow-colored horn still sat at the back corner, and her pink unicorn bedding hadn't changed. I'd half-expected the room to be transformed into something entirely different.

Dainty white furniture embellished her room. The bed, the dresser, a desk, and a bookcase were all the same as before, only now there were photos on her dresser. One was of Bridget and a beautiful woman. She must be her mother. They both had the same blue eyes, blonde hair, and similar features. I'd thought the woman I had seen at the plaza was his wife, but the women looked nothing alike.

The second photo was of the three of them, Bridget, Leonardo, and the woman. They were at the beach, and they looked so happy. I wondered what had happened.

Most couples shared custody after a divorce, shuttling the kid back and forth from week to week. Not a word about Bridget going to her mother's within the two-week span I had been hired to stay.

I needed to stop being nosy. None of my business. Take care of the kid for two weeks and that was all. Simple enough.

I startled when my phone vibrated silently in my back pocket. I had forgotten I had put it there. It was a text from my sister. She said she had something to tell me and that I should message her back. She knew I'd be annoyed with her for checking up on me so soon.

The never-ending dots indicated she had a lot more to say. Why didn't people just pick up the phone and call? I was guilty of it too. So I sat on the edge of the mattress and called her.

"Hello. Kate?" She sounded hesitant.

"I'm calling to let you know I'm still alive."

"Uh hum." My sister cackled through the phone.

"What's so urgent? But I have something to tell you too, so you first."

She sighed like she had a mouthful to say, something I wouldn't like. "Okay. Don't get mad, but I did some snooping around."

Starting with "don't get mad at me" didn't bode well. I wanted to tell her she had to stop meddling with my life, but she was my older sister. She always had my back. And grieving her husband might make her even more overprotective of those she had left. So I listened.

She continued, "Anyway, one of my friends, who knows Jessica

Conner—"

"Jessica Conner. Seriously?"

"Just listen," she groaned. "Anyway, my friend, who knows Jessica, said her friend's friend went for the interview the day before you went."

She had lost me already. I rose and leaned my hip against the bedpost. "And?"

"Obviously, she didn't get the job, but she thought it was strange when there were no pictures of the family at their home. She also thought it was strange when there was no Roselyn Banks listed in any nearby school. So she did some digging and she thinks Mr. Banks is not Banks but Medici. Is she right?"

I laughed out loud.

"What's so funny?"

"I met Mr. Banks, all right. And yes, the friend is right."

"*What*?"

I had to pull the phone away. "That was my reaction too. It seemed they wanted someone genuine."

"Huh?"

I picked up one of the stuffed unicorns by the wall and set it by her pillow. "You know, someone who didn't want to get into Medici's pants … or his money."

"Ohhh."

She got it. "Yup."

"And Roselyn?"

"Yup, really Bridget."

"Wow."

I loved how Abby and I communicated with few words.

"So … are you staying?" she asked hesitantly.

"Of course I'm staying. Four grand, Abby. It's not like I have any other agenda. And do you remember my star painting you sold in New York? The one I named *My Soulmate*?"

"Yes. I love that one. It was one of your best," she said with a hint of pride.

I sat back on the bed again. "Do you recall who bought it?"

"I don't remember. I'll have to check, but I do recall I had to ship it. Why?"

"It's hanging in Leonardo's bedroom," I said, a bit too excited.

"His bedroom? What are you doing in his bedroom?" She sounded accusatory.

"I'm not. I'm in Bridget's. I snuck a peek, though." I went to her window and looked out to the beautiful backyard. The grand swimming pool looked tempting. It was probably heated and comfortable year-round.

"Kate." A warning.

"Oh. My. God. Abby, I'm not doing anything to get fired."

"That's not what I'm worried about."

I paced from the window to the door, back and forth as I spoke. "I'm not going to fall for him if that's what you're implying. Yes, he's very good looking, charming, but he's a bit annoying and quirky too. Besides, someone as rich as him has nothing to gain from someone like me."

"What do you mean someone like you? You're beautiful, kind, giving, and anyone would be lucky to have you. Jayden is an idiot, and besides, he wasn't good enough for you. Just because he cheated on you doesn't mean there's something wrong with you. Real men don't cheat. Real men know when they have someone worth loving and they hold on to it."

Her words unleashed some of the pain I shoved aside. I had been so angry with Jayden and myself that I hadn't had time to process much. Sometimes it was easier to bury feelings than face them. I plopped down on Bridget's white plush rug next to her bed.

"Is there anything else you need to tell me?" I asked when silence fell between us.

"I'm sorry, Kate. I didn't mean—"

"No, no. You're fine. Are you on your way to get Ty? I miss him." I pulled up my knees to my chest and leaned back on the footboard.

"Yes. I'm going to get him after I hang up with you. He misses you too."

"Give him a kiss for me. I'll come home when Leonardo comes back from his trip. I won't be staying here every night it seems."

Maybe it was Abby bringing up Jayden combined with being alone, but the tears wouldn't stop and I didn't want her to hear me. I also cried for my sister, who had lost her husband too soon. For Tyler, who would have to grow up without a father. Then for my brother-in-law, whom I missed dearly. I let the hurt, the frustration, the betrayal, the resentment, and even guilt out.

The thing about crying your heart out is you feel lighter. Somehow everything looks a little shinier.

I went back to the kitchen to read the detailed instructions Mona had left for me. Then I checked on the chicken baking after I tidied the house. Almost time.

The sound of the door opening echoed.

Bridget was home.

Chapter Seventeen – All the Sparkling Things

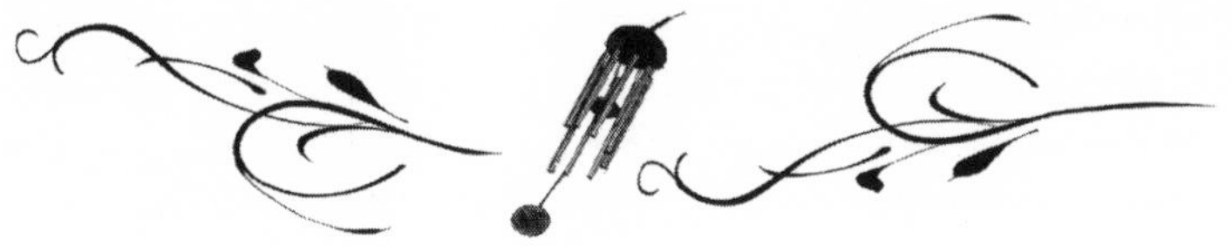

"Hi Bridget," I said.

She slid through the open door, a middle-aged man at her side.

"You must be Phillip." I extended my hand.

"Yes, Miss Chang. Mona told me you'll be taking over her position for two weeks. I'm sure Bridget is in good hands. If you need to go anywhere, please give me a ring. I'm at your service." He tipped his head and left, leaving Bridget and me in the quiet.

Bridget headed up the stairs without a word.

"Are you hungry or thirsty?" I said, following her.

She turned to face me halfway up. "No, thank you."

"Do you need help with anything?"

Was I supposed to go to her room with her? Mona hadn't written that part down. I tried to follow my instincts and not overthink it.

"No, I'm fine," she said in her cute, soft voice. "I'm going to change my clothes and come down."

"Okay. I'll wait for you downstairs." I watched until she was completely out of my sight and headed to the kitchen.

Talking to Tyler was easy, but I knew nothing about Bridget. I would have to see how much she'd open up to me.

The timer dinged. I opened the oven door and backed away as hot steam blew out.

I put on mitts, took out the baked chicken and sliced it into serving portions. After grabbing two plates, I arranged a drumstick, carrots, beans, and potatoes.

Just as I wondered if I should check on her, footsteps padded and she stood by the leather sofa where the family room opened up to the kitchen. She had changed into a pair of jeans and a T-shirt with a cute unicorn and the words *Follow your Dreams.*

"Are you hungry?" I asked, setting our plates down across from each other.

She jerked a shoulder and looked at the bookcase in the family room, avoiding my eyes.

When Bridget had come home, I'd thought I detected an attitude from her. Now it was evident. No Father, no Mona to keep her in check. Just a new person she thought she could run all over.

I grabbed two glasses of water from the kitchen and set them down on the table. "Mona said to have dinner ready for you by six. Are you ready to eat?" I pulled out a chair and took a seat.

"I guess." She crossed her arms.

I needed to find what we had in common and go from there.

"Well, you can try some of Mona's chicken, but if you don't feel like it then you can eat later. I'm not going to force you if you're not hungry."

"You're not?" She sounded surprised, relaxing her arms.

"Nope." I bit into the soft meat from the drumstick I held. "Mmmm. Hot out of the oven. This is so good. Mona makes the best chicken." I licked my lips. "I can taste the garlic, oregano, basil, and even mangos."

Bridget took a step away from the sofa, licking her lips.

"I don't think I've ever tasted something this good." I shoved a green bean into my mouth. "Yum. With butter. The beans are to die for, and I hate beans."

Bridget inched closer, tugging at the hem of her shirt.

"If you don't want yours, I'll be happy to eat them." I sucked my buttery fingers, one at a time with exaggerated delight.

She scrunched up her nose. "I think I'll try eating. Mona might get mad if she finds out I didn't eat on time." She took her seat across from me and dug in.

I forked a potato and nibbled on it. "I agree. You're very smart."

She sat taller and her eyes gleamed. "Mona says I'm smart too."

"Because she's right. And I also like your shirt."

Bridget lowered her gaze to her shirt, and then looked at me. "You do?"

"I love unicorns. My sister thinks I'm too old to like unicorns, but I don't care. I wish my room looked like yours."

Her lips tugged wider, and she gnawed on her drumstick.

"According to your schedule, you can have dessert after dinner.

You can have some fresh baked cookies Mona made this morning or some ice cream. Which one would you rather have?"

"Ice cream." She paused, staring at her food, and then peered up to add, "Please."

"Ice cream it is. Did you see Tyler at school today?" I took a sip of my water.

Tyler was something else we had in common. A safe topic.

She nodded, her mouth full of carrots. She wiped her lips with a napkin. "Yes, but I think he's mad at me."

"Why? What makes you think that?"

She blinked, looking unsure. "I think … because you're here instead of at his house."

"Oh. We can set this straight. How about we call him after dinner?" I took another bite of the chicken.

She shook her head, her voice high pitched. "No. I don't want you to ask him."

I put my drumstick down and wiped my fingers on the napkin. "It's okay. I'm not going to ask him if he's mad at you. I'm going to call him because today is the first day I'm not with him. I was going to talk to him, anyway. I promise I won't bring up anything you don't want me to. I wouldn't do that to you. I promise with all the unicorns, rainbows, and all the sparkling things."

Bridget giggled, the cutest sound. Well, second cutest, after Tyler.

"Unicorns, rainbows, and all the sparkling things." She cracked up like I had told her the funniest joke. She laughed so hard she began coughing.

My heart shot up to my throat. I sprinted around the table to pat her back and offered her cup. "Here, drink."

After she gulped some water, she eased her shoulders.

"You okay?" I asked and sat back down.

"Yeah. That was close." She sounded like a grown-up. "I like that you like unicorns."

"I like that you like that I like unicorns." I tossed a carrot in my mouth.

She giggled.

"That will be our mantra," I said.

"What's a mantra?"

"Something we'll say that has a special meaning just between us."

"Ohhhh. I like that."

After dinner, I cleared the plates and Bridget went to her room. I called her down for dessert, and this time she didn't hesitate. She sat on the counter stool instead of at the dining table.

"I know you said you wanted ice cream, but I'm double checking. Cookies or ice cream?" I had set both on the counter, along with bowls and spoons.

Her eyes bounced between them, sticking out her tongue. "I can't decide. I wanted ice cream at first, but now I don't know." She propped her forehead on her hand and sighed as if this was the hardest decision she'd had to make.

I wrinkled my nose and placed my chin under my fists, elbows on the counter. "Well … how about we have both?"

"Both?" Her eyes sparkled brighter than the kitchen lights. "Mona doesn't let me have both."

"Mona isn't here, is she? That means I get to make the decision. Just this once, I think you deserve both for being brave."

She blinked and her eyes rounded. "I was brave? How?"

"Well, two people you love are away and you are acting like a big girl by letting me watch over you. And I want to thank you for accepting me."

She dipped her head wordlessly. I could assume she felt guilty for giving me an attitude earlier.

"Maybe I wasn't that brave," she said softly.

"I think you are. So let's eat." I scooped small portions of chocolate and strawberry ice cream into two bowls and shoved a snickerdoodle in the middle. "There. One for you and one for me."

Bridget's eyes widened in delight as she picked up a spoon.

"Wait. We forgot something." I went to the fridge and took out a can of whipped cream. "Do you want some?"

"Yes." She jumped in her seat and clapped.

I shook the can and swirled the cream in both of our bowls. "There. Now it's perfect. Cheers." I raised my spoon.

Bridget clinked her spoon with mine and dug in. "This is the best."

"Oh, wait." I walked back to the kitchen cabinet next to the sink and nabbed the cake decorations I'd seen when I was snooping. "It's not dessert without sprinkles," I sang.

"I never had them on ice cream before, only on cupcakes."

"Well, now you have." I sprinkled the pretty pink dots inside the bowls. They fell like snow. "To unicorns, rainbows, and all the sparkling things," I said, holding up a spoon.

Bridget giggled, clinking her spoon against mine once more.

I think we'll get along just fine.

We ate until we were scraping the bowls.

Chapter Eighteen – Bedtime Story

Mona's instructions stated, in capital letters, that I had to help Bridget with her bath after dinner, but Bridget was not my child. Mona had been her nanny since she was a baby, but I was someone new. I had to be sensitive about the situation.

Bridget's bathroom was connected to her bedroom. Lucky girl. I tested the water temperature—not too hot or cold—then I told Bridget to get in while I had my back toward her.

Once she was covered in bubbles, I handed her a unicorn wash scrubber and set the pink towel by the tub for easy access. As she bathed herself, I sat on the toilet lid, glancing at her unicorn bath rug, toothbrush, and hand towels. After she was done washing, she put on her unicorn PJs and got into bed.

"Miss Chang, can you read me a bedtime story?"

"Of course," I said as I tucked her inside the blanket. "I was just going to do that, but only if you call me Kate. Do you have a book in mind or do you want me to pick one?"

She stuck her hand under the pillow and yanked a book out. "This one," she said excitedly.

I read the title and laughed. "I should have guessed. *Goodnight, Unicorn.*"

The cover featured a white unicorn with a rainbow horn running across a glittering rainbow.

"Is it okay if I sit on your bed?" I asked.

She scooted over and settled herself with cushions behind her. I rested on top of her soft, fluffy comforter and read aloud while she held the book.

About halfway through the book, the sound of soft and soothing wind chimes came from my phone, almost identical to the chimes I'd heard at Abby's gallery, when Leonardo stormed off after I got paint on his shirt. And I felt that same invisible hand caress down my back.

Strange. I hadn't changed my ringtone. When I grabbed my cell next to me on the bed, Bridget jolted up into a sitting position, her wide eyes twinkling.

"My mama. That's my mama!"

At Bridget's outburst, I ditched the call and swung my legs around, ready to greet her mother. Halfway to my feet, it hit me. Leonardo had said there wasn't a Mrs. Medici. I closed my eyes and listened, but the rest of the house remained silent. No footsteps strode toward us from the hall.

I eased back down next to her. "Bridget. What are you talking about, sweetheart?"

She fluffed her pillow and leaned back to the headboard. "When the wind chimes, an angel is near. That was my mama, I know it."

A quiver passed through me. "Can you tell me more about your mama?"

She didn't have a chance to answer. My phone chimed again and *Leonardo Medici* flashed on caller ID. I hadn't answered his call seconds ago, so I picked it up. My heart raced. This man caused my body way too much disruption.

"It's your dad. He wants to video chat with you." I brushed a thumb across and handed her the phone. Something about speaking to him face-to-face seemed intimate. He'd called for his daughter and not for me anyway.

Leonardo's face popped up. "Hello, sweetheart."

"Hello, Papa." She waved her small hand.

"I see you're ready for bed. Good girl. How was your day?"

"Good. And Kate—I mean Miss Chang—is very nice. And you know what? She loves unicorns as much as I do." She flashed me a smile, and then got back to the conversation.

"That's great. Remember you have a piano lesson tomorrow."

"I know." She puckered her lips and bounced once on the mattress. "You don't have to remind me."

"Yes, boss." He winked, making Bridget giggle. "Anyway, I called to say goodnight. I'll see you in three days. I love you, Unicorn."

"I love you, Skeleton."

"Can you give the phone back to Miss Chang, please?"

When Bridget handed me the phone, my heart thudded faster. I didn't like that he made me so nervous, so I clipped that feeling and presented my professional smile. I mostly resisted the urge to check my image in the corner and try for my best angle.

"Hi." I stared into the screen at his face … his thick eyebrows, his stunning chestnut-colored eyes, his sharp nose, and those lips that made you wonder what they tasted like. Then a horrifying thought came to mind. He could see every detail of my face, so I pushed back the phone.

"Miss Chang."

"Kate. Call me Kate, please."

"Kate …" He paused and seemed to have lost his words.

"Did you need anything?" I found myself lacking words and lost in his eyes.

"I wanted to thank you. If you need anything, please don't hesitate to call."

"You don't have to thank me. It's my job." I flashed a glance at his daughter and smiled.

His eyebrows drew to the center, like he was concerned. "I … Well—"

"Leonardo. Who are you talking to? I hope it's not business." A woman's voice.

The phone shifted. I got a glimpse of people at a table with candles shimmering. I bristled, my heart thundering. This situation reminded me of the night Jayden had cheated on me. He'd said he was away on a business trip, but he wasn't. He'd drunk too much and video chatted me. Some girl he was with had showed herself and made out with him.

"I'm talking to my daughter." His voice sounded muffled, like he didn't want me to hear, and then I didn't know what else he said.

"Mr. Medici?" I had to repeat his name.

"Miss Chang. Sorry about that. Anyway …"

I didn't bother asking him to call me Kate again. "Well, looks like you're busy. Please go back to your dinner. Bridget is fine. Everything is fine." I angled the phone so he could see his daughter one last time before we ended the call.

"Good. I'm not checking up on you. I know Bridget is in good hands. Thank you again."

"Goodnight," I said in a professional tone and pushed back into the headboard.

Bridget looked at me with her head tilted when I hung up. The way she crinkled her nose and scrunched her eyebrows reminded me of how Tyler looked when he was thinking over something intently.

"Is something wrong, Bridget?"

"Are you mad?" She pulled her blanket up to her chest.

"What? No. What made you think that?"

"You sounded mad."

I'd been sure I kept a steady tone. Had I raised my voice? "I couldn't hear well. Anyway, you want to continue?" I flipped back to the page we had left off.

The corners of her mouth turned down, her eyes wide with concern.

"What's wrong?" I wondered if I'd said something to upset her.

"Can you sleep with me? I get scared at nights. Sometimes Papa or Mona sleeps with me when I ask."

I smiled. "Sure. Not a problem."

She shifted to get comfortable among her pillows.

"Bridget, I promise I won't get mad, but did you do something to my phone? Like change the ringtone by accident?"

"No, I promise." She shook her head.

I wasn't even sure when she would've had access to it. The only time I hadn't had it was when I was in the bathroom. But it wouldn't be the first time my phone had done something strange on its own, so I brushed it off.

"Bridget, where's your mother?" I attempted to ask once more. I assumed from her previous words that her mother was dead, that she was an angel, but sometimes kids get their words mixed up.

It seemed like a simple question, but she didn't answer and pointed to the book. I began to read aloud. It was none of my business.

Just do your job. Don't meddle.

When Bridget fell asleep, I turned off the lights and called Abby as I lay in bed.

"Hey. How's it going?" Abby said.

"Fine. How's everything on your end?" I whispered and stared at the nightlight by the bathroom.

"The same. Nothing's new. I'm in bed."

"Can I speak to Ty?" I shifted to my side, facing Bridget.

“Sorry. He’s already asleep.” She sounded tired.

“Oh,” I dropped my voice. “Can you make sure he calls me tomorrow?”

“Of course.”

“Can you do me a favor?” I yawned and stretched my arms and flexed my bare feet.

“Sure.”

“Can you ask your friend that knows Jessica’s friend’s friend if they know anything about Bridget’s mother?”

“Huh?”

I snorted. That sounded confusing and crazy.

“Oh, gotcha. Sure. Is everything okay?”

“Yeah.” I stroked Bridget’s hair.

Everything was fine with me, but maybe not for this little girl. Kids her age would jump at the chance to talk about their mother, but she’d brushed off my question. It was probably a sensitive subject.

My heart hurt for her. I told myself not to get too involved when I was going to be a temporary fixture in her life, but I needed to be aware so I could be sensitive to her situation.

After I hung up, I slept next to Bridget as promised. I wished for her to dream nothing but unicorns, rainbows, and all the sparkling things.

Chapter Nineteen – Welcome Home Lee

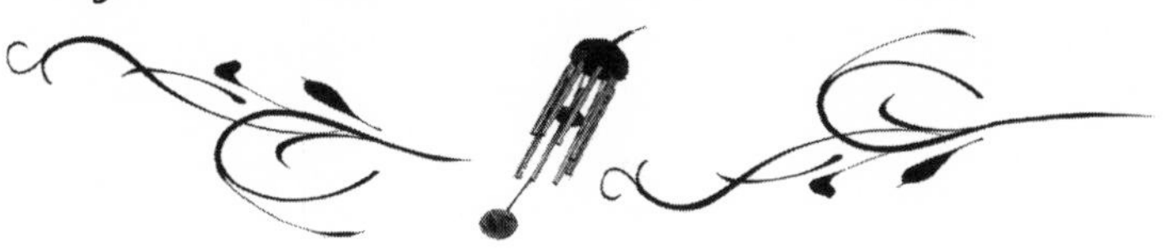

As Bridget and I were coming down the stairs together to eat dinner, the front door opened.

"Papa?" Bridget rushed ahead of me, her feet thudding down the stairs.

Under the crystal chandelier, down on his knees, Leonardo wrapped Bridget in his arms as he stood, giving her tons of rapid kisses on her head. He twirled her and brought her down. Her sweet laughter rang in the air.

I counted the days in my head. Lee had come home a day earlier than expected.

"The meeting went well, so I came home. Unless you want me to go back." He turned sideways, reaching for the door.

"No." Bridget yanked on his hand, and then she was swinging from his flexed arm.

I laughed as I hit the bottom step. So much love between them. I was seeing a whole different side of him—more playful and down to earth. Not the businessman I had met in the cab. Even his attire was causal—jeans and a black T-shirt.

The door opened and Phillip walked in with Leonardo's briefcase and suitcase. "I'll put them in your room, sir."

"I can do it. Just leave them there."

"Very well, sir. Goodnight." He tipped his head to me and walked out.

I cleared my throat and smiled. "Well since you're home early, I guess that means I can go home. Dinner is already set on the table." I waited for Leonardo to confirm, but he didn't say a word.

"No," Bridget protested, catching me off guard. "Can Kate stay for dinner?"

Leonardo raked his hair back. "Of course, but only if she wants to."

Bridget jumped up and down as she begged. "Please, please, *please*."

I didn't know what to do. I felt like I was intruding. Leonardo hadn't asked me to stay, Bridget had. I didn't want him to feel uncomfortable. After days away, he had come home to relax, not to entertain. However, the plea in Bridget's eyes could not be denied.

Eat dinner and leave. Simple.

"Sure. I'll stay for dinner. I didn't make anything special. Bridget wanted tacos, and it was on Mona's approved list."

"I love tacos" Leonardo said, and then turned to his daughter. "I think Bridget knew I was coming home." He tapped her nose with love in his expression.

She bobbed on her heels and giggled. Bridget grabbed my hand and then her father's, and pulled us toward the dining room.

While Bridget and I settled in our chairs, Leonardo set his phone down on the table and strolled to the kitchen.

"Go ahead and eat," Leonardo said, opening the fridge. "I'm going to pour some wine. Would you like some, Miss Chang?"

"Please call me Kate. And yes, thank you." I placed a tortilla on my plate and scooped some spiced chicken.

He came back with two glasses filled with red wine. He handed me mine and sat across from me. I took a sip, savoring the rich, fruity notes and cool sensation down my throat.

He tapped Bridget on top of her head. "So what did you do while I was gone?"

Bridget lightly slapped her forehead with a roll of her eyes "You already know. I told you everything on the phone." She picked up her hard-shell taco and nibbled the end.

"Geesh, already starting at age four." Leonardo shook his head, smiling, and lifted a tortilla onto his plate.

"I'm going to be five soon." Bridget held up her hand to me. "I'm going to have a party in four weeks and Papa said I could invite anyone I want."

"I bet it's going to be a unicorn theme." I scooped up some guacamole and layered it on top of the spiced chicken.

Bridget's lips parted in surprise. "How did you know?"

"Because that's the theme I would have."

"Papa." She clutched his shirt and shook him. "Kate loves unicorns as much as I do."

"She does? That's wonderful. You have someone to talk about it with." He chuckled.

His ears must be full of unicorn talk daily.

"Can I invite Kate, too? I'm going to invite Tyler."

My cheeks heated. I didn't want Leonardo to be put on the spot.

"Sure, If Miss Sum—"

I cleared my throat. "Kate."

"Kate." He nodded my way after he corrected himself. "Has time. I'm sure she's busy, but no pressure."

"I'll see, but I don't know if I'll be around." I rolled up the soft tortilla.

"Oh?" Leonardo set down his wine glass with a light clink.

"I don't live in Kauai. I'm here for the holidays with family. Unless I find a job I can't live without, I'll have to go back to Los Angeles."

"I see." Leonardo made another taco for himself, this time with a hard shell.

"Did you bring me something from work?" Bridget asked her dad with a mouthful.

"Oh, I almost forgot." Leonardo reached inside his front pocket and handed something to Bridget.

"It's beautiful." Bridget held up a magnet to show me—The Hollywood sign that had *I Love LA* on it.

"You were in Los Angeles?" I asked.

"Yes. I went to wrap up a business deal. My client bought a hotel in Santa Monica overlooking the ocean."

I could only imagine how much that cost. I wondered if that mysterious woman was the buyer who'd had her hand on his shoulder. I shook that thought away. None of my business.

"I don't know much about your company. Do you deal with only large properties?"

Leonardo wiped his mouth with a napkin before he spoke. "We have several sub-brands. We sell houses, apartments, commercial buildings, and land. My role is more executive oversight but I handle the clients that request me specifically."

Like that woman. *Again, none of my business.*

"Medici Real Estate Holdings belongs to your parents?"

I wanted to take the question back. It came out of my mouth before

I could stop myself. It was an innocent question, but I didn't want him to think I was fishing for information on his finances.

"Partially." He crossed his arms on the table and gave me his full attention. "My parents started the business, but they're retired. It's in my hands now." Leonardo poured more wine for me and then refilled his, all the while eyeing me suspiciously. "Are you interested in becoming a real estate agent?"

"Oh, no." I finished chewing and wiped my mouth with a napkin. "I'm a graphic designer, but if I could paint all day I would."

"Then why don't you?" Leonardo folded his hands, his elbows on the table.

"Painting doesn't provide a steady income."

"Well, an art piece is subjective. What is junk to one person is treasure to another. Your sister is a painter too. What an artistic family. Your parents paint as well?"

"My father is an accountant and my mother is a teacher. My mother painted, but more as a hobby. She's really good, though. She was the reason Abby and I got into art. We loved watching her paint and going to galleries when we were young. We both went to USC to study art."

"Oh yeah?" He added beef to a tortilla. "Great college."

"Thank you," I said.

"Any more siblings?"

"Nope. Just me and my sister. How about you?"

"I have a younger brother, who has been absent for a while. But that's a story for another day." He took a big bite that closed the subject firmly.

We chewed quietly for a few moments. Bridget pushed some tomatoes around her plate.

"You have a lot of art pieces in your house," I said. "You have an eye for it."

"I took lessons for a little while, but I'm not good at it. Besides, I don't have time for hobbies."

That piqued my interest, but again I didn't ask for details. Instead, I thought about my painting hanging in his bedroom.

"I was wondering why you bought the painting in your bedroom?" I handed Bridget a napkin.

He stiffened and his eyes darkened. I shrank in my seat. Had I said something wrong?

Bridget, who had been patient and glancing between Leonardo and me during our conversation, said, "Mona doesn't let anyone in Papa's room."

I flushed with mortification. I had to think of something fast. "Mona gave me a quick tour when I interviewed and I forgot. I'm sorry if—"

"It's fine." He offered a tightlipped grin. "You don't need to apologize. I'm grateful that you're here."

My heart regained a steadier beat, and silence took over when Leonardo checked his phone and texted someone.

"I'm finished with dinner. I'm going to put this magnet away." Bridget got out of her seat and opened a long cabinet.

I must have missed that one somehow. Magnets of all shapes and sizes were attached to a board fastened to the cabinet. "Do you collect magnets from every place you visit?"

He took a quick glance at his cell before meeting my gaze. "It's not for me. Bridget likes to collect them."

Bridget surveyed the board, trying to find a place for it. "I'll put it here," she said finally and climbed back in her seat. "My teacher said there's a family picnic at the beach this Saturday. Can we go Papa?"

Leonardo caressed Bridget's check. "I think I have a meeting that day, but I'll have to check my schedule to be sure."

Bridget groaned, turning her lips downward.

"If I can't go then Kate can take you." He looked at me to confirm.

I licked a drop of wine from my lip. "Yes, of course." I'd been hired for two weeks, weekends included.

"What time?" Leonardo asked.

She jerked her shoulder with a pout and crossed her arms. "I don't know."

Leonardo shifted his position to face her. "Do you remember what happens when you give me a mean face?"

Her lips parted wide and she raised her hands as if bracing for something.

"The tickle monster," Leonardo said in a deep, growling voice.

"Ahhhh!" Bridget jumped off her seat and ran.

Leonardo chased after her. Their running footsteps pounded

around the sofa, the tea table, and then the dining table before he caught her and swung her onto his lap. She laughed and squealed as he tickled her. He stopped, both of them panting as her giggles subsided.

"Okay, young lady. No more pouty face. I promise to do my best." He put a hand to his heart. "I'll pinky promise too."

"Deal." She curled her pinky around his.

I cleared my throat and then my lips tugged up at the corners. "Don't forget to make him say our mantra."

"Oh, yeah." Bridget bounced on her toes in front of me but faced her father. "Repeat after me. To unicorns, rainbows, and all the sparkling things."

Leonardo chuckled, his grin wide and beautiful. "To unicorns, rainbows, and all the sparkling things."

"Yah." Bridget clapped.

Leonardo turned to me, playfulness gone. "Kate, Phillip will take you home when you're ready. No need to call a cab. Can you come back tomorrow evening about five?"

"Sure. I'll leave after I clean up." I picked up my finished plate and rose.

"That's okay. I can clean it. It's getting late."

I assumed he wanted me out of his house so he could rest. "Goodnight, Bridget. I'll see you tomorrow." I headed toward the spare room where I had left my purse.

"Wait." Bridget rushed over and wrapped her thin arms around my waist. "Thank you, Kate. See you tomorrow. Say hi to Tyler for me."

"I will." I patted her back in a steady rhythm.

Her gratitude and her hug were a nice surprise. I wanted her to be comfortable with me, but she had warmed up to me faster than I'd expected.

When I peered up, Leonardo held a small grin, watching us. I offered a quick smile and left.

Chapter Twenty – Sisterly Bond

I texted Abby, letting her know I was on my way home when I got inside the black SUV with tinted windows. Leonardo must have given Phillip the address, since he hadn't asked for it.

Phillip wasn't much of a talker, and neither was I. In the quiet, I stared out the window. Nothing but darkness aside from the occasional streetlight, and then my heart bloomed.

Countless twinkling stars filled up the black canvas of night, anchored by the two brightest, reminding me of my painting *My Soulmate*. In reality, the soulmate stars were light-years apart. They would never meet.

My mind drifted to Bridget's mother as the grassy hills became a blur in the darkness. Dead? Divorce? Separated? Though I reminded myself dozens of times to mind my own business, I couldn't help but wonder. The questions would probably nag at me until I found out.

I thought about asking Phillip, but instead I leaned my forehead against the cool window, not looking at anything particular the whole ten-minute ride home.

"Auntie Kate." Tyler tackled me by the entryway table after he shut the door. "I'm glad you're home. You've been gone so long."

"I missed you, too." I rubbed his back, his PJs soft on my hand.

I ruffled his hair and planted a kiss on his forehead. He clutched my hand and led me to the dimly lit family room.

"Come." Abby patted the cushion beside her and sipped a cup of tea. "Do you want some?"

"I'm fine. I just had dinner." I dropped my purse and my phone on the tea table and slumped beside her.

The lit Christmas tree twinkled in front of me with a few wrapped presents underneath. Abby must have put them there. The lights were not as bright as the Medici's tree, but this tree was perfect for this house.

Tyler, smelling of his vanilla and honey shampoo, snuggled beside me.

"Bridget told me you're nice. She likes you." His brown eyes glittered along with the tree's lights.

I draped my arms around Tyler, bringing him closer. "That makes me happy. She's a good girl. Are you guys planning to go to the beach picnic this Saturday?"

Abby snorted. "I'm the coordinator. I have to go."

I poked her shoulder and snickered. "No way. You?"

But I wasn't surprised. Abby had been the Associated Student Body senior president at our high school. She liked organizing things. In college, she'd helped her professor with the last showcase for the senior class. It had been a lot of work, but it had paid off when she'd gotten an internship at the gallery in New York, where she eventually was hired.

"Are you going?" She placed her mug on the table and crossed her legs.

"If Leonardo can't make it, I'll have to take Bridget."

"And if he does take her, you come with us, okay?"

"Sounds like a plan." I had nothing better to do, and spending time with my family was the whole point of being in Kauai.

Fast asleep in my arms, Tyler hadn't moved or said a word. I debated whether to tuck him in bed, but decided to wait.

Abby leaned back into the sofa cushion and put her feet up on the coffee table as she closed her eyes. "I forgot to tell you, Mom and Dad called earlier."

"From the cruise? Are they okay?" I whispered sharply. Now that Tyler was asleep, I lowered my volume and I didn't want to move, afraid I would wake him up.

"Everything is fine." She patted me lazily on my arm with her eyes still closed. "They wanted me to say hello to you. I told them you were out. I didn't know if you wanted them to know about your nanny position."

"No, I don't." Not that I was ashamed of my job, but I didn't want them asking me a bunch of questions. Ever since they'd found out Jayden had cheated on me, they questioned me about my friends and what I was doing on weekends. Made me feel like they didn't trust my judgment anymore.

"They'll arrive on Christmas Eve."

"I didn't ask you this before, but should I stay at a hotel? You don't have an extra room for them."

She tilted her head to face me. "No, you don't have to leave. They're going to stay in my room. I'm going to sleep on the sofa."

I felt horrible. "I have a queen-size bed. You can sleep with me. Or have Ty sleep with you and I'll sleep on Ty's twin bed."

She swatted her hand in the air with a deep sleepy sigh. "Whatever. We'll work it out."

"Like we always do," I said.

Abby leaned her head against mine. Her voice cracked as she said, "I miss Steve."

My throat tightened and my eyes pooled with tears. I had no words of comfort. I glanced at the family portrait of the three of them that hung over the mantel, wishing Steve were with us.

Her breath fluttered. "I miss him every day, but more so now. Steve loved Christmas music. He would turn up the volume and sing along. Now, our house is quiet."

I dabbed the liquid at the corner of my eyes before it could fall. "We should play Christmas music for Steve, okay?" I squeezed my sister with the arm that wasn't holding Tyler.

She wiped away a tear. "I'm so happy you're here."

"Me, too." I swallowed my sorrow. I refused to cry in front of her.

"Oh," she said as if suddenly remembering something and faced me with her eyes wide. "I asked my friend if she knew anything about Bridget's mother …"

Under different circumstances, I would have brushed her off, but this distraction was welcome.

"And …?" I dragged out the word.

"Well." She rubbed at her temple. "They don't know anything about her mother."

"That's weird." I paused when Tyler shifted in my arms and waited for him to settle. "Medici is well known in the community. Everybody is in his business, right? Well, not everyone, but the single women, from what I saw."

"That's true. I always hear about so-and-so trying to catch his eye. He's a big fish in any pond, but on an island this size, he's a whale. If my source is correct, he's been here just as long as I have, and he's a private man. I was surprised when you told me he attended the Movie and Popcorn fundraising night. He's never been to any of the gatherings."

Tyler's head drooped to the side awkwardly. I carefully pushed it up. "Maybe she left him and he's heartbroken."

"A mother would never leave her child behind." She caressed Tyler's cheek.

"We don't know anyone who did that, but many have, Abby."

She shrugged. "I guess you're right. So, what's he like? I've only met him at the gallery."

I scrunched up my nose, thinking. "He's … he's very good with Bridget. The way he interacts with her is endearing and sweet. But he can also be stiff and so professional. I get that he's a businessman, but I don't know. He's fine. Why? You interested?"

I tried to make my voice light and teasing, but I couldn't picture them as a couple. Worse, I didn't want to. I didn't want to see him with anyone.

Dear God, I didn't need that thought.

"No. Don't be silly." She glared at me. "Maybe for someone I know."

"Oh," I said, trying to not sound disappointed. "Anyway, have you sold anything?"

"No." She pressed her back against the sofa. "Speaking of Medici, he hasn't picked up Cupid yet."

"I'll take it to him tomorrow. I don't have to be at his place until late afternoon."

My phone flashed brightly on the table. Abby handed it to me since I couldn't move with Tyler in my arms.

I had turned off the volume and I had missed a text.

"It's Leonardo." I stared at the message, my heart drumming faster.

"What did he say?" My sister leaned closer to me to read the message.

> Leonardo: Phillip will pick you up tomorrow
> at four. See you then. Goodnight.

Then the dots rolled in. I waited, watching and waiting, but no words came. Whatever he wanted to say, he hadn't.

"It's regarding work," I said and flipped the phone over on my lap.

"Of *course* it is." Her tone suggested there was some secret.

While Abby tucked Tyler into bed, I sat on my mattress and texted Leonardo back.

Me: Thank you. See you tomorrow. Goodnight.

Dots followed immediately. I waited patiently, but then they stopped.

Chapter Twenty-One — Unwelcome Visitor

The next morning, I went to the gallery with my sister. I helped her out until Phillip picked me up. When Phillip looked at the Cupid in my hand, I'd told him it was for Mr. Medici. He nodded with a carefully neutral expression. No doubt he was used to seeing Leonardo with statues and paintings.

"All I Want for Christmas Is You" filled the house when Phillip opened the door for me.

"Bridget," I called.

When she didn't answer, I headed up the stairs. She would likely be in her room. I stopped after a few steps when I heard laughter coming from the family room. Instead of rushing in, I tiptoed and peeked in to see what they were doing.

Leonardo sat on the sofa with a tablet on his lap, his finger touching the screen, while Bridget sat next to him.

"Hurry. The skeletons are going to get you." Bridget covered her eyes and then leaned in eagerly.

"You're going down. Pow. Pow. Pow." Leonardo's arm darted from side to side.

His playful tone made me smile and I wanted to take back what I had said about him being too stiff to my sister.

"Eat it. Eat it. Eat it." Bridget pumped her fist in the air.

Ah, they were playing *Unicorns versus Skeletons*. I knew Bridget played, but I hadn't known Leonardo did. They had called each other *Unicorn* and *Skeleton*, but I'd thought he was humoring her.

There was something sexy about a man who played with his child.

"Oh, no." Bridget shook her head. "They're coming too fast. My poor unicorns."

Leonardo ran a hand down his face. "Poopers. That's the end of that round."

Poopers? Too adorable.

"Poopers." Bridget crossed her arms, frowning. "Can we play again?"

"After I eat my unicorn." Leonardo jolted up and curled his fingers into claws, growling.

Bridget screamed and ran, her little feet scurrying on the hardwood floor. They ran once around the sofa and then Leonardo halted with wide eyes. They both finally saw me, looking like they had been caught red-handed.

"Kate." Bridget's feet pounded across the gap between us.

Air left my lungs in an *umph* as Bridget careened into me, almost knocking Cupid out of my hands.

"Kate." Leonardo rubbed his nape and straightened his short-sleeved button-up shirt.

Was he embarrassed? Nervous? I had expected him to be wearing a suit and going to a business meeting, but he wore slacks. Not for work, then. So why had he asked me to come over?

"I would have rung the bell, but Phillip let me in." I hiked a thumb behind me.

"Of course. You're welcome to come in. I didn't recognize you at first. You have your hair up."

He noticed. I'd put on a comfortable cotton dress and tied my hair into a ponytail.

"Oh. I brought your Cupid. I had to stop by my sister's gallery, and since I was going to see you today, I picked it up. I hope that's okay?"

"That was thoughtful of you. Thank you." Leonardo took it from me and walked around the room as if unsure where to place it. He finally shelved it between the photo frames.

"Were you playing *Unicorns versus Skeletons*?" I asked Bridget, who was still holding onto me.

"Uh huh. Tyler told me you play. He said you're the best. Can you help us?"

"Ohhhh, I don't know if I'm the best. I don't think I'm at your level." I ran a hand down her soft, silky hair.

Bridget let go of me to grab the tablet and plopped on the sofa. "Come sit down. Can you show Papa? He's not that good."

Leonardo's eyebrows lifted in the middle in a pained expression as he watched me ease next to his daughter.

He chuckled lightly. "I guess Kate will have to show us if she's better than me."

I gave him a sly smile. "Challenge accepted. We shall see."

Leonardo stood behind us, watching. My pulse thumped a few times from the attention, but I eased into the game.

"Wow, you're good," Bridget said.

"Back up a little, Unicorn. Kate can't see the board if you put your face in front of it." Leonardo guided Bridget with his hand on her shoulder.

"She's almost past level ten." Bridget squealed with her fingers curled to her chest.

I bit my bottom lip when Leonardo came around and sat on the coffee table directly in front of me. Watching me play was not the problem. His eyes were not on the screen, but on me. Heat fused through my veins and my concentration faltered. My heart hammered when his knee brushed up against mine.

I tried to ignore the way he shook his leg and cracked his knuckles.

"One more row." Bridget's high-pitched, excited voice brought me back.

I had played level ten so many times that I could do it with my eyes closed, but they didn't need to know that. I wanted to look cool.

"The trick of the game is not to panic and to concentrate only on the flowers that are in front of the unicorn," I repeated what I had to Tyler.

"That's exactly what I told Bridget." Leonardo tapped his daughter's nose to get her attention, but her eyes were glued on the screen.

"Kate's on level eleven now. Ohhhhh." Bridget squealed.

Level eleven might show the limit of my skills in this game. The skeletons were closing in when the sound of wind chimes came from my phone. A familiar invisible hand caressed down my back and I shuddered a breath. I stilled, my heart thumping.

"Papa, that's Mama. When the wind chimes, an angel is near. It's her." Bridget jumped into Leonardo's arms.

My heart went out to both of them. The pain must still be so raw because Leonardo never talked about her. And that poor little girl, growing up without her mother. I couldn't even imagine. Like Tyler growing up without his father.

I bit the inside of my lip as my heart flipped. It was such a sweet gesture about the wind chimes, but one day she'd know it wasn't true and then what?

Leonardo stiffened. "Yes, she is." He caressed Bridget's back and kissed her forehead.

Leonardo and I locked eyes for a heartbeat again. I saw grief and sadness in them. Bridget jumped out of his arms and returned next to me.

"Oh, well." I threw up my hands when I lost the game.

Bridget's lips fell downward into a pout. "We almost finished level eleven. Can we try it again?"

"Maybe after dinner?" I met Leonardo's gaze to confirm, but we were interrupted by the doorbell.

He rose and straightened his shirt. "That's for me."

Bridget trotted behind him, and I followed. I stopped short when he opened the door to a tall, lovely woman. They exchanged hugs and he kissed her cheek.

My gaze lowered to the woman's black, form-fitting dress with black heels that accentuated her long legs. A small purse was clutched between her chest and arm. Her makeup was a little bit heavy for my taste, but she was stunning.

He'd wanted me to come back so he could go on a date. He had every right. A single man had needs.

"Hello." The pretty lady looked shocked when her eyes landed on me and Bridget.

Had she not known he had a daughter?

"Cassie. This is Kate, and you've already met Bridget."

"Hello. It's nice to meet you," I said.

Holding my hand, Bridget backed away without a word toward the Christmas tree.

Cassie assessed me from head to toe and turned away. She didn't seem impressed. "Well, shall we?"

"I'll be back soon." Leonardo kissed Bridget on the forehead and left.

As soon as the door closed, Bridget's shoulders eased, but she held her frown. "I don't like that lady." Her grip on my hand tightened. "She's not nice."

I agreed with her though I didn't know the woman.

"How many times have you seen her?" The nosy question left my mouth before my brain caught up.

She held up four fingers and then angled her lips to the side. "No." She brought one finger down. "I think three." She crinkled her nose. "I don't know."

"That's okay. Some people seem mean, but they're just shy." I led her back to the family room to have dinner.

After dinner, Bridget washed up and I tucked her in bed.

"Which book would you like for me to read to you?" I sat up with pillows behind my back.

"This one." She handed me a book from under her covers, stretched her arms to the ceiling, and yawned.

"*Unicorn Goes to School.* This should be fun." I ran my hand down the colorful, glittery cover. The unicorn was dressed like a child with a backpack.

I opened the book to read. About half way through the story, Bridget's eyes fluttered and then finally closed. I should go downstairs to my designated room, but I wasn't sure if I was supposed to spend the night. Leonardo and I had forgotten to talk about that detail. I had to wait for him to come home either way, so I closed my eyes, intending to wait there until Leonardo came home.

I'll go home when he gets here. But between Bridget's soft breathing and the warm glow of lamplight next to me on the nightstand, I dozed off.

Footsteps echoed in the hallway. Leonardo must be home. I tried to pry open my reluctant eyes, but they were too heavy.

The door creaked and then more footsteps. When no other sounds came, I tried to talk, but exhaustion dragged me back toward sleep.

Something warm covered my body. I shifted slightly to see a blurry image of Leonardo, looking at me, or Bridget, or both.

I should get up. Go home or go to the spare room. Groggily, I pushed the cover. "I'll be on my way," I murmured.

He rested his hand on my shoulder and I sagged back into the pillow, unable to resist.

"No, stay," he whispered. "I mean, it's late. Spend the night."

In my state of mind, his words sounded more intimate than they should. "Anything for you," I mumbled breathlessly.

"Goodnight, Bridget. Goodnight, Kate," he said.

The sincerity and the tenderness in his voice made me picture a husband coming home from a late night at the office and kissing his wife and daughter goodnight.

A girl could dream.

Some words tumbled out of me through the fog of sleep, and I had no idea what I'd said. A light chuckle filtered through my almost-dreaming state. I hoped I'd said goodnight back to him and didn't ask about his date. I knew I should stop talking, so I surrendered to the night.

Chapter Twenty-Two – The Next Morning

The sunlight beamed through the shutters. I turned to my side to escape the brightness. Yawning, I stretched my arms and bumped into the headboard. A giant unicorn with rainbow-colored horn came into focus. Bridget's room. I wiped drool off my face and sat up.

For a heartbeat, I thought I'd slept at a stranger's place. I had the same sense of disorientation as when I'd once stayed too late at a college party.

I was safe. And … wearing the same clothes I had worn last night. Worse, no Bridget on her bed.

I shuffled out to the hallway. The smell of eggs and bacon drifted up the stairs. I went into the kitchen to see Bridget sitting on the stool, a fork in her hand, and Leonardo cooking eggs. Plates and utensil were all set on the counter, along with a plate of toast.

"You're awake. Have a seat next to Bridget. Grab some toast if you like." Leonardo shot a glance my way and flipped an egg over on the frying pan effortlessly, like he had done it a hundred times.

"Good morning, sleepyhead." Bridget giggled and spread strawberry jam on the bread she held. "That's what Papa calls me."

"Good morning." I ran a hand down Bridget's hair and eased onto the stool next to her.

My gaze extended to Leonardo dressed in a pair of shorts and a plain T-shirt, but he looked beautiful, perfectly put together.

"I'm so sorry," I said. "I didn't know you were awake. I should be making breakfast."

"Nonsense." Leonardo frowned, waving a spatula at me. "You're not my cook. In fact, I don't have a cook. Maybe I should hire one." He winked at Bridget and snorted. "Mona's job is to take care of Bridget. I don't expect her to take care of me, but bless her heart, she does."

"Yup, she does." Bridget nodded, showing off all her pearly small teeth.

Leonardo poured coffee into a mug and handed it to me. Then he passed me a small tray with sugar, honey, and cream. "Scrambled, sunny side up, or …"

Too busy watching his muscles flex as he moved effortlessly from the sink to the stove, and about the kitchen, it took me a second to realize he was talking about eggs.

"Over easy, please." I dumped plenty of sugar and cream into my coffee and stirred.

"I'm not surprised," he commented and got back to frying.

I stopped the cup halfway to my mouth. "Excuse me?"

"Your coffee. You liked the chocolate-covered popcorn. You like sweet things."

"I sure do." I raised my mug to him and took a hot sip. I released a long sigh. "Don't tell me. You like it black."

Leonardo planted his hands on the counter, leaning toward me. "I like the taste of coffee. If you add sugar and cream, it takes away the flavor. You might as well eat chocolate. However, sometimes a little sweet is good." He winked.

Oh, that wink. I paused for a second to compose myself. "You have a point."

He puffed out his chest a little and gave me a smug grin. His gaze lingered and I wasn't sure if I should look away. But he broke away first and went back to the stove.

"Papa is going to take me on a helicopter ride. You should come too." Bridget scooped up eggs with her fork and shoved them in her mouth.

I was thankful for the interruption.

I thought Leonardo would come up with an excuse as to why I shouldn't go, but he said, "Have you been, Kate?"

"On a helicopter?" I felt queasy at the thought. "No, and I'm not sure if it's a good idea. I get motion sickness."

"You can take something for that. Besides …" Leonardo handed me a plate of eggs and bacon. "I'll be driving." Then he poured oil into the pan and cracked two more eggs.

I took a bite of eggs, processing his words. "What? You're flying the helicopter? Then I'm definitely not getting in."

He chuckled as he used the spatula to scramble the yolk. "Don't worry. I have a license. And Kauai isn't a busy island so you're safe with me. I'm a good driver, right, Bridget?"

"Yes. The best," she gushed through a mouthful of toast.

"The view is spectacular," Leonardo said. "It's the best way to get a tour of the island. And the best part, it'll be free and you'll get the best view. You'll regret it if you don't. It's a once in a lifetime offer."

His persistence was adorable, but I wondered why he wanted me to come along. Surely, he would rather take that woman. What was her name? Cassie. Or some other date.

"I don't know. Can I think about it?" I nibbled on a piece of crispy bacon.

"Of course." Leonardo sounded disappointed. He took a sip of coffee and slid the eggs onto a plate.

He came around and instead of sitting next to Bridget, sat next to me. His tension eased, his mood livelier. Something had changed in him, but I couldn't put my finger on it. Perhaps I was the one looking at our interaction in a different light. Maybe I had lightened up.

Having never worked as a nanny before, I didn't know what I could and couldn't do. I had to rely on Mona's list and ask when I didn't know.

"I … last night … should I have gone home? We didn't discuss whether I was supposed to spend the night."

Leonardo tilted his head, squinting in confusion, and then his eyes shot wide open. "Please don't worry about it. I wasn't sure what would happen last night." He cleared his throat.

What had happened last night?

"I meant …" His eyes drilled into mine. "It's fine. I came home past midnight. I wouldn't have let you go home that late anyway. I'm glad you stayed. I mean … You should for safety reasons … and Bridget."

I broke away from the trance that held us together. Or maybe it was one sided. Normally, I didn't have trouble reading guys, but having Leonardo as my employer made me doubt everything.

"I have a question." I rubbed at my temple. "Did I say anything weird last night when you came home?"

He drew his chin toward his chest with a snicker and then gave me a side-long glance. "Do you remember what you said?"

I furrowed my brow. "No. That's why I'm asking you."

He stabbed the fork through his eggs and shoved them in his mouth. He was buying time. *Ugh!*

"Well?" I tugged at his shirt and then stopped when I realized what I was doing.

"I don't remember." He took a drink from his mug to avoid my gaze.

"So does this mean you're coming with us?" Bridget had her elbow on the table, resting her chin on her fist, looking bored.

"When is this trip?"

"Sunday, or I can arrange it for another day if that doesn't work for you," Leonardo said, grabbing a toast and spreading jam on it.

I was technically on his payroll, so my time should be saved for him just in case he needed me. But the helicopter ride was a leisure thing, and from the sound of it, he wasn't going away for business.

"I didn't make any plans since I promised to watch Bridget. I figured I should be on call in case you needed me—in case Bridget needed me. In case you needed me to watch Bridget." Oh dear, I was rambling. "Now that I know you're not going away on a business trip, I—"

"I'm on call," he said. "I mean, I might have to fly out Sunday evening."

"Don't worry, I'll be available, but I'm still not sure about the helicopter." I tapped my mug nervously and glanced over to the shelf in the family room. No Cupid there.

It wasn't only the helicopter ride, but getting close to Leonardo and Bridget on personal time might not be a good idea. For so many reasons.

"Of course. I understand. You can let me know later." His mug landed with a light thud on the table.

"You moved Cupid." I changed the subject to take the focus away from me.

Bridget jumped off her stool, raced to the sofa, and picked up the statue on the end table.

"I moved it," she said. "I put it on the table because it's so cute. I wish it was real. Mrs. Fong said Cupid shoots magical arrows at two people when he wants them to fall in love. Is that true?" She hugged the Cupid in front of her.

"Shoosh. Shoosh." Bridget pretended to shoot imaginary arrows at

Leonardo and me, and I didn't know what to think of that.

Leonardo got out of his seat and walked toward her. "Cupid is the son of Venus, the goddess of love and beauty. It's Roman mythology. Something you'll learn more about when you get older."

While he went on and on about mythology, I picked up the plates and took them to the sink. I turned on the faucet to let the water run for a bit. When I turned, I jerked. I nearly ran into Leonardo, who held our mugs like an experienced waiter.

"You need to make some noise, Mr. Medici." I let out a breath, resting my hand on my chest.

"Call me Lee, Kate." He placed the mugs on the counter. "Mr. Medici makes me sound old. I wanted to help. Like I said, you're not here to take care of me. You shouldn't have to clean up my mess."

Jayden had never lifted a finger to help me. We'd mostly eaten out, but the times I'd cooked for him, he'd sat in front of the TV while I did all the work. The two men were so different.

"That's sweet of you, but I don't mind."

It was difficult to come back to reality when sparkling chestnut-colored eyes stared back into mine with something unreadable. That piercing gaze seemed longing or predatory, but I didn't know if I was imagining what I wanted to see. Heat blazed through me as if his eyes were hands caressing me. Touching me in places that happened only in my dreams.

The cab driver had said only people close to him could call him Lee, so what was he trying to tell me?

A sweet, hesitant voice broke our spell. "Can I get some water? I'm thirsty."

I flinched out of my daze.

Lee spun like he'd been caught doing something he wasn't supposed to do. "Sure, sweetheart. Here." He grabbed a cup and handed it to her.

As Bridget got water from the refrigerator dispenser, Lee turned to me and whispered, "Can you teach Bridget how to paint? I would pay you for her lessons. She's been asking, but I haven't had time to find a teacher. And since you're a painter …" He rubbed the back of his neck. "You don't have to give me an answer today. But—"

"I would love to." I smiled.

"You will? Are you sure? I hope I haven't said anything to pressure you. I mean, I'm good at talking business and I get what I want and get things done, but—"

I put a finger on his lips to hush him, and another wave of dangerous heat exploded inside me. "I said yes."

His lips parted into a broad grin, and then something else crept into his expression. I felt that sparkle of something brewing and growing between us. My finger on his mouth felt way too intimate, and I liked it a bit too much.

Bridget came between us, breaking the trance, and peered up at us with innocent eyes. "Kate is going to teach me?"

"Yes," Lee said, his eyes never leaving mine.

"Yah!" She jumped up and down.

I laced my fingers through my hair and slipped out of the kitchen. "We'll start when I get some supplies."

"Oh, wait." He grabbed my arm gently, then let go. "I have to show you something."

Bridget went running first as if she already knew where we were headed. I kept up with Lee at first but fell behind. We went past the stairs, past the Christmas tree, past the garage door, and down the hallway to another room I hadn't even known existed.

Bridget stood in front of an easel, holding a paintbrush in either hand.

"Look." She hopped in place, waving the brushes.

Canvases of all sizes rested against the wall on the left. A table lined with paintbrushes and paint tubes was on the right. Two empty easels, stained with different colors, stood in the middle of the room. Several finished paintings hung on the walls.

I went closer to the nearest one by the door—a painting of Bridget when she was about two years old, sitting at a park, looking at ducks. She wore a simple pink dress with a matching bow tied in her hair. On the bottom right was a signature that read *R. Banks.*

The walls began to close in and I couldn't breathe as I zeroed in on her name. Lee must have noticed.

"R for Roselyn," he said. "Roselyn was Bridget's mother."

It became clear why he had initially used Roselyn as Bridget's fake name. And Banks must be her maiden name. I was going to apologize for his loss, but then I realized I had no idea what their story was. I wanted him to tell me more, so I thought of a task for Bridget.

"Bridget. The best way for a teacher to know where to start is by knowing what the student already knows. Can you paint something for me?"

"Okay." She sat on the stool and wiggled with excitement.

I grabbed a medium-sized canvas leaning against the left wall and placed it on the tripod. I handed her a paint palette after dabbing on some acrylic paints.

"Go ahead and paint anything you want," I said.

Lee watched his daughter with tenderness and turned back to the painting by the door. I stood next to him.

"This was Roselyn's last painting." He dropped his voice to a whisper. "She wanted to memorize her daughter and give her a gift to remember her mother by."

"This is precious." I paused to admire the pink hues on Bridget's dress, and then asked hesitantly, "What happened to your wife?"

"My wife?" He jerked his head back, his eyes rounded with surprise.

Did he forget who we were talking about?

He furrowed his brow. "I'm sorry. I guess I forgot to tell you." He glanced over his shoulder at his daughter. "Roselyn was my younger sister."

"Ohhh." I leaned my back to the wall beside the painting. "I'm sorry. I thought … So Bridget isn't your …" My perspective shifted and several things made sense.

He shook his head, shifting to stand in front of me. "Bridget is my niece, but most people assume she's my daughter. I don't bother correcting them. They'd only ask more questions." His face stiffened. "It's none of their business. The only people who know the truth are those I trust."

He trusted me?

"Thank you. I won't tell anyone."

"I appreciate that." He smiled at Bridget when she turned to him. When she went back to her painting, he murmured, "Roselyn passed away a little over two years ago."

"I'm so sorry." I stared into his somber eyes. I knew that expression too well, and I wanted to hug him, but I clasped one hand around the other wrist to hold myself back.

"Thank you, but we knew it was coming." He scrubbed at his stubble and wrinkled his nose. "Roselyn had stage four breast cancer. It spread so fast that by the time she found it, it was too late. It attacked all her organs too. Bridget was only two, and it was so difficult when her mother was gone from her. She cried every night for her."

I blinked the pooling tears away and peeked at Bridget. She was smiling and humming the upbeat theme music of *Unicorns versus Skeletons* as she painted. She looked so happy. It probably seemed like a lifetime ago for Lee. Sometimes it seemed like that to me about Steve.

I understood his pain. I'd dealt with my own grief when my brother-in-law had passed away, but Abby and Tyler lived through worse. I wanted to tell Lee that I understood, but this was about him opening up to me, about his and Bridget's loss.

"You said you had a brother. Where is he?" I stepped away from the wall and walked over to admire the second painting of roses in a vase.

He followed me. "Liam lives in New York. He's a stockbroker, didn't want to get into the family business. He left it all to me." Lee didn't sound thrilled about being the president of his company, but I didn't ask. "How about you? Just you and Abby?"

I turned back to him to meet his gaze. "Yes. My parents are on a cruise." I didn't know why I'd said that. I tried to make it sound natural and not awkward. "How about your parents?"

"They like to travel as well. They'll drop by here for Christmas, and they'll likely visit another country. My parents worked hard all their lives and recently retired. They want to travel the world before they get too old." He chuckled and shoved his hands in his pockets. "They have a better social life than I do. Well, I have some work to do." He took out his cell from his back pocket and glanced at it. "You're welcome to stay as long as you like."

I waved my hand toward the easel and paints. "Since you have all the materials I need, I'll stick around to give Bridget her first lesson. And please, this is my pleasure. You've already paying me more than I deserve. In fact, it's ridiculous how much I'm going to get paid for two weeks and I barely feel like I'm doing anything."

He rested a hand on my arm and then dropped it to his side. "You're helping me by watching Bridget. It was at the very last minute. We had many interested applicants, but Mona picked you. She did right. I trust her instincts. Always have and always will."

"Thank you." I tipped my head to the side and smiled. "Before you go, I have another question. Why does Bridget associate wind chimes with angels? Did you tell her that?"

"No." He furrowed his brow and stole a quick glance at Bridget. "In fact, I was going to ask you the same thing."

"I didn't. But …"

"But what?"

"Well …" I bit my bottom lip and rubbed my arms, contemplating how to say it. "When I was a little girl, my mom told me wind chimes were often hung in Asian temples because they were thought to bring peaceful spirits and ward off the evil ones. We always had a couple in our backyard because they reminded her of her childhood home. Every time the wind chimes tinkled, I imagined they were the sounds of angel wings flapping and they were visiting me. Protecting me, almost. The sound gave me peace every time I heard it, and that thought helped me through some hard times. It was a reminder that everything was going to be fine. That I was on the right path."

"That's sweet."

"Yeah, but those chimes drove our neighbors crazy, especially on windy days."

Lee burst out with a full belly chuckle, a heartwarming sound. I laughed with him until my eyes watered. It wasn't particularly funny, but his laugh brought out my own mirth. Bridget also giggled, but she lost interest and went back to painting. Then the room fell silent, but our gazes remained locked.

Desire bloomed inside me, but that was a place I didn't want to go. Unless I was reading his steady gaze wrong, Lee might be feeling it too.

I paced to the third painting to break away from whatever was happening between us. "Maybe Mona told her about wind chimes?"

Lee gave me a sidelong glance at first, and then finally understood. "I don't think so. The first time I heard Bridget say it was when we were playing the game. I didn't ask her about it because …" He glanced over to his niece, and then back to me, clearing his throat. He seemed to be struggling with words. "Maybe it's helping her deal with the loss of her mother. I would say anything, do anything to help her. I thought about sending her to a therapist, but Mona is very good with her and has helped her in many ways. All I can do is love her and let her know I'll always be there for her."

I raised my hand to touch his face, but stopped halfway and dropped my hand to my side. He was such an amazing person. It was a huge responsibility to take care of a child. Few uncles would do the same for their nieces.

"She's lucky to have you," I said, looking at Bridget.

He shook his head. "No, I'm lucky to have her."

My heart melted. "What about her father?"

He clenched his jaw. His expression darkened and he whispered sharply, "He walked out on my sister shortly after she got pregnant. He had another woman. I don't know where he is and I don't care. I would never let him get close to Bridget even if he wanted her back in his life."

I didn't blame him.

We had lowered our voices and kept the conversation away from Bridget, but when she turned to look at us, I flinched.

"I'm done. Want to see it?" She waved the brush toward her easel and flecks of paint splattered off the tip.

Bridget had painted stick figures of two people with long hair. Lee and I exchanged glances, and from the way he clutched his chest, I was certain his heart somersaulted like mine did.

Lee went to her and placed a tender hand on her back. "Who did you paint, sweetheart?"

She pointed with her brush. "The little one is me, and the big one with wings is mommy. We're holding hands. Sometimes I dream about her."

Lee kissed her forehead and caressed her face. "Your mother is always thinking of you. She's right there, always." He patted her heart. "And I am right here. Always." He tapped his chest.

"I know." She nodded with her head lowered and looked up. "Can we play *Unicorns versus Skeletons* now?"

If Bridget hadn't suggested something fun, I might have. We needed something uplifting after the somber conversation. Gloom seemed to fester in the air and just like how I was here to make Christmas the happiest time of the year for Tyler, I was going to do the same for Bridget.

Lee glanced at the time on his cell and paused. Then his gaze went from Bridget to me and lingered on me. He said the unexpected words, "Well, I do need to catch up to Kate's level."

"You can try." I arched a single brow, with a hint of challenge in my tone. "What about your work?"

"Work can wait." His voice went guttural and his fingers bent into claws. "I'm hungry. I think I'll eat some unicorns."

I grabbed Bridget's hand and we ran screaming out of the room.

Chapter Twenty-Three – Picnic at the Beach

"Don't forget to grab the napkins and the cheese tray," Abby hollered from the back of the car, the soft breeze tousling her hair.

"I got it." A bit annoyed, I put on my sunglasses and tied my hair back. Then I hefted a beach bag over my shoulder, and slammed the passenger door. She had already asked me three times since she parked on the curb.

Abby had organized the Picnic at the Beach event. Like many times before when she'd taken on too much responsibility, she let out her stress on me.

What are sisters for?

I wanted to tell her to get back in the car and start over.

"Ty, please grab the blanket beside you." My sister shut the trunk and came around to her son. "Make sure you don't drag it. And please don't wonder off by yourself. I'm going to be busy, so stay close to your auntie, okay?"

Tyler glued his eyes to the ocean and didn't answer. I was sure he'd heard only half the things his mother had said to him.

Abby closed his door with her hip, her arms filled with trays of cookies made from a bakery. My sister had never liked store bought ones. They had to be freshly baked, and that was why we were on time and not early. Being on time was being late for her, especially if she was in charge.

With the wind in my hair, I inhaled the fresh sea breeze as my sandals slapped on the concrete. The sight of the water glistening like sparkling diamonds, waving in and out on the shore, filled me with serenity, but then my pulse quickened when I thought of Lee. He was bringing Bridget to the picnic—the reason he had sent me home last night.

Even though I'd only known Lee for such a short amount of time,

I felt like we'd moved to a new level of friendship after he shared about his sister. I liked knowing something about him that most people didn't know.

The way he'd been taking care of his niece the previous two years said everything about the kind of man he was. I could tell through their interactions how much they loved each other and what a fine job he had done raising her.

Abby shot a glance over her shoulder. "Ty, hold on to the handrails and be careful," She led us down the uneven steps, palm trees swaying on either side. "Look for tables with blue canopies. The school rented them."

When we hit the shore, three large blue canopies stuck out like sore thumbs, pitched in the sand. A long banner attached to the middle canopy read: Poipu Preschool. Tables were arranged in a square, closer to the rocky hill. A few families had already claimed their space, beach blankets and lounge chairs laid out on the white sand.

"I'm sorry I'm late. I had to pick up a few items," Abby said to the ladies arranging containers of food on the table. She gave them each a quick hug and introduced me.

Afterward, Abby took me to the side. "After you settle Ty, if I look like I need help, can you come? Ty will be fine. He knows not to wander off and you'll be able to keep an eye out for him from here."

"Sure," I said and led Tyler to claim our space.

My sandals dug through the cool sand, fine powder lifting up with every step. The warm sun felt good on my face, the breeze light and soft. I tucked my tank top inside my shorts so I didn't expose too much skin.

I hadn't planned on going swimming and I wasn't the type to parade in my bathing suit around people I didn't know. I noticed the other mothers wore hats and long-sleeved, sheer garments over similar attire or a swimsuit.

Tyler squinted up at me, the sun hitting him directly in the eye. "Jace isn't coming, but I think Bridget is. Can we save a spot for her?"

"Of course." I dropped the bag at a perfect spot and took out Tyler's sand toys—a bucket, shovel, rake, and plastic sand moldings. Then I anchored the blanket with a few of his things.

More families were coming down the slopes. I searched for Bridget and Lee in their midst, but so far, no show. After I took out the sunscreen, I spread the cool thick lotion that felt like acrylic paint on my palms, and lathered up Tyler with a second layer. Abby had made him wear a long-sleeve protective swimming top and shorts so the only parts of him exposed were his legs, neck, and face.

"Yuck." He fidgeted and shook his head as I rubbed in stubborn spots.

I wiped the remainder on my arm and closed the lid. "There. It's done. Ty, stay right here, okay? I'm going to see if your mom needs help."

"Okay." Tyler dug into the dry sand with a shovel and poured it into the bucket.

I adjusted my sunglasses and went to find Abby under the canopies. My sister introduced me to a few more families as they arrived. They asked me a bunch of questions, mostly about living in Los Angeles.

This was the part I didn't like at social gatherings. Uncomfortable small talk with people I didn't know. We didn't have much in common—I didn't have a kid in preschool yet—and I wasn't much of a talker.

I pulled Abby to the side. "Do you need me?"

I didn't want to be sitting comfortably and soaking up the sun while my sister was doing all the work. Several of the mothers who were supposed to be helping her were now chatting amongst themselves. And Abby would rather do the work than ask them for help.

Abby nodded and she sighed with relief. "Can you open the ice bags and dump them inside the ice chest for me?" she said and then went to the next canopy.

"Oh, hi there."

I turned to that familiar, sultry voice just as I opened the cooler. Jessica Conner wiggled her fingers at me, having obviously forgotten my name, but at least she acknowledged me. Though she wore the same type of beach garment as the other mothers, she had on a stunning red bikini underneath that hugged her curves.

"Hi, Jessica," I said with an amiable tone, ripping bags of ice open.

I assumed she'd come to me because everyone else was in their cliques.

"What are you doing?" she asked.

She could *see* what I was doing.

"Abby asked me to spread the ice. I'm going to put the drinks in there. Do you want to help?" I didn't need help but offered, anyway.

She looked at her curled fingers. "I just got my nails done. I'm not sure if that's a good idea."

I rolled my eyes as I grabbed the cans and bottles and nestled them in the ice layer. *Be nice.* Better not to say anything, so I kept my mouth shut.

"Oh, I heard from someone that you're working for Leonardo Medici. Is that true?"

I closed the ice chest, frowning. That explained why she'd made a point to talk to me.

"Who told you?" My words came off a bit harsher than I meant to.

"Oh, a friend of a friend," she said nonchalantly with a flop of her hand.

"Is this friend-of-a-friend Leonardo's friend?" I crossed my arms and scowled. Good thing she couldn't see my glare pinning her behind my dark sunglasses.

She blinked, looking flustered. "I suppose, but that's not important."

And neither is your question.

"Would you like anything to drink?" I grabbed a small bottle of water, drank all of it, and tossed it into the trashcan a few feet from me. I hoped she would dismiss the conversation when I changed the subject, but she didn't.

"Well?" She followed me to the table where families were fixing their lunches.

I glanced over to Tyler to make sure he was where I had left him and then grabbed two paper plates and picked out some bread slices.

"One of those is for Ty, right?" Abby said in passing and went to the next table before I could answer her.

I wasn't going to eat two, that's for sure. It was her polite way of asking me to feed him, which I would have done, anyway. When I reached over to grab a few slices of turkey, I bumped into Jessica's shoulder. She glared at me.

"Maybe you shouldn't stand so close." I flicked my finger like I was waving bugs away.

She frowned and backed away. "Well, you haven't answered my question."

Geez. She was persistent.

I squeezed some mustard and piled on lettuce and avocado, then I added some tomatoes on my sandwich. Tyler didn't like tomatoes.

"Yes," I finally said to her when she kept staring at me. "I'm working for Mr. Medici. I'm watching Bridget for two weeks."

"Oh, so it is true." She said it more for herself than for me. "Is that all? What else do you do?"

Is that all? Doesn't she know taking care of a child is a lot of work? Where is her kid, anyway?

"Jessica ..." I looked at her squarely in the eyes, mustering as much patience as I could. "I'm Bridget's caretaker and nothing else."

I hope she didn't think I slept with him. Even if I had, it was none of her business.

Jessica shadowed me to the next table, whispering, "Does he bring home different women to his place? I heard he dates around, a different woman practically every week. What happened to his wife?"

Now I understood Lee's caution about nosy people. He had gone out with that Cassie woman, though I couldn't be absolutely sure it had been a date.

Who was I kidding? Of course it had been.

"What?" I frowned, snatched two chocolate chip cookies, and put them on Tyler's plate.

When I didn't answer she added, "What's his place like?"

She had gone too far.

I whirled and narrowed my eyes at her. "Look, Jessica. I take my job seriously. I'm not going to tell you any personal information."

I shoved one cookie in my mouth. This should buy me some time from answering her next question. But Jessica wasn't looking at me. In fact, she focused on something over my shoulder, and she wasn't the only one. The ladies froze in place and gawked. Some tried to hide grins.

With the cookie still in my mouth, I spun to face the glaring sun. My sunglasses hindered the brightness, but I couldn't see anything interesting. Then...

"Hello, Kate."

I'd know his smooth baritone voice anywhere.

With sunglasses hooked on his head, Lee looked younger and playful in swim trunks and a white tank top. The temperature suddenly spiked hotter. I'd noticed the gym setup at his home, but out of his jeans and T-shirts, he showed more of his toned body.

At least half the women there were undressing him with their eyes and probably having thoughts they shouldn't have—like I was. His presence made my pulse thunder. Perhaps it wasn't as much him as the way everyone shifted their stares to me.

He finally acknowledged the others with a dip of his head. "Good afternoon, ladies."

"Hello Leonardo," numerous voices chorused back.

Lee ignored them and took a step closer to me. His lips slowly curled into a smirk.

"You might want to either eat it or take it out," he said chuckling.

I dropped my cookie to my plate. If he only knew why I had it in my mouth in the first place.

He learned closer as if he needed to tell me something important. "Kate. I hope you don't mind, but I left my things next to your beach blanket. Bridget insisted on sitting with Tyler."

"Yes, of course. We were expecting you."

His grin grew wider. "Can I help you with those plates?" He lowered his eyes to my hands.

Before I could answer, he took them from me. He jerked his head to the side for me to walk with him. I grabbed two water bottles and followed.

"When did you get here?" I matched his pace, but it was more like he slowed down for me.

"Few minutes ago. I heard what you said to Mrs. Conner …"

I stiffened. I hoped he'd heard enough to know I wasn't gossiping. "I can explain. I—"

Lee weaved around families sitting on beach blankets.

"I appreciate what you said. I'm sure she won't be the last to interrogate you," he said. "I apologize ahead of time. Like I said before, people like to get into other people's business in a small community. I like the quiet pace here, but I don't socialize much unless I know the person is genuine."

"I can understand that. Is Jessica married?"

"I don't know much about her, but I do know she's divorced. Not because I wanted to know. Jessica made a point to tell me. I just want to make that clear."

I laughed inwardly.

When Lee stopped at a white beach gazebo, I glanced around for Abby's blanket. "I don't think we're at the right place." I had been too focused on our topic that I'd just followed blindly.

He chuckled. "Check the front."

I shuffled through the sand to see Tyler and Bridget making a sandcastle. They both waved at me and got back to digging.

"Where did this come from?" I motioned to the tent.

"Me. Do you not like it?" He looked concerned as he handed Tyler his plate, then set mine inside the tent on a small round table that separated two lounge chairs.

"I love it, but how did you get it here and when?" I'd been so busy helping Abby and fending off Jessica's questions that I hadn't noticed.

"You can rent it through the hotel. Please have a seat and eat."

"Where's your lunch?" I sank into the lounge chair, took a bite of my sandwich as I watched him spread out his long legs, and leaned back.

"Bridget and I had a late breakfast, but thank you for asking." After a short pause, he asked, "Where's your brother-in-law?"

It took a few seconds for me to realize he was asking about Abby's husband.

"He—um—Steve. He died recently from cancer."

Lee had been watching Bridget, but his head snapped back to me. "I'm so sorry, Kate. Why didn't you tell me?"

I sighed, rubbing my thighs. "I didn't tell you because you were talking about your sister. It was your story and your grief. I didn't want to take that away from you, if that makes sense."

He swung around in his chair to face me, his bare feet touching the sand. "That was very considerate of you. Thank you. How's your sister doing?"

Not well, I wanted to tell him, but instead I said, "She's fine. She has to be for Tyler. She has her bad and good days."

He nodded. "I'm sorry about Steve."

Afterward, I ate my sandwich while Lee read on his tablet. A comfortable quiet grew between us.

While I listened to the hypnotic sound of the waves, I stared at the water, glistening like crystals when caught in the sun's light. My eyes became heavy and peace filled my soul.

"Papa!" Bridget yelled.

We both jumped up.

"What? What's wrong?" Lee ran over, looking around Bridget for any sign of danger.

"Look what we made," she said excitedly.

"It's a castle." Tyler pointed.

They had piled on wet sand, molded from the buckets. The sides were crumbling and the front tilted. It looked more like a hill than a sandcastle. Not bad for a couple of four-year-olds.

"That's awesome, you two." I picked up Tyler's paper plate, weighted down with a pile of damp sand. "Ty, are you done with your lunch?" He had eaten everything except the crust, as usual.

"I'm done."

He was too busy to even look up at me.

"Can I have a cookie like Tyler?" Bridget tugged on Lee's leg.

"I can go get it." Taking care of Bridget had become second nature.

Lee gripped my arm before I could take a step. "That's okay. You stay here. I'll go get it."

While Lee treaded back through the sand, I helped the kids with the castle. They didn't ask me to leave. In fact, they passed me a shovel and a bucket. I took a brief break and texted Abby.

Me: We are in front of the huge gazebo.

Abby: I know. Lee told me.

Lee? She had never called him Lee before. Maybe he'd told her to call him Lee like he had me. A little jealousy pricked at me, but I squashed the ridiculous feeling.

Me: Do you need my help?

Abby: I don't, but Lee might.

Me: Why?

When I didn't get a text back, I got back to helping with the sandcastle. A minute later, my phone tinkled like wind chimes. That same familiar invisible hand caressed down my back. And I wasn't sure if I shivered from the sound or the sudden breeze catching my breath.

Bridget's head shot up and she gazed at me. Her grin tugged at my heartstrings. I smiled back and checked my phone. A text from Lee had come through and my pulse quickened.

Lee: What are you doing?

I bit my lip. A text shouldn't make me melt into the sand. Maybe I should cool down by dipping my feet in the water. He had texted me before, but this felt different. And the wind chimes? *Strange.*

Me: Building a sandcastle

Lee: I want to help.

Me: Come

Lee: I can't.

Me: Why?

Lee: Help!

He couldn't be physically in danger, but I wasn't sure what warranted that *Help*.

"Tyler. Bridget. Stay right here. I'll be right back."

They were perfectly safe. Only our party was here. When I rushed over, parents surrounded Lee. He nodded and smiled at them. He seemed perfectly fine, like he was enjoying himself, but he wanted out and was only being polite.

I marched right through the crowd to Lee. "Bridget is asking for you. Can you come right now?"

"Excuse me." He gave a polite nod.

His admirers broke the circle. Lee and I headed back together, a cookie wrapped in a napkin in his hand.

"Thank you," he said, weaving around families sitting under beach umbrellas.

I didn't understand why he'd needed my help to walk away, but I didn't ask.

"Sure. Anytime," I said.

"I didn't want to be rude. I rarely attend these events. It was the first time meeting most of the parents. They were asking me personal questions and I couldn't figure out how to deflect any more without hurting feelings."

"It's okay, Lee. I understand."

He halted a few feet away from the kids and the gazebo, so I stopped too. The sunlight bounced off his sunglasses but I could tell his eyes were pinned on mine.

"Thank you again," he said. "I didn't mean to put you in that position, but you're easy to talk to. I'm glad we got the chance to be friends. If you need anything, please don't hesitate to ask. So … will you be joining us for the helicopter ride tomorrow?"

The question threw me off. We hadn't talked about it for a couple of days. But we were friends. He'd clearly stated that, so I didn't see the harm in it.

I planted my fists on my hips and leaned to one side. "On one condition."

"Name it."

"Can you help with the sandcastle? It's a lot of digging."

He threw his head back and let out a joyful sound. "Of course. It's a deal."

Lee handed Bridget her cookie and we got down on our knees.

Jessica stopped by to chat, but when Tyler accidentally flicked sand on her, she left in a hurry. Lee and I laughed at that.

Others came by to admire our sandcastle and took pictures. The creation wasn't perfect, but it was perfect in my eyes. And so was everything else about the day.

Chapter Twenty-Four – Tour of Kauai

Phillip picked me up from Abby's house and took me back to Lee's. I scooted over for Bridget in the car and belted her in while Lee hopped in the front.

"Good morning, passengers." Lee twisted his body to face me, grinning. "Phillip is going to drive us to the hangar, and we'll get on the helicopter from there. Here. Put this on and take this. These will help with the motion sickness."

He handed me a wristband, a pill, and a bottle of water.

I had already purchased a wristband, but since he'd gone out of his way to get one for me, I didn't want to refuse. It was sweet of him to remember I got motion sickness.

"Don't be scared, Kate. Papa is a good helicopter driver." Bridget patted my knee in a curiously grown-up way.

Bridget was observant for a child her age, and so was Tyler. As if the tragedy in their lives made them mature faster.

Abby had been against me going. Not because she didn't trust Lee, but because she felt I was getting too attached to both of them. I told her we were friends, but she'd scowled and shook her head.

I wasn't sure how I'd given her the impression that I couldn't handle myself. Lee had clearly stated he was glad we were *friends*. His expectations were clear. Mine were too.

There was the fact that he had never seemed remotely interested in me more than as a friend. Sure, we had the occasional moment, but sometimes sparks fizz out without ever igniting. And the job search hadn't gone well, so I needed to go back home.

As silence took over the small space in the vehicle, I looked out the window. We passed through the town where locals and tourists were busy at restaurants and shops, and then through the tree tunnels. Outside the tunnel, tall grasses skirted the areas that had not been developed yet.

Before I knew it, we had arrived. Countless helicopters were stationed in their designated parking area. All the helicopters looked alike and I didn't know which one belonged to Lee.

My door opened just as I tugged at the handle. Lee popped a hand in front of me, and I graciously took it. He also took out my camera bag and carried it for me.

Bridget and I followed Lee to the helicopter, its propeller already lazily spinning. I ducked my head into the front with Lee while Bridget sat in the back.

"Here, put these on." Lee handed us headsets after he put on his. "This will block out noise and we'll be able to hear each other." He flipped switches on the control panel, the blades picked up speed, and the helicopter lifted off the ground. "Ready? Here we go."

My muscles tightened and I folded my hands onto my lap. The farther up he went, the faster butterflies swarmed in my center.

"Yah!" Bridget's laughter filled my earpiece.

People, cars, homes, and the town shrank to little dots, while we lifted higher into the sky with scattered white clouds. Then Lee banked left toward the vast ocean. So beautiful in its simplicity from up high. As he got closer to the mountain, waterfalls sporadically appeared here and there.

I took out my camera and took pictures of my view.

"There's the Wailua Falls." Bridget pointed, her forehead pressed to the window.

A painting of this waterfall hung in Abby's gallery. Lee had admired it that day he purchased Cupid.

"It's beautiful. Where are we?"

"North of Lihue," Lee said. "Did you know this waterfall is famous?"

"Really?" My curiosity was piqued.

"It's most recognized from the opening credits of the old TV show *Fantasy Island*. But I've never seen it."

"Now I have to see it." I snorted and took more pictures.

Lee began to lower the helicopter. "We're going to land soon and have lunch."

As I continued to admire the breathtaking view, I'd expected some hidden gem of a restaurant in the mountains, but there was nothing here.

I supposed he meant picnic.

While Lee landed the helicopter on a flat area atop a mountain, I gaped at the waterfall. Crystal-clear water cascaded from a dizzying height, droplets shimmering in the air, and splashed into a small pool lined with boulders and shrubs.

Lee helped us out and grabbed a picnic basket and a big blanket. We climbed down a steep slope in a single file between glossy green leaves. Mist dampened my face from the waterfall like soft kisses and I let them dry on their own.

Lee led the way to a grassy area, and I helped him spread the blanket. I backed away and snapped pictures of him and Bridget with the waterfall background, a few with the boulders and tall shrubs behind them, and then the waterfall itself.

Exquisite. Perfect.

"Don't tell me this is your property?" I placed my camera down beside me on the blanket.

Lee chuckled, taking the water bottles out of the picnic basket. "No. I wish. I found this spot while flying around aimlessly. It's secluded and no one comes here."

Lee took out a stack of aluminum containers next. He handed me one and then one to Bridget. He opened the silver lid and stream rose.

"Bridget picked the restaurant. It's Chinese food, and it's warm. Please, eat away."

I eyed the dumplings, hot buns with meat inside, and noodles with beef. "I didn't know we were having lunch here. I would have brought something as well."

"No need. I asked you to come." He took a bite of the hot bun.

I took the chopsticks he handed me and twirled the noodles around. "Do you come here often?"

Bridget held out two fingers, her little mouth stuffed with dumpling.

"We came twice this year," Lee used the chopsticks to pick up a dumpling. "It depends on how busy I am. My business slows down in December. I also take Bridget to see snow."

"Here?" It sounded ridiculous after I had said it. It didn't snow in Kauai, or any of the Hawaiian Islands.

The corners of Lee's lips tugged. "No. Not here."

I flipped open the water bottle cap and took a drink. "I would love to go where it snowed one day. I've never been."

Lee swallowed. "Really? What's so special about the snow?"

"The sight of snow always fills me with peace, the way the sound of wind chimes does. Snow also reminds me of Christmas and all the magical things. Christmas is about family and friends. Helping your neighbors and strangers. Giving and receiving."

"I agree with you, and I can take you to see snow whenever you like, but before it melts."

I let out a light laugh. I hadn't been hinting at Lee to take me, but it was nice of him to offer, and if our friendship continued, I just might accept.

I took a bite of my dumpling and the other half fell on my plate. "You must travel a lot with your line of business."

He nodded, slurping noodles into his mouth. "I used to enjoy it, but when things happened"—he jerked his head toward Bridget—"I didn't enjoy it as much. I feel a sense of duty and I don't like to be away. But I took on business responsibilities as well, and I need to honor those commitments. It's difficult juggling both. I'm hoping my younger brother will take some business responsibilities off my hands."

I figured there were some issues with his brother, but I didn't ask. Lee had opened up to me, more than I'd ever expected, so I wasn't going to push him. He would tell me if he wanted to share.

"How about you? Have you traveled much?" He took a long drink from his water bottle.

"Not internationally, but hopefully one day. I'd like to visit Asia since my family comes from there."

"It's an experience. You would love it. I'm going to take Bridget when she's old enough to handle long flights."

Bridget, who had been eating quietly, frowned. "I can handle it now. I'm a big girl."

Lee chuckled. "We'll see. Maybe next year."

Bridget got up and dusted the front of her shirt. "I'm done. Can I have dessert?"

"I almost forgot." Lee reached inside the basket and took out another container. "Fresh-baked chocolate chip cookies from the local bakery. These are the best."

My mouth watered. "This must be my lucky day, Lee. Thank you."

I let Bridget take one out first and then grabbed my own. I didn't bother finishing my plate of noodles as I sank my teeth into the soft cookie, the chocolate chips melting in my mouth.

"You're right, Lee. These are the best," I said with a mouthful.

"Yummy." Bridget stuffed the cookie in her mouth so fast crumbs fell all over her shirt.

Lee and I laughed.

"Slow down, sweetheart," Lee said. "You'll choke. Drink some water." Lee shook his head and handed her a water bottle. "You would think she'd never had cookies."

"Can I go over there?" Bridget pointed to the waterfall.

Lee gave her a pointed look. "Do you remember the boundary?"

"Don't pass the fifth boulder and stay by the small rocks."

"Good. Yes, you may go." He watched her and then turned to me.

"So …" I washed down the last bit of cookie and picked out a little white flower growing within the grass. "You've been taking care of Bridget for the past two years. Do you get to go out with friends or date much?"

I wanted—needed—to know if what Jessica had told me about Lee having many lovers was true, and I hoped the relaxed setting would make my question sound less invasive.

He rolled back his shoulders and anchored his hands behind him. His hair was slicked back and his face clean shaven. He looked like a model posing for an outdoor adventure magazine photo shoot in his jeans and a form-fitting T-shirt.

"When I adopted Bridget, I spent all my spare time with her. We needed to get comfortable with each other. Bringing someone else into the family and dividing my time didn't seem right. To be honest, some women were turned off I had a child. They didn't know she wasn't my own."

"I could understand. It can get complicated." I stretched my legs and closed my eyes. We sat in the shade of the mountain, but just the sight of the sun's halo around the peak filled me with warmth.

"What about you? Is there someone special back home?"

My eyes flew open at the unexpected question. I tried not to think of Jayden, and I'd been good at forgetting him, but what he'd done still hurt. I didn't want Lee to see the pain in my face, but I wasn't good at hiding my emotions. Though, I knew he would understand since his sister's husband had left her for another woman.

I cleared my throat. "My ex-boyfriend, whom I dated for almost two years, cheated on me."

I didn't want his pity and I didn't want to sound pathetic either, so I left out that Jayden had cheated on me twice.

Lee frowned. "I'm sorry that it happened to you. It's his loss, Kate. I don't understand people who cheat. Act like a grown-up. Break up first and then go on your way."

"I couldn't agree with you more."

"Was it recent?" He sounded hesitant.

He wanted to know more about my private life. My stomach lurched, and I told myself to calm down. *Talking about relationships is just another level of friendship.*

I peered up to the puffy clouds and then met his gaze. "It happened about a year ago, the day after Christmas. So I really hate that 'Last Christmas' song." The second time had been more recent, but I wasn't going to go there.

Lee laughed. "I'm sorry. That's not funny, but your comment was."

I shrugged. "The song fits my situation though."

"It does." Lee picked up the empty containers and shoved them into the bag.

I tried to help but he swatted my hand away.

"He wants to get back together." He didn't need to know that, but I'd said it. Too late.

"Oh." He halted briefly. "Are you planning to?"

"No. He lost my trust, and trust is everything in a relationship, right?"

"Yes, it is. I couldn't agree more."

We sat in silence as we watched Bridget carefully maneuver on the boulders.

"Look, Papa. Butterflies." Bridget leaned forward to get a closer look.

My chest tightened, something inside me tugged in warning. She was standing too close to the edge. I was about to say something but Lee beat me to it.

"Bridget, get back." Lee raised his voice and bent his knees, poised to jump up.

"Okay, but—"

In truth, it was over in a couple of seconds, but it felt like a lifetime. Bridget's left leg slid, causing her to fall on her butt. Then she plummeted over the side.

I had never been so scared in my life.

"Bridget!" Lee hollered from the top of his lungs, bolting toward the water.

Heart thundering, I raced behind him.

"She just learned how to swim," he said in a frenzied tone, tossed off his shoes and dove in.

I searched for Bridget, panic beating against my ribcage. *Please, let her be fine. Hurry, Lee.*

Seconds passed. And more seconds passed. Every second seemed like minutes. Too long. Too long. It was taking too damn long to find her.

A head popped up. Lee spat out water, panting, trembling. "I can't find her. Do you see her?" He whirled around, calling her name again and again with desperation.

Oh, God. Oh, God. Oh, God.

I frantically scanned every inch of the ground around the pool, from the trees and shrubs to the left and boulders to the right. No Bridget.

"Bridget!" I hollered. This could not be happening. Lee had lost Roselyn. He could not lose Bridget too.

Lee splashed out of the water again without his niece, the pain in his eyes palpable. I didn't have time to think how cold the water would be, nor did I care. Nor did I care my jeans would weigh me down. I took off my shoes and jumped in.

The drop in temperature stung my bones, my muscles constricting. My teeth rattled and I nearly sucked in a lungful of icy water. I resurfaced and dove underwater again. If I'd fallen and wasn't a good swimmer, where would I find shelter?

Lee dove under the deeper water, which made sense if she didn't know how to swim, but Bridget did. The teacher would have taught her to go to the edge of the pool or find something … anything to hold on to.

Oh, please, please, please. I swam away from Lee, struggling against the frigid water threatening to pull me under as I searched the lower grounds. Icy fingers wrapped around my lungs, squeezing tighter and unyielding the longer I stayed. Every stroke was a torturous effort. Every breath I took out of the water without Bridget had me in tears.

Then … small splashes.

There. She was there. I inhaled a deep, excruciating, thankful breath and happy tears pooled in my eyes.

Bridget clung to a root that draped over the giant rock, her body halfway out of the water, in the fetal position and trembling.

"Over here, Lee." I waved at him from the other side of the boulder.

"Bridget. I'm coming." I swam, flapping my feet, pushing my arms, fighting against the jarring stiffness.

"Kate." Her teeth rattled and she could hardly speak, but her eyes were teary with relief.

"I've got you, Bridget. Thank God I found you." I held her tightly and stroked her hair, tears streaming down my face from relief. "You're okay." I repeated the words to keep her calm and to reassure her, and myself.

When Lee reached us, I moved away for him. He squeezed her in his arms, and just held her to compose himself, and then finally swam back.

The cold was even more unbearable when I got out, my movements stiff and robotic. The breeze stung like needles. Every step took great effort, and my body might as well have turned to ice.

Bridget was still in Lee's arms, her legs anchored around his waist. She whimpered. Her lips shook and her voice cracked as she spoke. "I'm sorry. Please don't get mad at me. I fell. I was so scared." She sobbed in his arms.

I shoved everything off the blanket and covered them, water dripping from their clothes. Before I could step back, Lee folded me into his spare arm under the blanket, the other still holding onto Bridget. The warmth of our three bodies pressed together finally calmed my pounding heart.

"Thank you." His voice was low and rough. "I don't even know … I don't think …"

I nodded, overloaded from the cold, Lee's proximity, and the thought of almost losing Bridget.

I put my finger on his lips. He didn't need to thank me, and he didn't need to think about what could have been. Bridget was safe in his arms, and that was all that mattered.

In the silence with our eyes locked, and with more assurance than I normally felt, I wiped away the water dripping from his face and caressed his cheek. And then I turned to Bridget and stroked her hair.

Lee met my gaze again with a smile that said a thousand words and pressed his forehead to mine. Then he brought all of our heads together. We stood in the quiet, taking in the warmth, taking a moment to breathe and be thankful.

"Can I have another cookie?"

Lee and I broke apart, laughing and still shivering.

Lee planted a tender kiss on Bridget's cheek. "You may have as many as you want. Let's go home and drink some hot cocoa. We've had enough swimming for today."

Chapter Twenty-Five – Never Again

"Kate. I've got you." Lee took me out of the car when we got back to his place.

My nonsense reply was muffled against his chest, my eyes closed. Lee had his arms wrapped around me, my front pressed to his side and my arms around his middle.

The bright sun made my nausea worse. My knees buckled with every stumbling step, but Lee's strong hold on me kept me from collapsing.

"What's wrong with Kate?" Bridget said, opening the front door.

"Kate's going to be okay. She needs to sleep it off. Can you be a big girl for me? I need you to grab a bottle of water and a T-shirt from my dresser."

Bridget's footsteps shuffled on the marble and faded the farther she went.

We were on the move again, my feet dragging up the stairs. My body felt as heavy as the boulders at the waterfall. I had been fine with the first half of the helicopter tour, but on our way home, motion sickness had hit with a vengeance. My breathing had quickened, sweat had dampened my forehead, and I'd wanted to vomit.

I had wanted to keep Bridget from thinking about the almost-drowning experience, so I'd sat in the back and talked with her. It turned out that wasn't a good idea. Dry heaves racked my body every few minutes.

Lee assisted me to bed. "Kate. I know you feel horrible right now, but you're going to be okay. I'm going to take care of you."

Lee laid me over the comforter, and he took off my shoes.

I groaned, unable to open my eyes. Clutching the pillow, I prayed the room would stop spinning.

"I'm sorry." I squeezed my eyes tighter, clenching my teeth. Even talking made my head throb. The urge to puke rose again, and I would do anything so Lee didn't watch me throw up.

"Why are you apologizing? You did nothing wrong. I'm the one who should feel horrible, and I do. I wish I could have done something more to prevent you getting airsick."

"It's not … your fault. No … pill," I managed to say, unsure if I made sense.

I wore the wristband Lee had given me, but I hadn't taken the motion sickness pill. I had taken one once when Jayden and I had gone on a boat ride with some friends. The medicine had made me groggy and ruined what should have been a fun date.

I hadn't wanted the same thing to happen today, so I'd shoved the pill inside my pocket. The wristband might have been enough had I not sat in the back with Bridget.

Light footsteps padded into the room. "Here. I got the water and a T-shirt for Kate. She doesn't look good."

"She's going to be fine. She just looks pale." His reassuring, soft voice made me feel better for a second, but then the room spun again.

A dresser opened. Something crinkled. Then the dresser shut.

"Kate, I'm going to lift you up a bit so you can take this medicine and sip some water."

Lee cupped his hand under my head and tilted it up. Then he put a pill inside my mouth and placed the open water bottle to my lips. With my eyes still closed, I gratefully drank.

"Thank—" I lunged off of the bed and slapped my hand on the wall for support. I parted my eyelids just enough to make out the location of the bathroom and stumbled toward it.

Had Lee not held me, I might have fallen into the bathtub.

"Bridget, go to your room. I'll be right there soon to help you shower."

"But—"

"No but. Just do it." His stern voice rang in my ear.

I was glad Lee made Bridget leave the room. Not only did I not want her to see me like this, I didn't want her to witness what I was about to do.

I hugged the toilet in a hurry, the damp jeans hard and scratchy on my skin. Horrendous sounds escaped my mouth as acid charged up my throat. My lunch spewed into the toilet in a multicolored fountain, and a few drops splashed onto my face.

So gross. I hope I didn't get any on Lee. But I felt so relieved. The urge to vomit went away and I finally felt like I was on the road to recovery.

Nope. False alarm.

I clutched the toilet again, but this time, Lee held my hair away from my face. Such a sweet gesture, but I was mortified.

Why did I have to get airsick? Lee didn't need this right now. He shouldn't be the one taking care of me. This was so unprofessional.

"I'm sorry. Call my sister." My voice echoed inside the toilet, my body trembling.

I heard running water from the sink and then it shut off.

"Are you done, or do you think—"

I plopped on the cold marble floor and rested my head on my bent arm on the toilet. "I'm done," I murmured, energy drained from me.

Something warm and soft brushed the side of my cheek. Lee dabbed a warm cloth on my face. Then he hefted me up and guided me to the bed.

"Your sister doesn't need to be here. You have me. You might want to take off those damp clothes. They're somewhat dried but you might not want to sleep in them. I would take them off for you, but I don't think you want that. Here's a clean T-shirt. I'll turn around."

I pulled my shirt over my head, but my jeans peeled reluctantly from my skin. I slipped on the T-shirt he'd left on the mattress and hugged a pillow, nestling my head with a sigh. Something soft and warm covered me. I needed to shower, especially after falling into the water, but it was the least of my concerns. How could I face Lee in the morning?

Abby was right. If Lee, my boss, whom I barely knew, took the time to take care of me better than my ex-boyfriend, someone who had supposedly loved me, I shouldn't have any problem finding someone better. Right?

During the boat trip, Jayden had been busy drinking with his friends instead of taking care of me when I'd gotten sick. In fact, he'd mostly left me alone.

"Thank you … Lee," I said, drifting in and out of sleep. "You're a good … and …"

My words came out incoherent and jumbled. Hopefully he

understood.

In my dreams, Lee and I were a couple. After the helicopter ride, the three of us had dinner in his gorgeous backyard. He grilled steak and chicken while Bridget and I made salad and some side dishes in our fabulous kitchen.

We talked and laughed during dinner, and afterward we swam in the giant pool. Then after we put Bridget to bed, Lee and I drank wine and made love in our bedroom.

When I opened my eyes, the white walls and the dark, closed shutters slowly became familiar. I was in the room next to Bridget's. Everything that happened the previous day came crashing through my mind. The helicopter ride, the waterfall picnic, the conversation with Lee, Bridget almost drowning, my nightmare of being airsick, and then the too-good-to-be-true dream.

I got out of bed and checked my cell on the bedside table. Ten in the morning.

Holy cow. I had slept more than twelve hours.

My hair reeked of old water, but worse, I had no pants. I wore only a T-shirt. Lee's shirt?

I began texting Abby, but I called her instead, seeing that I had several missed calls. Lee must have turned off my phone.

"Are you okay?" Abby asked.

I plopped on the bed and ran my fingers through my tangled hair. "It's a long story."

"I know. Lee called me."

I heard Tyler in the background. "He did?" I recalled asking him to call Abby. Then why was I still here?

"Yes. He told me how you got airsick and that you wouldn't be home. I offered to come pick you up, but he said he had it all under control and that you just needed to sleep. He was very sweet about it. See, this is what a real man—a man with a good heart—does. Do you remember when you got sick on the boat with Jayden?"

I sighed sharply. "Yes, I do. You don't need to bring it up. I get it." I didn't need a second mother.

"Okay, fine, but are you okay? Are you coming home or do you need to watch Bridget? Do you need my help?"

Abby hadn't given me a chance to respond, but I couldn't say much, anyway. I was still shocked by what I was wearing.

"I'm wearing his T-shirt." I sniffed the fabric—pine. "It smells like Lee—sweet and fresh laundry."

"What? What happened?" I could picture my sister's shocked face.

I laid back in bed, glancing up at the recessed lighting. "Nothing happened. I'm just making a comment. I'll let you know if I'm coming home. I'll call you later."

I bit my bottom lip, contemplating if I should put on yesterday's clothes. Surely they were dried by now. I got out of bed and searched the bathroom, then on top of the dresser. Where could they be?

Lee must have them if I was wearing his shirt. Had I taken off my clothes in front of him? At least I had my bra and panties on.

There was only one way to find out. Brave it and leave the room to find him.

I inhaled a deep breath and opened the door. Well, I didn't need to find him. Lee stood in front of me with my clothes neatly folded.

"Hi?" My greeting came off like a question.

He gave me a once over and produced a devilish grin, and then with a straight face, he handed me my clothes. "I hope you don't mind but I washed them except for your"—he cleared his throat—"undergarments. You didn't take them off."

Heat flushed through me. I rubbed the side of my face. "Did I … did I take my clothes off in front of you?"

"Yes," he said.

My eyes widened, shock rendering me speechless. No hesitation there.

His cheeks turned color. "Oh. I meant, you did, but I turned around. I didn't see you. I would never take advantage of you. I hope you don't think—"

I exhaled with relief. "No, no, no. I don't think that. I'm just grateful, that's all."

Lee's chest rose and fell with a long sigh. "I'm glad we cleared that up. Anyway, you must be starving. I have breakfast ready. After you change, please join us."

"Sure. Thank you, but let me take a quick shower."

"Of course." He took a step, but then turned. "Before I forget to tell you, I need you to come back tomorrow morning about eight. I'll be gone the rest of the week, but I'll be home Friday afternoon."

"Sure. No problem." I gave a wobbly smile.

When he turned, I gently laid my hand on his shoulder, recalling that day he had done the same to me in the cab. Life was strange. I couldn't believe I was working for the man who had given his taxi to me, whom I'd thought I would never see again.

"Lee?" My heart fluttered in my stomach.

"Yes." His voice was tender and hypnotic, like his eyes.

"I'm sorry you had to take care of me. I'm so embarrassed. This is so unprofessional. I hope you don't think less of me or that I'm incapable of watching Bridget, and—"

He brought a finger to my lips, parting them. I sucked in air as something warm grew in the center of my belly.

Lee lowered his darkened eyes to my mouth, then met my gaze with intensity. His voice became rough and deeper. "I don't think that at all, Kate. If you knew what I was thinking at this moment, you would think *I* wasn't being professional."

I had no idea how to process that as I watched him walk away.

Chapter Twenty-Six – Painting Room

Lee never failed to call twice a day during his business trips—in the morning before Bridget went to school and then before she went to bed. He also texted me daily, asking if I needed anything.

Sometimes, our conversations were about his work, and sometimes he would send me random paintings he saw at the hotel or at the restaurants and ask my opinion. We were acting like a couple.

Four days passed and Lee came home. He had asked me to keep Bridget home from school, so I arranged a lesson with her swimming teacher. I'd thought it was a good idea to get her back into the water as soon as possible.

From where I stood by the pool, I could see Lee through the double glass doors, sitting at the dining table with his laptop open. Occasionally, he would look out toward us.

The swimming lesson had ended about half an hour ago, but Bridget wanted to stay in the water longer. When I thought she had enough, I wrapped a towel around her, and we walked back inside.

"Kate, can you stay tonight?" Lee kept his eyes on the computer screen, moving his fingers along the keyboard and continuing without a glance my way. "I have a meeting after dinner and I'm not sure what time I'll be home."

"Yes. I can stay."

Lee closed his laptop and rose. "Great. I ordered pizza from World's Best Pizza. I hope you don't mind."

"I love their pizza. It's the world's best." Bridget clapped, her pool towel slipping off her shoulders.

I covered her up again. "Before pizza, you need to take a shower."

She nodded and ran off.

Lee followed her halfway and watched her climb up the stairs. I didn't know what he was thinking, but I could assume.

"She's fine, Lee." I stroked his arm to get his attention. "Kids bounce back faster than adults. You can talk to her about it if you want, but the swimming instructor did a good job helping her feel comfortable swimming again. I bet she's busy thinking about the pizza and not what had happened at the waterfall."

Lee pressed his lips together, his eyes soft and vulnerable. I understood his concern. Being a parent wasn't easy. Abby had talked to me often about Tyler. She regularly tied herself in knots worrying that she was doing too much or too little of everything.

"Thank you. I needed to hear that," he said, meeting my gaze.

"Good." I pointed my finger upward. "I need to go and help her."

After Bridget washed up, we gathered at the dining table. While Lee passed out the plates of pizza, I gazed at the lit Christmas tree and the lights dangling around the room. It gave a warm and cozy feel—a reminder Christmas was soon.

Bridget, sitting next to me, held her pizza and picked off the olives. She tossed them in her mouth before she sank her teeth into the dough.

Lee squeezed his eyes shut and stopped chewing, as if remembering something terrible. "I'm sorry, Kate. I forgot to ask you what toppings you wanted."

I was just about to take a bite, but stopped to answer. "That's okay. I like everything on it, so you did good."

Bridget stuffed her mouth, kicking her legs under the table. "I like everything on it too."

"Don't talk with your mouth full, young lady. It's bad manners and you might choke." Lee shook his finger at her from across the table, his voice firm but soft.

Bridget huffed out air. "You told me that like one hundred times."

"Oh, is that all?" Lee laughed and took another piece from the box. "I'm worried what she'll say to me when she's a teenager."

"You don't want to know." I sank my teeth through the warm dough and cheese-drenched toppings.

I moaned into the pizza while Lee and Bridget stared.

"You're both right. It's the best pizza in the worrrrrllld," I announced with exaggerated enthusiasm.

"*Yah*." They cheered, giving each other high fives.

Bridget bobbed her head from side to side to the melody of "Feliz

Navidad" playing in the background as Lee poured soda in cups and sang along.

I liked this playful and relaxed side of Lee. He seemed to show it more around me lately.

"What do you want for Christmas?" I asked Bridget.

She pushed her pizza crust aside. "I don't know. I don't need anything."

"She has everything." Lee snorted and passed me a cup.

"That's not her fault. Someone spoils her." I gave him a mock scowl and drank.

He smiled sheepishly. "How about you?"

"I don't need anything. I mean, there's a lot I wish to have, but … Oh, I know—chocolate chip cookies."

I threw in a bit of humor because the things I wished for would never come true. Like wishing Steve and Roselyn had never had cancer.

"Chocolate chip cookies?" Bridget's giggles filled the room.

I continued eating and said, "Maybe I should ask Santa for pizza?"

Bridget laughed harder.

I wasn't trying to be funny. I didn't have anything else to say.

Lee and I flinched and I sucked in air when Bridget dropped her pizza and burst into a fit of coughing, like she was choking. She finally stopped and drank water.

Lee and I exchanged horrified glances and then relaxed with an exhale at the same time. He put a hand to his forehead and shook his head, and I did the same. We rolled our eyes when we made contact.

When a text came through, Lee got up and wiped his mouth with the napkin. "I need to leave, but I'll be back as soon as I can."

His words were meant for Bridget, but he was looking at me.

"Take your time. Go do your business and come home. I'll be here." I got up to clean the table.

Lee went around the table to Bridget and kissed her on the cheek. He then turned toward me, as if he'd been about to kiss me by reflex but stopped and retreated. Our gazes locked a heartbeat too long.

"I-I'll see you later, Kate," he said quickly.

"Be safe and have fun."

Have fun? Lame—he was going to a business meeting. But what if it wasn't? He might be going on a date. And he had every right to go out with whoever he wanted.

Irritated with myself, I shoved the thoughts aside and cleaned the table with Bridget's help. After we played a couple of games of *Unicorns versus Skeletons*, she brushed her teeth and I read her a bedtime story.

I got into bed with Bridget, snuggled under the blanket. It was only nine, but she was exhausted, and so was I.

"Would you like me to stay with you or would you rather me leave?" I asked.

"Stay," she said, her eyelashes fluttering.

"Okie dokie. Then I'll read you another book."

Bridget wrapped her thin arms around my neck and pulled me closer. "I know what I want for Christmas." Her words were soft and hardly audible.

"You do?" I whispered, using the same quiet tone.

She nodded, her big eyes glistening like blue diamonds.

"What is it?"

"You." She tapped my chin. "I wish you could stay with me forever."

I melted into a puddle. Abby was right—I was getting attached to Lee and Bridget more than I should. In only two weeks, we'd bonded strong and fast.

Secretly, I was playing house. Lee, my amazing loyal husband, who would never cheat on me. Bridget, my sweet daughter. We were a happy family. But I was down to the last few days. Mona would be back soon and they wouldn't need me anymore. When I left, Bridget would have to make another adjustment.

Kids are resilient. They bounce back fast. I'd miss her more than she would me.

"We will always be friends. No matter what happens." Liquid pooled in my eyes.

"Promise?" Her lips turned downward into a pout.

"Let's pinky promise."

She curled her small delicate pinky into mine and said, "Promise to the unicorns, rainbows, and all the sparkling things."

I laughed and repeated.

Bridget fell asleep about halfway through the second book. I shelved it and called my sister and we talked until my phone flashed with a text.

Lee: What are you doing?

I blinked. Jayden used to ask me that, so it seemed more intimate than something you'd text your employee.

Me: Bridget is sleeping.

Lee: That's good. Thank you.

Me: You're welcome. What are you doing?

I pictured him surrounded by beautiful, well-to-do women, and I almost didn't want to know.

Lee: Boring stuff. You'd fall asleep.

I laughed.

Me: Is that why you're texting me?

Lee: Maybe.

Me: Well, I hope I don't bore you then.

Lee: You're not boring.

I didn't know what to think of that.

Me: You're not boring either. Maybe. Sometimes.

Lee: What? I think my ego needs stroking.

Me: I think …

I itched to text something naughty about something else that needed stroking, but I sternly reminded myself who I was speaking to.

The three dots rippled for a few seconds and then stopped. They came up again and then stopped. When he didn't finish, I figured he'd gotten busy with his meeting, so I went to the painting room and continued a painting I had started. I wanted to leave Lee and Bridget a parting gift for welcoming me into their home and filling my life with joy.

Jayden was no longer in my thoughts and I harbored no bad feelings toward him. Abby, Tyler, Lee, and Bridget had filled me with gratitude that overpowered the residue of what he'd left behind. My heart had no room for past inconsequential things. No room for hurt and hatred, just love and happiness.

We are reminded life is fleeting when tragedy strikes—or almost does. That moment of fear that we had lost Bridget had jolted and reset my system.

As I listened to a Christmas playlist with my earphones on, I stroked the canvas with the paintbrush. I added details to the hair, lightening it a bit. Then I shaded along the cheekbones.

After I selected another tube, I squeezed it onto the palette. I added white to the pink and dabbed it on the canvas. Afterward, I swirled the brush into a jar of turpentine, and then blended brown with the blue on top.

There.

Perfect.

I put that away and replaced it with a new canvas I'd already primed. I changed the medium to acrylic and dabbed colors on the palette.

When my eyes began to droop, I looked at the time. Midnight. Lee wasn't home yet. Not that I'd expected him to come home early on account of me.

I got up. My muscles felt tight from sitting for hours. As I listened to "Rocking Around the Christmas Tree" singing and painting, I zoned into my creative world.

My piece looked like a unicorn had gotten sick and thrown up a rainbow. But that was how I thought all of my paintings looked at the beginning stage. I laughed at that thought and swung my arms back to stretch.

The walls around me were several feet away so I shouldn't have hit anything, but I did.

Not again. I swallowed and turned slowly. Lee held a blank expression with blue paint smeared across his black and white dress shirt. He must be infuriated. Twice I had done this to him.

"I'm so sorry, Lee." I covered my mouth, trying not to laugh.

I thought he was going to react the way he had the last time, so I mentally prepared myself for a scowl and a scolding. But instead he took the paintbrush out of my hand and swiped it across my shirt with a smirk.

Astounded, I gasped and lowered my gaze to the blue streak. I took my brush back, dipped it into pink and splashed it on his black pants. Lee furrowed his brow, scooped up white paint from the palette, and slopped it on my hair.

"You—what's that for?" I took two paint-drenched brushes and made circles on both of his cheeks.

Lee grabbed a tube and squirted it on my neck. "For making me think of you all night. You didn't text me back."

What did he mean by that? I only recalled how he hadn't finished and left me hanging. I laughed off his words and abandoned myself to the adrenaline rush.

He thought that was the worst I could do?

"Well, you should have stayed home, you big baby." I grabbed the canvas with wet paint, smeared it on his head, and ran.

The canvas thudded on the hardwood floor and tumbled to the side.

Lee growled playfully. That sound gave me the shivers in more ways than one. With his hands drenched in gobs of paint, dripping on the floor, he went after me.

"No, no, no." I went to the left of the standing easels and then the right.

His wide grin made me smile bigger as he continued to chase me. We circled around the easels, our laughter bouncing off the walls. Lee gripped my shirt from the back and I slipped on a smear of something cold and gooey.

I dropped sideways and he fell on top of me, his forearms keeping him from crushing me. The playfulness evaporated, air leaving our lungs in heavy spurts.

Our eyes locked with something much deeper than before. His gaze slid to my lips and his eyes darkened. He inched toward my mouth, torturously slow, as his finger brushed my cheek.

Lee, what are you doing to me?

My heart ricocheted inside the cavity of my chest as fast as his thumped against me. As we exchanged panting breaths, my treacherous muscles began to ease, surrendering to him.

I wanted him, and there was no denying he wanted me too. Not in this position. And I didn't want a one-night stand either. I had sworn off men, especially men at Christmas time, but this man had weaseled into my heart without even trying.

We would never work. I was going back to Los Angeles and he lived here. Besides, he likely wanted to be with someone of his caliber. Someone who moved in wealthy, powerful circles instead of the Poipū Preschool. The most I could be to him was fun with the nanny.

I was oil; he was acrylic, and we could never mix on the same canvas.

"I-I—" He swallowed hard.

His serious tone made me nervous. I didn't want him to tell me this was a mistake, that I was a mistake. I wondered if he was thinking of Bridget, that we were a bad idea. It certainly was unprofessional.

I had to listen to that warning in my head and not my heart or my body. I had to do something because as much as I wanted this kiss, in the end, I would be the one left heartbroken.

My hand already coated with paint, I patted his face with a wet squelch. The tension shattered.

Lee widened his eyes and opened his mouth in surprise. Then he poked my sides, tickling me as he smothered his cheek wherever it could touch me.

"Lee." I curled into myself, unable to stop laughing and he did the same.

We laughed for a good minute until the door opened.

"What's going on?" said a sweet, sleepy voice.

I sat up to see Bridget rubbing her eyes, holding a stuffed unicorn.

"Papa? Kate?" She giggled, pointing at us.

"Bridget, I can explain." Lee stood and almost fell on his knees when his foot slipped, but he caught himself.

Bridget laughed harder and so did I.

Lee continued, "I spilled paint and we fell. So you have to be very careful, too."

Lee was trying to make our mess into a learning lesson, but it wasn't working. Bridget couldn't stop laughing, turning her eyes on me, to Lee, and then sweeping over the floor. Her mouth dropped open with a small gasp.

The tile was layered with colors and our clothes were a gaudy acrylic patchwork. We'd made a mess that was going to take forever to clean up.

"Bridget, go to your room," Lee's said with a stern tone. "I'll stop by to tuck you in after I help Kate clean up."

"Okay," Bridget sang and left.

Lee took off his shirt and looked at me.

I narrowed my eyes, heat fizzing through my blood as I tried not to stare at his toned, smooth chest. Tried not to remember my first day here, when I had touched those warm, sculpted muscles. The familiar warmth tingled, so I shifted my gaze to his hands.

I didn't know if he was trying to imply we should get naked, but I didn't think he would be that bold. He had been a perfect gentleman thus far. Well, until he'd smeared paint on me.

"I'm not taking off my shirt. You're not expecting—"

He blushed. "I didn't ask you to, Kate. I'm going to turn around. Take them off and go wash up. I'll start cleaning up the mess."

Lee turned his back to me, facing the standing easels, patiently waiting. Taking clothes off that were stuck with wet paint on them was harder than taking off wet jeans. Finally, my shirt and pants thudded behind him.

"I'm done, but give me a second."

"Kate?" Lee's voice went from playful to tender.

"Yes?"

"There's a charity event tomorrow night. We raise money for cancer research. I thought you might want to go. I mean, would you like to go?"

Was he asking me on a date?

I glanced at the panting Roselyn had painted of Bridget when she was about two years, and said, "Yes. Thank you for asking me, but what about Bridget?"

He craned his neck to the side. "I could hire someone."

I contemplated what he said, but I had an idea. "No, you don't need to. Abby can watch her. Bridget would love that, and so would Tyler."

"Great. I'll pick you up at six." He paused and added, "It'll be easier. That way I can drop off Bridget."

That made sense, but the way he said it confused me, like he was reassuring me that it was a practical matter. I didn't know if this was a date or if he was being nice.

I picked up my clothes and approached closer, his back still to me. "What do I wear?"

"You can wear what you're wearing now."

I laughed inwardly and I lightly smacked his arm. When he tried to turn, I poked his back.

"You stay right there, mister," I said with a stern voice, but then I snickered softly.

His body shook with laughter. "Go take your shower."

If we were a couple, we would be showering together.

"I might take a while. You got paint in my hair," I ground out playfully and dropped my clothes to the side of him.

Lee's laugh echoed in the room. Then he said, "Wear a cocktail dress."

Chapter Twenty-Seven – Charity Gala

"Kate, you look beautiful. Wait 'til he sees you." Abby zipped up the back of my black strapless dress in her bathroom.

"Thank you. I love your dress, and I think I should keep it." I posed with a flash of my teeth in the mirror.

I hadn't had time to shop for a dress, so I'd borrowed one of Abby's. Abby didn't have many to choose from. She rarely went to galas where she had to wear fancy dresses, so I was thankful she had a few from her college years. Also, she was practical when she went shopping, just like me. The one we chose from her closet was perfect.

Abby fluffed my hair she'd helped me curl. "You can keep it. I don't have any use for it."

She said it like it was no big deal, but I read into her meaning. Steve was gone and she didn't imagine needing it again.

"Don't say that. You never know." I draped my arms around her shoulders and kissed her cheek.

I was about to tell her she would eventually move on and find someone else, but she wasn't ready for that. How long she would wait would be up to her.

"I don't know, Kate. I don't want to talk about it. Tonight is about you." Abby unplugged the curling iron and faced the bathroom mirror. "So, are you coming home?"

"Of course I am. What kind of question is that?" Warmth traveled up my neck. "I'm going to a charity event with him. He didn't ask me out on a date. And even if it was a date, I would still come home."

"Sure." She sounded like she didn't believe me.

My nephew peeked in, holding a tablet. "You look pretty, Auntie Kate."

"Thank you, Ty. Are you playing—"

"Nope." He frowned with his shoulders slumped. "I'm doing

homework. Mom is making me do some phonics sound thing. It's not as fun as *Unicorns versus Skeletons*, though."

I patted his back. "I'm sure it's not, but you can make it fun. It's all in the attitude, Ty."

His big eyes softened and nodded. "When is Bridget coming over?"

As if on cue, the sound of a car door slamming reached us.

Tyler ran to the window and peeked through the shutters. "Wow. It's black and very long. I've never been inside one like that."

Abby dashed out and stood beside Tyler. "See. It's a date."

Abby liked to be right, even if she was wrong. Though secretly, I wished she was right.

The doorbell rang.

"Stay right there." Abby narrowed her eyes at me to stress her point.

I felt like I was going to the prom and I was stealing a glance at my date. And Abby was my mother.

"Lee. Bridget. Come in." Abby moved to the side to give them room. "You look very nice, Lee."

Lee looked more than nice. He wore a dark navy suit with a flower-printed tie. His hair was slicked back the way I liked it. From his head to his polished black dress shoes, he was perfect.

"Thank you." His voice dipped softer. "This is Bridget's bag. It has her toiletries and PJs. I'm not sure how late we'll be."

"That's okay. Take your time. In fact, Bridget is welcome to spend the night. That way you can stay out with Kate as long as you'd like."

What did she say that for?

Before she could say something else, I stepped out.

"Hello." I waggled my fingers in a wave. I suddenly became nervous, especially when Lee's eyes brightened, taking me in.

Bridget wrapped her arms gently around my waist. "You look pretty, Kate." She peered up at me under those long eyelashes.

"Thank you." I tapped her nose.

"Well, you two should get going." Abby clasped her hands under her chin. "Have fun."

I grabbed the black clutch purse I had also borrowed from the entryway table and we were out the door. I tried to relax. Not a date. I was out with Lee, my friend. Bridget's father. My employer. We were on our way to a charity event—practically a work thing for him.

"A limo, Lee? The Poipu Grand Hotel is fifteen minutes away," I teased as my heels clicked on the front walk.

He rubbed his clean-shaven chin and chuckled lightly.

Lee and I chatted mostly about Bridget on the way to the function, but he never brought up the almost kiss. I supposed it wasn't the right time to talk about it in the back seat with a stranger in front.

For the next few minutes, we talked about some of my favorite artists and Lee's work, until the twinkling lights snaked around the palm trees on either side of the path leading to the front of the hotel.

Lee offered his hand to me after he got out of the limo, his gaze meeting mine with serious intensity. I wished I could read his thoughts.

When I touched his hand, it felt different—like we had reached a new level of intimacy and comfort. I wondered if it was one-sided. Then I linked my arm through his.

When we entered through the double glass door, I sucked in a breath. Lush, vibrant poinsettias were arranged in tiers and designed in a giant wreath. A Christmas tree embellished with red bows and gold star-like ornaments almost reached the high ceiling.

Fake snow coated the walkway with various sizes of snowmen. On the left were nine reindeer and Santa Claus on his present-packed sled. The village houses behind the sled reminded me of the North Pole.

"Too bad it's not real snow. It's beautiful." I wished I could see snow this winter. Every year I tried, but never got the chance.

"I agree," he said. Our footsteps echoed on the marble floor.

Something about his tone and the way he looked at me made me think he wasn't talking about the snow.

Just as we'd reached the grand ballroom, a small crowd bombarded him. I didn't know if they were friends or acquaintances until they called him Lee. As I watched him greet the others, I fished my phone out of my purse and scrolled through social media, feeling awkward and out of place.

A man tilted his head toward my direction. "Who's your beautiful date?"

Lee finally looked my way. His eyes widened, like he felt bad he had forgotten me. I smiled, hoping he'd see that I didn't mind that he hadn't had a moment to introduce me.

"Kate, this is Ted and Nance. Scott and Jill. And Donald and

Cindy." Lee introduced me to more people. Some of them called him Mr. Medici and some called him Lee.

Waiters came around and handed us champagne. I took a glass and sipped, savoring the bubbles on my tongue. Then we entered the ballroom.

Instrumental Christmas music bounced off the walls, from a band set up on the stage in the back. Ribbons of snowflakes hung down from the ceiling and swayed. A Cinderella-like carriage was parked at the photo station with white, barren trees. Blue and white baubles were filled to the brim in clear tall vases next to lit candles on the back tables. I felt like I was walking in a winter wonderland.

"Let's go find our seats." Lee snaked an arm around my waist and guided me.

A white linen cloth covered the table. Red and white roses and green and blue leaves were intertwined inside the vase. Snowflake candles circled the centerpiece.

We sat at our assigned table with our name cards on empty plates. Donald, Scott, Ted, and their wives sat with us.

Someone tapped my shoulder. I twisted around to greet Jessica, clad in a low-cut strapless red dress. She looked stunning.

"Hello." Jessica's high-pitched voice over the loud music hurt my ears. "I thought I saw you. And your date is … oh. Leonardo." Her lips parted and if she opened her eyes any wider, they would pop out of their sockets.

"Good evening." He gave her a curt nod and got back to his conversation with Donald and Cindy.

Jessica's hand went to her chest as if she was trying to hold in her shock. "When did this happen?"

"When did what happen?" I asked.

"You and Leonardo."

"Oh, we're not … It's not what you think," I said.

Lee turned to me with his eyebrows pinched inward, looking confused, and then back to Donald.

That was weird.

"Oh, that's good." She let out a breath. "Anyway, talk to you later."

That was weird too, but coming from Jessica, I wasn't surprised.

The band stopped playing. Silence filled the room and the light dimmed.

A middle-aged man walked onto the stage. "Good evening, everyone. You all look beautiful. Welcome to the Roselyn Medici Annual Charity Gala. I'm one of the four speakers for tonight. This year, our proceeds will go to the foundation Mr. Medici has set up for cancer research. Don't forget to place your raffle tickets in the basket of your choice. The winners will be announced later this evening. You do not have to be present to win. Dinner will be served as soon as I leave the stage. Thank you for your time and thank you for your generosity."

Clapping echoed in the room. The band picked back up and waiters came out with trays.

Oh, my heart. This was Lee's event? When he invited me last night, he never mentioned it was his charity named after his sister.

"Lee…" I leaned closer so he could hear. "Why didn't you tell me about the raffle tickets and the baskets? I feel horrible. I should contribute."

"That's okay." He placed a hand over mine, resting on the table. "I asked you to come yesterday. Please, don't worry about it. And I ordered you salmon. But if you prefer chicken or beef, you can let the waiter know."

"I'm fine. I like salmon. Thank you."

"There's someone I would like you to meet as soon as I find him." He glanced around. "Anyway, let me know what you think of him."

Had he asked me to come with him to set me up with his friend? I didn't want to assume, so I agreed politely.

While we ate, I made small talk with Cindy, who sat next to me. She showed me pictures of her son and her cats. Lee and I didn't talk much, but that was to be expected. At least he didn't leave me alone. After dessert, people mingled about, but we stayed seated at our table chatting away.

Lee waved. A man, possibly late twenties, came to our table. Lee rose and they exchanged a manly hug, a quick pat on the back.

"Where have you been hiding?" The man's dark eyes gleamed.

"Hiding?" Lee chuckled. "Stop trying to blame this on me. You were late."

"As usual." The man laughed and took a drink from his glass. "Who's this beautiful woman? She can't possibly be your date."

"Not a date. Kate, this is my good friend, Ian Bordonaro. We grew up together."

I rose to greet Ian and extended a hand.

Not a date. Well, that answered my question. Unexpectedly, his words stung. *That's what you get for getting too attached.* Abby was right. I was grateful today was the last day. Yes, I had told my sister Lee and I were just friends, but a part of me wanted more. I just hadn't wanted to admit it.

Lee didn't want me. Maybe for a romp in the art room, but not for charity dinners and the like. He wanted someone like that Cassie woman he'd gone out with. He'd only asked me to be polite, a spur-of-the-moment thing. He knew about Steve, so he was involving our family in his cancer research foundation. Lee was being nice, paying it forward.

Ian kissed the back of my cold hand and let go. The candlelight glistened against his pretty brown eyes, sharp nose, and strong cheekbones.

"Nice to meet you." I gave a cordial smile.

"It's my pleasure," Ian said.

"Did you come alone?" Lee asked Ian.

"I did."

"Good. You can join us." Lee indicated the chair next to him.

Everyone else had left to mingle with others so there were plenty of empty seats.

After Ian sat, he leaned forward, his voice almost drowned out by the music. "So, Kate. Lee told me you're visiting from Los Angeles. Are you planning to go back?"

Not a date, Lee had said.

"Yes. I haven't quit my job, but if I don't go back, they'll fire me." I let out a light laugh.

"Well, that's unfortunate." He chuckled.

Five minutes later, Lee excused himself to get more wine.

Ian scooted to Lee's chair. "Are you having fun?"

His question threw me off. I took a sip of wine to delay my answer. "Yes. How about you?"

Ian shifted, leaning his elbow on the table. "To be honest, I don't like going to these events. I'm only here to support Lee. He's like a brother to me. We went to the same preschool, and we even went to the same college just so we could be together."

"That's sweet," I murmured.

"Lee is a great guy. He's always thinking of others before himself. He doesn't have anyone special in his life and he's always trying to set me up."

"He's the pay-it-forward guy." I wondered why I said that. It came off a bit sarcastic.

"Excuse me?"

"Oh, nothing. Are you a businessman like Lee?"

"Yes."

As Ian talked about work, his words went in one ear and out the other. Lee hadn't come back. It felt like he'd purposely left Ian and me alone. There was no doubt Lee had invited me to set me up with Ian.

I slid back my chair to excuse myself when I spotted Lee. A woman had her hand planted on his arm, and another woman stood beside him, giggling and sipping wine.

Lee said he wasn't *dating* because of Bridget. Perhaps it was partially true, but maybe he didn't want to be with one woman, like Jessica had implied. A different woman for every event.

Not a date, I reminded myself. But as many times as I told myself that the scenario shouldn't remind me of Jayden, I needed out.

Jessica crossed my vision. She strutted her hips to the basket table. I was certain she had lots of rumors to share. Maybe she could clear things up for me. Some rumors were born in truth.

I shouldn't bother since I planned to head back to Los Angeles. I had already told Abby that I was going home after Christmas to figure out what I wanted to do with my career. She wasn't happy about it, but she knew it had to be my choice.

"Excuse me, Ian. I'll be right back." I rushed over to Jessica, my heels clicking in a steady beat across the tile floor toward the Cinderella-like carriage.

"Hello, Jessica," I said.

She jerked back, startled. She was placing her raffle tickets in the baskets. "Oh, you. You scared me."

I rolled my eyes. "What are you doing?"

She hiked an eyebrow. Okay, lame question, but I wasn't sure how to start the conversation. But of course she went right to it.

"Where's Lee?" She looked to the table where I had come from. She didn't give me a chance to answer and continued. "I'm sorry. He must be with another one of his women then. Cassie is my friend's friend. I heard they went out on a date. She told my friend he took her on a helicopter ride by a waterfall. How romantic is that? I think they're going to take the next step in their relationship. So I was surprised to see you with him tonight. Maybe Cassie couldn't make it and you were his second choice. I mean, Lee can't be seen alone."

His second choice.

My chest caved in like a balloon that had suddenly lost its air, my heart crushing and knees buckling. What was I doing here?

I'd heard enough. Lee was a friend, and I didn't need to know any more. I went back to my table, leaving Jessica to wonder at my abrupt departure.

Ian was sitting alone, drinking wine. "You're back," he said, sounding happy to see me.

I managed to give him a tight-lipped smile, searching for the right words. I didn't want to act unprofessional, but today was my last day. If I could be honest with myself, I never enjoyed socializing at these types of charity events. I'd rather be home painting than making small talk with pretentious people I didn't know.

I'd only gone because Lee had asked me and I found myself unable to turn him down. Like, against my better judgment, I'd gone on that stupid helicopter knowing I would likely get airsick.

"Ian, I'm not feeling well. Can you tell Lee that I took a taxi home?" I drummed up a simple but perfect excuse.

I felt horrible for leaving Ian alone. If I had met him under different circumstances, I might have felt differently. He seemed like a good guy. At least he hadn't brushed me off for other women.

I wasn't mad at Lee for speaking to other women. He had every right. Though I told myself we were friends, I had wished for more. I just didn't realize how much until now. This jealousy confirmed I was falling hard for him. Leaving now was a good thing—the only option.

Ian rose and gave me a hug. "It was really nice meeting you. I hope you feel better."

I grabbed my clutch from the table and offered him a genuine smile. He deserved one. Then I got out before Lee saw me leaving.

If he tried asking questions, I wouldn't have a good explanation. He wouldn't have believed me if I tried the same excuse I'd given Ian. But I doubted he was looking.

Chapter Twenty-Eight – After

"Back so soon? Where's Lee?" Abby looked up from the sofa when I entered the house alone.

My urban fantasy novel about the Greek gods rested on Abby's lap, the children fast asleep on the spare mattress by the Christmas tree.

"I came home alone." I kicked off my heels, padded to my room, and tossed my purse on the dresser.

"Why?" Abby followed me down the hall.

I sighed and slumped on the bed. "Apparently, you know me more than I know myself. I got attached. Unwisely."

"Oh, Kate." She threw her arms around my shoulders and sat next to me. "I'm sorry. What happened?"

I pulled back to the headboard and dabbed the tears pooling at the corners of my eyes. "It's not Lee's fault. There's no one to blame except myself. He told his friend Ian, I wasn't his date. In fact, I think he asked me so he could set me up with that friend."

"Oh," Abby's voice dipped lower. "Well, forget about Lee. You're going back home, and you don't have to see him again."

"It's not his fault." I wanted to stress that point. I didn't want my sister to have a bad impression of him.

"Well, then he shouldn't have tried to kiss you."

I had confessed to Abby what had happened in the painting room last night. If we had kissed, would today have turned out differently? No, I doubted it. I would have been an even bigger mess. I didn't take kissing lightly as some people did.

I stiffened when my cell rang like wind chimes. Stupid phone. I'd thought I had changed the ringtone, but it made me think of Bridget and Lee, and my heart ached. This was not how I imagined our goodbye would turn out.

"It's probably Lee. I'm not going to pick it up."

"He might want to know you're safe. You should let him know."

I at least owed him that much. He would worry about me. He was a perfect gentleman that way. I walked to the dresser and took out my cell out of my purse.

Lee: Are you safe?

Me: Yes. I'm home.

Lee: You left. Why?

I flinched, shocked the response had come fast.

Me: I'm not feeling well.

Lee: I'm sorry. Is there anything I can do for you?

Me: No, thank you.

Lee: I hope you feel better.

Me: Thank you.

Lee: Will I see you tomorrow?

I wished he had asked that question because he missed me, but I knew better.

Me: Isn't today my last day?

Lee: Yes, but I need to pay you and I believe you have your things in the room.

Me: I'm busy tomorrow. My sister will pick them up for me, if that's okay.

Lee: Of course. Get well. Please tell Abby I'm on my way to pick up Bridget. Thank you.

Why was he leaving so soon? Perhaps his duty was done. I tossed my phone on the bed and turned toward Abby who still sat on the mattress.

"Lee said he's on his way to pick up Bridget. Can you get my things from Lee's place tomorrow?"

Abby crossed her arms and raised an eyebrow. "Are you sure? I think you should do it."

I sat back down next to her and hugged a pillow. "I don't want to see him. Besides, it's not like he'll care. I was there to do a job and that's all. Mona will be back tomorrow night, and everything will be back to normal for them."

"Well, if that's what you want, I'll do it. I'll have to swing by before I go pick up Mom and Dad at the airport. Watch Ty for me. If you change your mind, let me know."

"Thanks, Abby. I really appreciate this." I hugged my sister, and then we said goodnight.

After I washed up, I lay in bed with my door closed. I couldn't sleep knowing Lee was on his way to pick up Bridget.

Would he ask to see me? I didn't think so, and if he did, Abby would tell him I was asleep. A part of me wished he would come to my room and tell me he was in love with me and that I should stay in Kauai.

I was a fool. A fool in love or whatever I was feeling. I needed to put distance between us. It was a good thing I'd be going back to LA soon.

The front door opened. Lee must have messaged Abby instead of ringing the doorbell. I heard feet shuffling and murmurs. Then quiet. The door shutting felt like closure somehow, like it was the last time I would see Lee and Bridget.

Chapter Twenty-Nine – Parents

"Grandma. Grandpa." Tyler dashed out of the house when Abby pulled her car into the driveway.

My parents got out of the minivan and hugged and kissed their grandson.

"Wow, look at you. You've grown." My petite mother held him with love twinkling in her brown eyes.

"I'm a big boy," Tyler said and pulled away.

"Kate." My father wrapped his strong arms around me, towering over me by six inches, and then my mother hugged me next.

"Go inside," I said. "I'll help Abby."

"Look at the beautiful door," Mother's sweet voice projected from the front porch.

I smiled when Tyler said with pride, "Auntie Kate did that."

Abby popped the trunk open and she took out a smaller suitcase from the backseat.

As I hefted their suitcases out of the trunk, Abby said, "I have your bag in the front. And I have your check in my purse. I'll give it to you later. Remind me."

I could buy one of her paintings anonymously instead of giving her the cash. That way she wouldn't know it was from me. But if she ever found out, she would get mad. I had to think about my options.

I took my bag out of the car and slammed the door. I was glad to have my parents join us. Aside from the obvious reasons, they were a perfect distraction.

Inside, I dropped my parents' suitcase in Abby's room and tossed my bag in mine. When I came out, my mother released a long sigh, sitting on the sofa next to my father and Tyler.

"That was exhausting," Mother said.

"That's because you hardly slept." My father gave her a pointed look, his dark eyes twinkling.

Mother frowned. "I couldn't sleep because you were snoring."

Father ran a hand through his salt and pepper hair, his eyes wide, looking innocent. "I didn't hear it."

Mother shook her head with a smile. "That's because you were sleeping and I wasn't."

Laughter filled the air.

Abby came from the kitchen and handed them each a mug of green tea. "Tell us all about your trip." She sat on the opposite sofa with me.

Father smacked his lips after he drank. "There's not much to tell. You see one island, you've seen them all."

Mother took a sip and let out a long sigh. "That's not true. I loved it. On the Hawaiian cruise, you get to island hop. You can clearly see the difference between the islands. Honolulu is busier, geared toward tourists, whereas the Big Island and Kauai are toned down. It's less crowded here. We should go on a cruise together soon."

"Can we, Mommy?" Tyler gave her puppy dog eyes.

"Someday." She gave a faint smile.

"Oh, we got something for Ty." My mother reached inside her big bag and took out a cruise ship about a foot long, and handed to him.

"Thank you, Grandma, Grandpa." Tyler moved the ship up and down as if it were riding the waves. "I want to go on this one."

Abby's phone beeped from the kitchen counter.

"We'll see." Abby got up to check her phone and thumbed a reply.

Who she was texting?

"I love what you did to the house, Abby." My mother's eyes crinkled at the corners with her smile.

My mother had amazing, ageless skin. She looked easily ten years younger than she was. People said my sister and I looked like her.

"It was a lot of work, but I'm glad I did it." Abby wasn't looking at our mother when she spoke, but at the phone.

Again? Who was she texting? Work? I didn't think so. She hadn't sold any artwork since the last one.

When I went closer to her, she flipped her phone over. *What are you hiding from me?*

Tyler walked away from the sofa and turned in a circle with the boat near the tree. "Do you like our Christmas decorations, Grandma? I helped Auntie Kate and Mommy."

Mother pushed off the sofa, walked to the mantel, and looked at the portrait of Steve, Abby, and Tyler. Then she glanced down at the red stockings and squeezed her eyes. She must be thinking of the missing stocking. Of course she would be missing her son-in-law. She was grieving too. Then she turned to her grandson.

"I love the tree." Mother stroked his hair. "You did great. Since your dad is in heaven, you're the man of the house."

Abby stiffened and stopped texting.

Tyler halted and pointed at himself. "Yup. I'm the man." He lifted his chin and pushed his chest outward in exaggeration.

I couldn't be prouder of him at that moment.

"Tomorrow is Christmas Eve," Father said and placed his half-drunk tea on the table. "What are we eating?"

Abby weaved around the counter and stood behind the sofa. "You haven't changed a bit, Papa. Always thinking about food."

Father was still lean, toned, and healthy for his age, expect he had high blood pressure. He had always stayed fit and worked out as far back as I remembered.

"I'm too old to change. And food is a necessity. You can't blame me. I've been eating the same buffet for the past week."

"Any particular food you want, Mom?" I already knew what Dad wanted.

Mom smiled. "I'm okay with whatever your dad wants."

Dad flashed all his teeth. "Let's get some steak. I'm buying."

Chapter Thirty – Christmas Eve

"This is nice." I admired the wooden floor and the lit candles on the tables as we passed them by. "Why didn't you bring me here before, Abby?"

"Because it's too expensive," Abby said over her shoulder, following the waiter to our table.

"I hope I can afford it, or you'll have to wash the dishes." Father chuckled behind us.

When we were young, one of my father's favorite jokes had been that we might have to wash dishes to pay for dinner. Abby and I had caught on to his teasing eventually, but once in a while, in true dad style, he still made that comment.

"This is your table." The waiter set the menus down and then another waiter filled our water glasses. Shortly thereafter, he returned with a basket of assorted warm bread and took our orders.

"What do you want from Santa Claus, Ty?" My mother asked as she set a piece of sourdough bread on Tyler's plate and then passed the basket to Dad.

Tyler was so preoccupied with the model ship that my mother had to ask him twice.

He jerked a shoulder. "I don't know. Maybe my own tablet. I always have to ask my mom for hers."

"What happened to wanting toys for Christmas?" Father shook his head and spread butter on his bread. "Times have changed."

"What do you want for Christmas?" Tyler glanced between his grandparents.

"I already got mine," my mother said. "I'm here with my two lovely daughters and my only grandson. I wonder if I'll get another one." Mom looked at me.

My mother never pressured me to get married, but once in a while she would make comments like that.

I raised my hands in surrender. "I'm not married so don't ask."

"Anyone special?" my father asked.

Before I could answer, Tyler tugged my mother's blazer. "Where do babies come from? How do you make a baby?"

The four of us looked at each other and laughed.

"Ty," I said to distract him. No one was going to answer him, anyway. "Did you see the Christmas tree? Isn't it beautiful?"

"I like the lights hanging down the windows." Tyler pointed with his ship. "We don't have those at our house."

"Maybe next year."

"Are you coming next year?"

"Of course. Last year was different. I was really busy at work. But I promise to see you every Christmas."

"Promise?"

"I pinky promise to the unicorns, rainbows, and all the sparkling things."

The latter part came out without thought. Tyler pinched his eyebrows, looking baffled. Bridget would understand. My heart hurt more than it should.

I just needed time. Time would mend all things.

The waiter brought us our meals, left, then came back with a bottle of wine.

"I don't think we ordered that," Father said hesitantly to the waiter.

"You didn't, but your friend told me to open the finest wine for this table."

"Who?" Mother asked. With her fork in one hand and her knife in the other, she looked dangerous.

"Mr. Medici."

I shot my gaze to Abby and then glanced around from the front to the back of the restaurant. Many tables were occupied, but he was nowhere to be seen. I wondered if my sister messaged him to let him know we were here. She had been suspiciously texting someone. But why would she? He didn't care what I was doing tonight.

"Is Mr. Medici here?" I asked.

"He's in one of the private rooms." He waved a hand toward the back.

"Well, you can take it back and tell—"

Abby covered my mouth. "Please tell him we said thank you."

The waiter poured the wine and left.

"Who's Mr. Medici?" Father took a bite of his steak. "This is delicious."

"Slow down." Mother patted his arm.

Father ignored Mother and drank his wine and smacked his lips. "Wow. This is very good. Who is Mr. Medici? Did you already answer that?"

"No one," Abby and I answered hastily at the same time.

"How can he be no one?" Father scooped up some mashed potatoes into his mouth. "Is he Kate's latest? Is he that guy who cheated on her?"

"No, Dad." I ran a hand down my face and turned to Abby. "Can you go thank Lee? I don't want to see him."

Abby glared at me and whispered, "Are you sure he was trying to set you up with his friend? He wouldn't have sent wine over if that was the case."

"It doesn't matter." My chest rose and fell with a deep breath. "I'm leaving in three days. I need to get back to Los Angeles."

I also didn't want to know who he was having dinner with. If he were there with Bridget, she would have seen Tyler and would have wanted to stop by.

My sister pinched her lips, contemplating. "Fine. If you don't care then what's so hard about thanking him?"

To be honest, I didn't have an answer.

"Did you say who Mr. Medici is?" Father gulped his wine down and poured himself another glass.

I wanted to change the topic. "Did you take your high blood pressure medicine, Dad?"

He sliced another piece of his steak. "Yes. This morning. Your mother always reminds me." He stroked her cheek, his loving gaze tender and sweet.

My parents had been married more than thirty years. Yes, they'd had their ups and downs like all couples, but their love was strong. I hoped to find a love like theirs one day. I wished that for Abby as well.

"I'll be right back. I'm going to the restroom." I placed my cloth napkin on my seat and left.

As I passed by the Christmas tree, past the window with pretty lights, and passed tables occupied with couples having romantic dinners, I prayed I wouldn't run into Lee. As long as Lee didn't come out of his private room, all would be just fine.

I halted short of the restroom when a door opened, blocking my way.

Lee stepped out. My heart somersaulted. I felt like I was going to have a heart attack. Either he had seen me coming this way or it was pure coincidence. But the way he rushed indicated it was likely the first.

"Kate—" he began, but I unintentionally cut him off.

"Hello, Lee." Nervousness took over me. *Act natural. Steady the pulse. You can do this.* "Thank you for the wine. That was very sweet of you, but you didn't have to do that. I was going to stop by to thank you at your table, but I didn't know where you were seated."

"I'm in that room." He pointed to the closed door. "You can't see me from the outside, but I can see out. Anyway, it's my pleasure. Your parents?"

"Yes. They just got back from the cruise. They'll be here for another week."

Why did he close the door? Does he not want me to see his date?

I had to stop torturing myself. I'd only known him for two weeks, and I couldn't believe I had fallen for him. I kept replaying the painting, playful fight incident, and that almost-kiss.

Our eyes locked briefly in the silence that fell between us and I looked away. He had such soulful, beautiful eyes. I could lose myself in them.

Lee took a step closer. When I retreated, my heel touched the wall. He took another step, his eyes darkening with something I couldn't understand. But his expression reminded me of our almost kiss in the painting room.

"Bridget misses you," he whispered, his gaze piercing.

If he had said *he* missed me, I would've kissed him. But I wasn't sure if I was reading this situation right.

"I miss her too," I said breathlessly.

A man walked out of the restroom, breaking our moment. Then a mother and her toddler shouldered between us to pass by.

Lee stood closer than before, our feet inches apart, with his hands shoved in his front pockets. "Would it be okay if Bridget calls you? She didn't get a chance to say goodbye."

The ache knotted tighter and I swallowed hard. "Yes, of course. Mona is coming tomorrow?" I tucked a lock of hair behind my ear just to do something with my shaky hands.

"The day after. Tomorrow is Christmas. When are you flying back home?"

I blinked. "That's right. I'm getting my days confused." I rubbed the side of my head and released my gaze from him. "I'm leaving in three days."

Lee's eyebrows pinched. "So soon."

I looked back up at him and the dagger in my heart twisted even more. I needed to end this. The longer I was with him, the more I didn't want to let him go.

"I need to get back to work," I said. "My vacation time is over. Thank you again for the wine. Enjoy your dinner."

I stepped to the side, but Lee mirrored me, and said, "I was surprised you got sick so suddenly. I'm glad you're feeling better."

My cheeks flared hot. His tone indicated he knew I had lied. It was a perfect opportunity to tell him the truth. But what did it matter? We were never going to be a couple. It was best to leave on my terms.

I held up my chin, refusing to show him any weakness. "Actually, I was slightly under the weather that day and I'd thought I would feel better after I took some medicine. But I'm sure you didn't miss me. You had all those beautiful women to entertain you." A fake laugh escaped me. "Anyway, I really need to use the restroom."

He furrowed his brow and parted his lips to say more, then shut them. If he didn't believe me, he would have pressed for further explanation. And if I meant something to him, he would have said something.

When Lee didn't budge or move out of my way, I walked around him. I took a peek when he opened the door and got a glimpse of a woman in a dress with black heels.

Cassie or perhaps someone new. Some other sophisticated beauty who'd make him forget about his temporary nanny. I shouldn't care, but it stung.

He was turpentine to my oil-canvas heart.

Chapter Thirty-One — Christmas Day

Abby cooked breakfast while Father made coffee. The aroma filled the house with warmth and love. I loved having all of us together under the same roof. It reminded me of the days when we'd lived with our parents. How fast time flew.

"Should we wake up Ty?" Father placed his steaming mug of coffee on the dining table and took a seat.

"Maybe we should. I can't believe he's still sleeping." Abby slid the scrambled eggs onto a large plate and passed it to me.

Tyler and I had played *Unicorns versus Skeletons* until he had conked out on my bed. I would never tell Abby. What else are aunties for?

Mother spread jam on the toast and then sliced the mango into a bowl.

After I set the plate of eggs down, I went back to the kitchen to help Abby. "If Ty doesn't come out soon, I'm going to wake him up."

On cue, Tyler entered the dining room rubbing his sleepy eyes, still wearing his PJs. "Is it breakfast time?" he said groggily.

I went up to him and kissed his head, then I pointed to the tea table. "Look, Ty. Santa Claus ate his cookies and drank the milk."

Tyler must have forgotten it was Christmas morning. His eyes shot wide and he ran to the tree.

"Santa Claus brought all these presents?" His voice rose to a new level.

Last night, Abby and I wrapped presents for Tyler and our parents. Ten more boxes were added under the tree.

"Hold on a minute." Abby rushed over from the kitchen and turned Tyler to face her, but his eyes were gleaming and locked on the gifts. "You need to say good morning. Eat your breakfast first, and then we'll open presents."

Tyler nodded and sat next to Abby at the dining table with plate of eggs in front of him.

"What's our plan today?" Mother asked, enjoying a bite of toast. "Yum. This mango jam is delicious. I need to buy some to take home with me."

Abby's mug clanked on the table after she finished drinking. "How about we go to the beach after we open presents. We can have a picnic there. I was going to take you all to a luau tomorrow but you have already been. Instead, let's go to Princeville which is on the other side of the island for lunch."

"Sounds perfect." I sighed.

Outside the window, palm trees swayed in front of the plush green of the neighbor's front lawn. A hen and her little chicks dashed across the street. Then a cab passed by. Thoughts of Lee and Bridget reeled through my mind.

Lee hadn't called, even after he had asked if Bridget could call me. I supposed he would after Christmas. I wondered how they were celebrating and what they were doing.

Last week on one of my days off, I'd gone shopping to buy presents for my family and, for Lee and Bridget. I had purchased a stuffed unicorn and had a T-shirt custom-made that said, "All the sparkling things."

For Lee, I'd had no idea what to buy, so I'd preordered chocolate cookies from his favorite bakery to be delivered on Christmas Day.

On the card, I'd written: *To the man who has everything. Hope your days are as sweet as these cookies.*

I'd also painted a portrait of him and Bridget, from a photo I'd taken of them by the waterfall. A perfect moment when they were smiling and looking at each other. But I hadn't let him know yet. It was still hidden in his painting room.

"Right, Kate?"

"Sure, Dad."

I hadn't been paying attention to their conversation. I had no idea what they were talking about. I must have given him the right answer to earn a pat on my back.

Abby gave me a sad face from across the table. She wasn't mocking me—she felt sorry for me. It was nobody's fault but mine. I got attached to a man who had no reason to love me, and a girl that wasn't mine. It was best Bridget and I didn't talk. Just the sound of her voice might crack my broken heart even more.

After breakfast, we sat around the Christmas tree. Tyler and I sat on the hardwood floor while my parents opted for the sofa.

Abby handed Tyler a box with reindeer wrapping paper and a big red bow. "This is for you, Tyler. It's from Grandma and Grandpa Chang."

"What is it?" Tyler shook the box.

Father waved his hand, chuckling. "Don't shake it, Ty. Open it."

Tyler tore the wrapper and his jaw dropped. "It's my own tablet. Thank you." He jumped up and down and hugged his grandparents.

"You shouldn't have." Abby scowled. "You'll spoil him."

Mother clucked her tongue. "Like he isn't already. That's what grandparents are for."

"Let's open these next. They're from Auntie Kate." Abby smirked at me. She handed one to my parents, Tyler, and then picked up hers. She sat next to me on the floor while she opened it.

The sound of crisp paper ripping filled my ears.

"Oh, Kate, this is beautiful." Mother held up a sixteen by twenty-four photo I'd had framed. "When did you take this?"

"I had an opportunity to take a tour around the island in the helicopter." I left out who I had gone with. They didn't need to know. More questions would be asked.

"I see the camera we bought you last year was put to good use," Father said.

"I love mine, Kate," Abby said. "I'm going to hang it on that empty wall." Abby pointed near the television.

I had blown up a picture of Abby and Tyler at the Poipu Shopping Plaza, taken the day we'd eaten shaved ice. The sunlight had hit them perfectly from behind. The clouds white and fluffy, the sky blue—it looked like someone had painted it.

"I also stuck a gift card behind the frame. I didn't have time to shop." I leaned into Abby and said quickly, "Can you please take some photos to Lee's house later today or tomorrow?"

I wanted to include the photos I had taken randomly of Lee and Bridget as part of his Christmas present, but I hadn't had time. And I didn't plan on seeing him. Bumping into him at the restaurant last night had confirmed it was best I stay away.

"Look what I got," Tyler exclaimed. "It's a *Unicorns versus Skeletons* coloring book, lunch box, and a T-shirt. Thank you, Auntie Kate." Tyler tugged off his shirt and replaced it with the new one.

"Open this one next, Ty. It's from …" Abby read the tag and swallowed. "From Grandma Fuller. When did we get this one?" She looked at me and then to my parents.

Mother glanced at her slippers, then cleared her throat when she met Abby's gaze. "I didn't want to tell you over the phone, but your father and I swung by to see Peggy in Miami before we went on the cruise. She was going to mail the presents, but we offered to take them for her. You should call her."

Steve's father had passed away from a heart attack shortly after Steve had. Abby's mother-in-law, Peggy, had moved from New York to Florida to be closer to her daughter, Michelle.

Abby nodded, her eyes pooled with tears. "I was going to after we opened presents. I sent Peggy and Michelle gifts as well." Abby cleared her throat as if she was trying to hold back a sob and added, "I asked them if they wanted to visit, but they said hopefully next year. Peggy has arthritis and tires easily. I'm thinking of taking a vacation soon and taking Tyler to see her."

"That'll be nice." Mother smiled. "She'll love that."

Talking about Steve and his family made me think again about how fleeting life was. I debated messaging Lee to wish him Merry Christmas, but he would receive his gift soon and that would be enough. Some people were meant to stay a while and some were meant to be in passing. Unfortunately, he happened to be in the latter.

"Look. I got two swords that light up." Tyler jumped in front of me, showing off the present from Grandma Fuller. He tossed me one. "We can play."

"Hold on a minute." Abby held out a hand. "Wait until we finish. You have more presents. Unless you want me to take them back to the person who gave them to you."

"No. I'll be good." Tyler stilled, and then, as if he remembered something, he rushed to the box and gave Abby an envelope. "I don't think this is mine. It doesn't have my name on it."

Abby shifted her legs on the floor to get comfortable. With an inhale of a deep breath, she opened the envelope. As she read, tears streamed down her face.

I dragged my butt on the floor closer and wrapped my arms around her. Sympathy tears dampened my own cheeks. "What's wrong?"

Abby's voice cracked. "Bless her heart. My mother-in-law wrote me a check. She said some of the money came from friends and people from her church for Steve's funeral, but she added to it." She sobbed, taking a moment. "She wants to give it to Tyler, for his education."

Tyler kneeled on the other side of Abby and hugged her. I wiped away my tears and so did Mother. Father had his head lowered. The silent moment lingered for a bit, and somehow it felt like Steve was with us, telling Abby that everything was going to be okay.

The doorbell chimed, breaking our somber thoughts, and I couldn't help but think of Bridget and her mother, and also Lee.

I looked through the peephole and cracked the door halfway when I saw a uniform. The deliveryman held three boxes, two large and one small. The largest had *Handle with care* written on the side.

After I signed on the square tablet, Abby helped me bring them in and placed them on the tea table in front of our parents. She gave me a suspicious look and handed me a cutter from the kitchen drawer.

"It's not from Jayden." I cut along the tape and glared at Abby. "He wouldn't do things like this. It's probably from my friends."

"Which friend? Do I know this person?" Father sipped at his second cup of coffee, which had to be cold by now.

"I don't know, but let me find out and I'll answer your question." I flipped the top, annoyed and exhilarated all of sudden, and I didn't like the two mixed together. "Oh ..." I carefully took out a Santa's sleigh vase filled with red roses, lilies, bird of paradises, green stems, and baby's breath.

"That's beautiful. Who sent it?" Mother leaned closer, examining the arrangement.

I opened the sealed envelope.

To the woman who deserves everything. ~Lee

Not fair. How dare he write those words? He destroyed me without even being here.

I might deserve everything, but it doesn't seem like I deserve you.

"What does it say? Who is it from?" Mother asked again.

"From a friend." I handed Abby the card for her to read and I unsealed the next box.

Abby hiked her eyebrows and nudged me with her elbow. "Call him," she whispered so only I could hear.

I shook my head.

"What's that smell?" Father sniffed. "It smells like chocolate."

"Chocolate chip cookies?" Tyler's face peered over the box I had opened. "Can I have one?"

"Of course. You're my favorite nephew." I wrapped him in my arms and rubbed his head.

He squirmed as he laughed. "But I'm your only nephew."

I picked up a cookie and shoved it in his mouth.

"Open the last one." Abby handed me a box from the table.

I picked off the bow and tore through the wrapping. I laughed out loud, my heart swelling and aching at the same time. It was a large white unicorn with a rainbow-colored horn, a smaller replica of the giant one in Bridget's room.

"There's a card inside." Abby took it out and gave it to me.

Kate was written on top. The elementary handwriting told me Bridget had written it but when I opened it, the writing wasn't hers. It looked like Lee's.

"What does it say?" Tyler looked over my shoulder.

Dear Kate,

Thank you for watching me. I had the best time with you. You are pretty and nice. I hope you have the best Christmas. I miss you.
To the unicorns, rainbows, and all the sparkling things always.

Love,
Bridget

"It's from a friend. It says Merry Christmas." I didn't want to read it out loud and tear up in front of everyone, so I shoved it inside my pocket.

Something inside me crumbled. I hadn't thought letting go would hurt so much. It had only been two weeks. How had I let this happen? Because … it was easy. Being with him was easy.

As I bore the pain of my bleeding heart, I wondered if I should call Bridget. I didn't want to talk to Lee though. It was better this way.

Then a text came through my silent phone. I had forgotten to turn it on with all the excitement of Christmas morning.

> Lee: Thank you. Bridget and I love our gifts.
> But you're wrong. I don't have everything.

I stared at the message until Abby took my phone to read it.

"Call him," she ground out, a bit annoyed this time.

I shook my head. I didn't know how to answer so I tucked the phone inside my back pocket and enjoyed the cookies with my family while silently thanking Lee and missing him madly.

I was going home soon. The distance between us across the ocean would heal my heart.

Chapter Thirty-Two – Soulmates

"I don't understand why we have to dress up." I narrowed my eyes at Abby who stood next to me in front of her bathroom mirror. "We're going to dinner, not a ball."

Actually, I'd rather stay in. We'd had a wonderful Christmas dinner two nights ago and I wanted to spend my last night in the comfort of home.

Abby ignored me and smoothed out her simple crimson dress that rested on her curves—not too loose and not too tight. She looked sophisticated and stunning. Her makeup brought out her brown eyes.

I finished curling my hair in silence, then fluffed it with my fingers. Then I twisted from side to side to examine the black dress I had borrowed from my sister.

Abby glided on lipstick and smacked her lips together. "There. I'm ready."

"Can we go now?" Tyler walked into Abby's room clad in a navy suit with spit-shined dress shoes. He even wore a red tie to match his mother's dress.

Tyler's hair was parted to the side and slicked back, which I'd supervised earlier. He looked adorable, and he knew it from the way he held his head high, smirking.

"Let's go," I said and placed a hand on his shoulder and guided him out to the family room. Abby followed behind us.

My parents stood in front of the two paintings on either side of the hearth. Father had his back to me, pinning a sparkling palm tree pendant on Mother's black blazer while her hand rested down her long skirt. Then Mother dusted something off from Father's navy suit and adjusted his tie.

I loved watching the simple, loving gestures between them—and between older couples in general. It proved that love conquered all, even after their years together.

"Papa." I draped my arms around his shoulders. "Why are you taking us to an expensive dinner?"

They should be saving money for their retirement and not spend unnecessarily on us.

My father frowned and peered down at me. "Can't I buy my daughter the best dinner on her last day in Kauai?"

"Yes, but why Poipu Grand Hotel? There are so many restaurants."

Dad placed a tender hand on my cheek. "Abby told me they have good steak. And you know how much I love steak. Let's live a little and do something spontaneous."

"Ready? Say cheese." Mom had her phone in her hand and took pictures of Dad and me. Then she snapped one of Tyler and Abby.

I'd thought to bring my camera to dinner but I wasn't in the mood.

"Now I know where Kate got that habit from." Abby grabbed her purse from the entryway table and slipped on her heels.

"It's not a habit." I didn't appreciate her sly remark. Or perhaps I was being ultra-sensitive to anything anyone said to me the past few days.

"Oh wait. I almost forgot." Father went to Abby's room and came back with three pink hibiscus flowers. "One for each of you."

"That's so sweet, Dad." Abby took two and handed one to Mom.

"Thank you, Dad." I pressed my nose to its soft petals and sniffed the sweet fragrance before I slipped it behind my left ear.

Abby took the flower out of my hair and moved it to the other side. "You would be taken if you would just call Lee. Anyway, since you're not, you put it on your right."

I frowned but dismissed her comment.

The drive to Poipu Grand Hotel was short, but my heart pounded the whole ride. We were going to the same hotel where the charity function had been held. There was no reason to think I'd see Lee, but no guarantee I wouldn't.

After Abby handed the minivan keys to a valet, we passed through the double glass door. The lobby was just as beautiful as the first time I had seen it.

My family was so mesmerized by the poinsettias arranged in tiers and Christmas tree embellished with red bows almost reaching the high ceiling that we took our time going to the restaurant. Other families had the same idea, too. After we took pictures in front of the seasonal displays, we were on our way.

I sat before a spectacular view overlooking the beach and placed my black clutch purse on my lap. Although it was dark, the lights on the walkway allowed us to see the people strolling below us or dining at other restaurants.

"This is nice." My father peered over his glasses. He pushed them up and got back to reading the menu.

"There's so much to choose from." My mom flipped the page. "I can't decide. Should I have the beef or salmon?"

"It depends on—" I stopped and turned toward someone tapping my shoulder. "Jessica?"

She wore a purple silk dress, too formal for casual dining. But then again, it was Jessica.

"Hi." She lifted a hand and glanced about the table. "I thought it was you, but I wasn't sure. And your sister, Al … Ab—"

"Abby," I finished for her. "This is my father and my mother, and Abby's son Tyler. You remember him, don't you?"

I might have sounded a bit sarcastic but I didn't care. This woman always put me in a foul mood. Why was she always in my face?

My parents nodded in greeting and smiled.

Jessica let out a fake laugh. "Of course, I remember Tyler. Hello, Mom and Dad. Abby, you'll have to excuse me. I didn't forget your name. I've been working so hard. I've been busy helping Leonardo."

I bristled. I wanted to know what they were working on, but I should let it go. During the movie night, Lee hadn't seemed to want to work with her. Maybe he'd changed his mind. Maybe he'd finally given in. Sometimes persistence worked.

My sister gripped my arm. I hadn't realized I was holding the steak knife a bit too hard.

"What are you helping Lee with?" I asked.

"Well …" She bit her bottom lip, fluttering her eyelashes. "He asked me to—"

Abby's chair skidded on the hardwood floor when she pushed back. "I'm going to the restroom. Order the clam linguini for me," she said to me and grabbed Jessica's arm. "Come with me. Let's talk."

Something was going on between Lee and Jessica, and Abby must have known. Well, whatever. I had no right to be upset.

"Who is she?" my mother whispered, her eyes still on them. "She's pretty but she's … she's …"

I rolled my eyes. "I know. Where's the waiter? Let's order."

My father frowned at my tone and waved at the waiter. "Maybe you need to eat. You're grumpy when you're hungry."

I let out a laugh. If only he knew the true reason for my foul mood.

The waiter brought us water and a basket of bread, and took our orders. My mother put a warm sourdough roll on Tyler's bread plate and one for my father. Then she handed the basket to me.

I raised my eyebrow at Abby when she came back. "What was that all about?" I whispered so only she could hear.

Abby leaned closer. "You looked like you wanted to punch her."

"I did not." I lowered my head, ashamed at the truth of her words.

Abby huffed and placed the white linen napkin on her lap. "Anyway." She spread butter on a roll and took a bite.

"Is there something you're hiding from me?" I said around a mouthful of bread.

"I have no idea what you're talking about."

"Is Jessica with Lee at this restaurant?" I glanced behind me and I shook my head, upset with myself for caring. What was I doing? I had to let him go. "You know what, never mind."

Abby shifted her gaze away from me. "He's not. Don't be silly."

My sister was lying. She could never look me in the eye when she did, but I let it go. I was leaving tomorrow anyway, so what did it matter?

"Why are they whispering?" My father chomped on his bread.

"They don't want us to hear." Mother handed Tyler a glass of water. "Drink some."

Tyler shook his head. "No, Grandma. I'm not thirsty."

I kissed Tyler on the head and hugged him. He always made me think of what was most important in our lives—the people we loved and who loved us back.

After dinner, we took more pictures by the Christmas decorations in the lobby. I was ready to go home, but Abby wanted to check out the garden.

"Why are you walking so fast?" I fell behind Abby's swift steps pounding on the marble floor.

Abby rounded the corner and halted in front of a ballroom.

"This isn't the garden. Are you lost?" I looked over my shoulder at my parents, making their way to us with Tyler, and then back to Abby.

"Kate." She inhaled a deep breath, her hands clasped under her chin. "Your life is about to change. Don't be mad at me." She kissed my cheek. "I love you."

"Abby? What did you do?" My heart thumped faster and I reached for her arm, but she pushed the door open.

We stood in an empty room, but the walls were filled with twenty paintings and large, framed photos. They looked familiar. It took a moment for me to process that they were mine. *All of them.*

I walked up to the painting of Lee and Bridget I had wrapped and stored at the back of Lee's painting room. I hadn't messaged him about it yet. I had planned to after I left, but it was here. How?

And … oh goodness, the painting *Mr. Medici's Shirt* hung smack in the middle of the side wall, sticking out like a sore thumb. Not only from the grand size, but the muddy blobs of mismatched mixed together.

Who put it here? Abby? Why?

On the corner of the frame, a white tag said—*sold.* Price: $20,000. Name: Ian Bordonaro.

What? I blinked and looked at it again. Lee's friend bought that painting? What in heavens for? Then I went to the next painting of New York City buildings.

It had a white tag that said *sold* with the name of the person who had bought it, and a price of $5,000. I went to the next frame—a wine bottle on a stack of books. Depending on the size of the canvas and the framed photo, they were priced from $5,000 to $20,000.

I had meant to blow up the pictures I had taken and give them to Abby to sell, but she had beaten me to it.

"Abby, when did you do this? What's going on?"

I turned to find Abby when she didn't answer, but I was stunned to silence. Lee stood where I had expected her, and my family was nowhere to be seen. I had been so shocked to see all of my work that I hadn't heard anyone come in or out of the ballroom.

I wanted to cover up the photo behind me, one of my favorites. I had taken that picture of Lee by accident at the Poipu Plaza. The mistake turned out in my favor. He looked so dapper and natural, with his eyes directly at the camera.

"Lee. What are you doing here?" I swallowed and took a step back. Standing a few feet from each other had my pulse racing. Seeing him again brought back feelings I'd tried hard to suppress.

Lee took a step forward, his expression unreadable. "Why did you leave that night, Kate?"

His question and sternness intimated me a little.

"I wasn't feeling well. I already told you." I shifted my clutch purse to the other arm, needing something to do with my hands.

Lee's frown told me he didn't believe me.

His chestnut-colored eyes darkened and a hint of hurt came through his tone. "I think you were just fine. I think you ran away. I said something or did something that made you upset. Please tell me so I can explain. I'm not going to hurt you. I'm not like your ex."

I glanced down to my black heels. This was the moment of truth. Lee was right. I had run away because I didn't want my heart crushed again. After what Jayden had done to me, I had closed my heart and come up with reasons not to be with anyone else. But still, even with this revelation, I still made up excuses.

"I wasn't running away." With my chin up, I raised my voice a little, trying to sound strong. "It was my last day."

Lee shook his head. "There's something else bothering you. I thought …" He squared his shoulders and inhaled. "I thought we had a start of something special."

"I thought so, too." That slipped out too fast. His confession had chipped away some of the barrier I had built between us.

Lee's eyes grew wider. "Then what happened?"

"Ian. You were trying to set me up with your friend." Embarrassed from my outburst, I shifted my gaze to the closed doors on the other side. I wondered where my family went.

He pressed his lips, trying not to smile. "No, like I told you, I wanted you to get to know him because I thought he would be a good match for Abby when she's ready. Ian means a great deal to me, but when it comes to finding someone right for him, he hasn't had any luck."

"Oh." I felt like an idiot. Except … "You never told me that."

He rubbed the back of his head, his brow furrowing. "Yes, I did."

I crossed my arms. "No, you didn't. Believe me, I'd remember that."

His frown deepened, then he looked a little sheepish. "Well, I certainly *meant* to tell you."

I wasn't done. I wanted to get everything out in the open. "I heard you have lots of women." I arched an eyebrow in challenge.

He raked his fingers through his hair in frustration. "Some women spread rumors about me because I never pay attention to them. They have no idea who I am. What other women are you talking about?"

"Cassie?" I brought my clutch purse to my chest and hugged it.

Lee scrunched his features. "Cassie requested me for a real estate deal. I take on the requested projects and then I pass down the responsibility to someone else. I'm not going to lie to you. Cassie wanted more than a business transaction, but I didn't. Nothing happened between us and nothing ever will."

Either Jessica had gotten her information mixed up or her friend had. Or she had just made it up.

I didn't waste a second. I threw the next question at him. "Why were you with Jessica tonight?" I pierced my gaze into his, my toes tapping on the hardwood floor in a steady beat.

"Jessica Conner?" His eyebrows pinched to the center as he said her name like he couldn't believe I'd even mentioned it. "Unfortunately, I had to ask her to help me arrange your art exhibition. She's well known in our community and, believe it or not, some people respect her. Jessica has no idea you're the painter. She called people she knew and I did too. The people I contacted were business associates. Property owners purchase paintings or poster-size photos to display in their sample rooms."

I gave him a sidelong glance and parted my mouth. "*You* did this for me? Why?"

He inched closer. "I think you're an amazing person, and you're very talented. I didn't realize I had already bought one of your paintings. It's hanging in my bedroom, which you knew. I think you wanted to tell me when we had dinner that one day but you stopped. Why?"

I shrugged and glanced at the door again. "I don't know."

"I did this for you because I believe in you. I'm a businessman, and I know how hard it is to get ahead. But I don't want to take all the credit—your sister helped me. Don't go back to Los Angeles, Kate. You can make a living by doing what you love. Look at all the paintings you've already sold. You don't know this yet, but the clients already requested more from you and Abby. Your life is going to change."

I frowned, but my emotions fluttered like a trapped butterfly in my belly.

"When did this happen?" I lowered my purse.

"While you were eating dinner."

"Do my parents know anything about this?"

"Yes. Abby told them."

I was grateful for everything Lee and Abby had done. Arranging this art exhibit had taken a lot of effort and work in such a short amount of time. The reason she'd been texting a lot more frequently and recently. But a little part of me felt a little betrayed they had done this behind my back.

I released a long sigh and said, "Lee, thank you, but …"

"No but. And you're wrong, Kate." Lee grabbed my hand and pulled me closer with his other arm.

"Wrong about what?" I said breathlessly, staring into his eyes.

I was drowning in his voice, his smell, his warmth. This was what I'd tried to avoid. This was the reason I couldn't talk to him, let alone be face-to-face with him.

Lee pressed his forehead to mine. "You said I'm a man who has everything, but you're wrong. I don't have you. You complete my everything. Please don't leave. I want you. I want us. You painted the blank canvas of my heart with colors I've never seen or felt. Joy, laughter, and love. I want it all with you. And you deserve everything. Let me be the one that gives it to you."

I blinked in surprise and my heart combusted with happiness. I couldn't believe all that he was telling me. This man was too good to be true.

In the two years I'd been with Jayden, he had never expressed what he had felt for me. But Lee, he was an open book. He had poured out his heart and I knew without a doubt he meant every word. He made me feel important and that I was enough.

It was then when I realized that what I felt for Lee was much deeper and real than anything I'd felt with Jayden. What I'd had with Jayden wasn't love. With Jayden, it was all about him. But with Lee, it was all about us.

Relationships were complicated. And the love thing … What did I know about it? But with the right person, your heart explodes with pure bliss, and you feel like you can fly. Abby was right. Love was easy when it was right.

I loved his heart.

I loved the way he loved Bridget, and the way he paid it forward.

I loved how much he wanted me and the promise of tomorrow with him.

Pulling back enough to see his face, I said with conviction, "I want us, too. I want you to be the one to give me everything I deserve, and I want to do the same for you."

Lee gave me his gorgeous smile, but his eyes gleamed darker. As he wrapped one arm around my lower back and cupped the back of my head with his other hand, he pressed his lips to mine.

Thump went my purse. My arms went to his firm biceps.

The kiss was soft and sweet at first, until I moaned and my hands traced across his hard pecs.

He sucked in a breath and yanked me closer, my softness pressed against his hard chest. As his fingers laced through my hair, I parted my mouth and kissed him madly, tongues tangling.

We kissed with desperation, with all the pent-up momentum of longing we'd had ever since that time in the painting room. Perhaps even earlier, since the cab when I tossed my wet hair at him. He thirsted for me as I did for him, and I wasn't sure if we would ever be quenched.

When he kissed me even deeper, my body ignited with the sparks and this time they didn't fizz out. They burst with tiny fireworks, spreading to every inch of me until they exploded in a grand finale. I melted, evaporated, and drifted off into oblivion. And I'd swear I heard wind chimes tinkling.

I knew kissing Lee would be amazing, but I had underestimated him. I had floated off the stars and I'd thought I would never come down. Then Lee embraced me tightly like he never wanted to let me go, and finally released me. Breathless, his forehead pressed to mine, and he lowered his hands to my hips.

"I've been wanting to kiss you for a long time." He caressed my cheek, his eyes tender and gleaming. "I'm disappointed that I have to cut it short, but I think we should let your family back in now. Bridget is with them, too. They're waiting for us. And just in case you're wondering, Bridget loves the idea of us together." He took my flower off my hair and placed it on the left. "There. Now you're taken." He winked. "Should we tell everyone the good news?"

I frowned at him playfully, still catching my breath, and the feel of his memorable kiss lingering on my lips. "Only if you answer two questions."

He scrunched up his nose. "Okay."

"What did I say to you that night when you found me sleeping in Bridget's bed?"

A smug grin bloomed on his face as he shifted his weight from side to side. "You said … goodnight, husband."

"Oh, my goodness. I did?" I gnawed on my bottom lip, mortified.

"Don't be shy." He caressed my cheek. "I liked it. You didn't hear me but I said, 'goodnight, wife,' back to you. Your next question?" He seemed eager to move on.

"Why did you buy the painting in your room?"

He rubbed the back of his neck and hunched his shoulder as if embarrassed. "You might think it sounds silly, but I like to think that the star on the right is me and the one on the left is my soulmate. We're two stars drifting in the vast universe until we find our perfect match. After I found you, I knew you were mine."

I think I stopped breathing. Overcome with a rush of giddiness, I embraced him with all of me. I had stopped believing in soulmates, but my faith had been renewed.

The two stars finally joined as one at last.

Chapter Thirty-Three – Mauna Kea

I assumed Lee was taking the five of us to a picnic by the waterfall, but he banked the helicopter away from the island to a breathtaking view. The sun beamed high in the early afternoon, casting golden sparkles along the vast ocean, while the whipped cream-shaped low clouds scattered about the blue gave me the illusion I could reach out and touch them.

"Where are we going?" I asked.

"You'll see. It's a surprise." Lee's voice reverberated through my headphones.

I glanced behind me at Abby, Tyler, and Bridget for answers, but they were no help. Their wide grins told me they were in on the plan. I scrunched my face into a playful grimace and turned to focus back on the endless ocean to prevent from getting airsick.

"We're almost there. You feeling okay so far?" Lee squeezed my hand and that simple touch gave me all the comfort I needed.

"Yes, but I'll feel much better if you tell me where we're going." I had taken half the pill and worn my wrist band as Lee had suggested. So far, so good.

A sly grin unfurled on his lips as he veered the helicopter lower. "Kate, look."

My stomach dipped, but my heart soared. I pressed my nose to the window, unable to believe my eyes. "Is that …? It can't be."

A thick white blanket covered the mountain like a sea of clouds, the kind I'd only seen on a plane. The sight of snow always filled me with peace, exactly the way the sound of wind chimes did.

I glanced at Lee and behind to the trio, whose smiles grew larger as they cackled.

"Surprise!" the trio cheered.

"It's snow. It's real snow." I sounded like a child who had just met

Santa Claus. "Is that my surprise?"

"Yes," Bridget and Tyler shouted, clapping.

Lee lowered the helicopter. "We're at Mauna Kea Mountain on the big island. It's one of the places that snows in Hawaii. You told me when we were at the waterfall you wanted to see snow. I wanted to be the one to take you to see it. We didn't get to spend Christmas together so think of it as a second Christmas with me."

"Thank you, Lee. It's magical. How I imagined it would be." Tears pooled in my eyes. This man. He was too much. I loved everything about him. "But we're not properly dressed."

Abby rested a hand on my shoulder. "We're good. I've packed everything we need."

I twisted in my seat to get a good look at her. "You sneak. You told me that duffel bag was stuffed with a blanket and picnic food."

She shrugged. "What are sisters for?"

We shared a laugh, and then I smiled. A silent way of thanking her for always being there for me. She never failed to be the best older sister.

"I'm guessing Mom and Dad knew?"

"Yup. Lee offered to take them, but they declined. They said it was too cold."

It was the reason why my parents never took us to see snow in the mountains. Beach, yes, but never snow. It had worked out since Lee's helicopter transported five at the most, anyway.

After we landed, we took turns changing into snow outfits in the helicopter. When I stepped out, the frosty air nipped my nose and bathed my face.

"I can't believe I'm actually here." I reached down without my gloves and pressed my hand into the ice, the cold digging into my flesh. It made a crunch sound when I squeezed.

"Can we go over there?" Tyler pointed to the crowds about a hundred feet away, icy mists escaping from his mouth.

"Hold on, Ty. Put on your hat." Abby adjusted a backpack over her shoulder and fussed with her phone.

"The internet is horrible," Lee said, shoving his cell inside his jacket pocket. "And you'll have none after this point."

Lee wrapped his spare gloved hand around mine. The other one held a large backpack. As snow crunched from out steps, we left a trail of footprints behind us.

Lee took us to an area where it was less crowded, where families with smaller kids had gathered. I was surprised how packed it was considering it was New Year's Eve day.

"Let's stay here," Lee said, glancing from the barren tree to the fallen log. "This is a good spot."

I couldn't agree more.

"Look, I'm making a snow angel." Bridget flapped her arms and legs, her back on the crystalline surface. Her cheeks were rosy and she looked adorable in a pink beanie that covered her ears.

"Me too." Tyler snickered next to her, purposely puffing out breaths and watching cool mist float out of his mouth. "This is fun. Let's make a snowman."

The kids rose and dusted white powder off their legs. Then they gathered fresh, fine ice in their gloved hands and patted it into balls next to the tree.

Abby placed her backpack on the log. "Thank you, Lee, for inviting us too."

Lee flashed a quick grin and set his pack beside hers. "You're welcome. I do whatever makes Kate happy."

"Awww. I want you to be happy too." I caressed his arm, his words filling me with warmth.

"I'm happy when you're happy." Lee kissed my forehead and walked toward the kids.

That man. He made my world complete. He filled me up with hope and joy and made me feel like I was enough.

I sat on the log and pulled Abby into my arms. "Steve is smiling, watching his son having a great time."

"I know," she said softly. "And he's so happy you found someone who's worthy to have you."

Lee was everything I wanted and never thought I could find. "Steve is also proud of you and your new journey with me."

After my art exhibition at the hotel, we had gotten countless requests, as Lee had said we would. Abby and I were going to be busy filling orders for the next year at least.

I couldn't wait to start on this new adventure. It was a dream I hadn't thought possible. Lee had helped make it come true. I would always be grateful. He was my angel. And perhaps I was his angel too, in a different way.

"How was your date last night?" Abby adjusted her scarf and lowered the zipper on her blue goose down snow jacket.

When Lee and I had decided to give us a chance, he'd taken me out the next day and then last night again. We'd spent those nights talking and getting to know each other. Although he'd kissed me, he hadn't pressed for more.

"It was great." I played it off as if it was no big deal, shuffling my feet into the snow, giving me something to do besides look at my sister.

"Give me details." She lightly smacked my arm with her gloved hand.

I frowned and shrugged, watching Lee using his hands like a shovel to gather more snow. "We had fun."

"Anything else?"

"Abby," I drawled. "It was only our second date."

"You didn't come home, Kate."

I hadn't. I'd spent the night in Lee's arms. We planned to take our relationship slow. I had finally felt peace of letting go of Jayden so I thought it was best not to rush things. Currently, I lived with my sister, but one day soon I would be able to afford a place of my own. And perhaps in the future, I would move in with Lee.

When we had told Mona that we were dating, she could not contain her excitement. She'd hugged the both of us and told us she'd hired me hoping we would fall in love.

Mona was our living Cupid.

I picked up a bit of snow and splashed it on Abby's face. "I don't kiss and tell," I said quickly and ran.

"You—" Abby gave chase.

I sprinted in circles around Lee and the kids, leaving footprints, my leg muscles working harder. It was difficult to tread through the snow, especially with my heavy snow boots.

"Don't fall." Tyler opened his arms wide, protecting the snowman.

I stopped, panting, and something cold hit my cheek. Flakes fell into my mouth and I spat out liquid. I scowled at Abby. She was never the one to give up. While chasing me, she'd managed to scoop up a handful of snow.

"Truce." I stood behind Tyler, moving from side to side, using him as my shield, while Abby mirrored me with a snowball in her hand. "You won't dare hit your son, would you?"

Plop! A snowball smacked Tyler in the center of his chest.

"Mommy." Tyler squealed. He picked up a chunk of snow and threw it at her.

Abby had started a war. Snowballs flew in every direction between the five of us until we were spent and out of breath.

"Who wants hot cocoa?" Abby opened up her backpack on the log and took out a thermos and cups.

Steam rose from the thermos and my mouth watered at the sweet scent.

"Me," the two kids cheered, eagerly waiting in front of her.

I was just about to help Abby, when Lee draped his arm around my shoulder from behind and planted a kiss on my neck. "Abby is coming tonight, right? I invited Ian."

I had told Lee that Ian was perfect for my sister, but thought it might be too soon to set them up. Lee had suggested they meet at a casual gathering. Hopefully, they would become friends and perhaps it could turn into something more down the line, like how it had happened for us.

"Yes, she'll be there." I spun to face him and put my arms around his neck. "And you said my parents can come as well? They'll probably leave about nine and take Tyler home with them. Abby and I can stay longer."

"Of course. They should come. We can celebrate Eastern Standard Time and celebrate again at midnight."

"Sounds like a plan."

"Then perhaps you can meet my parents next month when they visit." He sounded hesitant, as if unsure.

"I would love that."

The way he looked at me with such tender eyes, I felt how much he cared for me. I fell more in love with him at that very second. He was not just Bridget's hero, but mine as well. I couldn't have asked for a better man to have a future with.

Plop. Plop.

Snow whacked Lee's left cheek, and something cold slapped my face. The kids had restarted the snowball fight.

"I … am … Skeleton!" Lee's voice went guttural as he curled his fingers like claws and chased after them.

"I'm Skeleton, too." I followed beside Lee, mimicking his monster expression.

We ran in circles around the log until Lee grabbed Tyler and I grabbed Bridget. We became tickle monsters and poked their sides as they squirmed. Giggles and snorts filled the air.

The kids rushed to work on their snowman by the tree while the three of us sat on the log and watched.

I recalled the first day when I'd arrived in Kauai and had seen a rainbow just as we pulled onto my sister's street. No sign that it had rained, except for the beautiful shimmering colors that arced across the sky. I'd had a feeling that Christmas was going to be special, and it was. But never had I imagined I would find Leonardo Medici.

Life was unpredictable and full of surprises. Sometimes fate intervened, and sometimes the people you love did. Like Mona hiring me, my sister owning a gallery, and me being Bridget's temporary nanny. Who knew all these coincidences would bring Lee and me together?

"We need help with our snowman," Tyler hollered and poked two sticks into the side for arms with Bridget's help.

"Coming," I said.

As Lee and I walked hand-in-hand, wind chimes tinkled on the chill wind. Despite the cold, a warm breeze brushed past me. Strangely, I didn't feel the invisible hand caressing down my back.

Turning my head, I searched for the sound, but I couldn't figure out where it came from. I thought I was hearing things until Lee stopped walking and looked at me with his eyebrows arched, silently asking if I'd heard it too. Then his gaze lowered to his jacket pocket.

There was no reception here. Bridget didn't notice the sound, as if it were meant for just Lee and me. When Lee pulled out his phone, the sound stopped. But even though there was no reception, the caller ID flashed: Unknown caller.

Lee and I exchanged a baffled look as I thought about all the times I had heard unexplained wind chimes on my phone. Perhaps it wasn't a fluke after all. Lee must have thought the same.

Lee smiled wide and beautiful, meeting my gaze with intensity, and said, “Sometimes angels come in human form.”

"I couldn't agree more.” I smiled the kind of smile I reserved only for him.

Then Lee kissed me, brushing a thumb along my cheek, and I knew with absolute certainty … Bridget’s mother was looking down on us.

About the Author

Mary Ting is an international bestselling, award-winning author. Her books span a wide range of genres, and her storytelling talents have earned a devoted legion of fans, as well as garnered critical praise.

Becoming an author happened by chance. It was a way to grieve the death of her beloved grandmother, and inspired by a dream she had in high school. After realizing she wanted to become a full-time author, Mary retired from teaching after twenty years. She also had the privilege of touring with the Magic Johnson Foundation to promote literacy and her children's chapter book: *No Bullies Allowed.*

www.AuthorMaryTing.com